TRADE SECRETS

Visit us at www.boldstrokesbooks.com

By the Author

Awake Unto Me

Forsaking All Others

A Spark of Heavenly Fire

Warm November

Two Souls

Taking Sides

The Last Time I Saw Her

Somewhere Along the Way

Trade Secrets

TRADE SECRETS

by

Kathleen Knowles

2020

TRADE SECRETS

ISBN 13: 978-1-63555-642-1

THIS TRADE PAPERBACK ORIGINAL IS PUBLISHED BY
BOLD STROKES BOOKS, INC.
P.O. BOX 249
VALLEY FALLS, NY 12185

FIRST EDITION: AUGUST 2020

CREDITS
EDITOR: SHELLEY THRASHER
PRODUCTION DESIGN: SUSAN RAMUNDO
COVER DESIGN BY TAMMY SEIDICK

Acknowledgments

Many thanks to my editor, Shelley Thrasher who always makes my books better. And thanks to the entire Bold Strokes team whose efficiency and precision never ceases to amaze and impress me.

Dedication

For Jeanette

Chapter One

The Moscone Convention Center exhibition floor in downtown San Francisco was populated with information booths belonging to over two hundred companies. Antoinette, "Tony," Leung scanned the map of the convention floor in her hand and considered where she should start. Wandering up and down random rows didn't seem like the most efficient use of her time, but she didn't have an obvious organization such as alphabetical-by-name or grouped-by-company-type to guide her. Tony was all about order and method; she had to be because of the work she performed. Blood testing allowed no room for error, because people's lives and health were at stake.

Tony didn't hate her current job at St Francis Hospital, but she didn't love it either, mainly due to her relationship with her supervisor. Clinical-lab specialists tended to have somewhat rigid, by-the-book personalities because that was part of the job. The problem arose when that lack of flexibility extended to their interpersonal relations. Not to put too fine a point on it, but Tony considered her supervisor kind of a bitch. She was looking for a new job, and a job fair would be a good place to start. Tony was a certified clinical-laboratory specialist, but she could do all sorts of lab work. Working for a private company, as she had once before, might be a nice change from the hospital-run, clinical testing labs.

A brown-haired woman in a conservative business suit stood in front of the sign reading *Global HemoSolutions* at the corner booth.

She might as well start there. She wrote the name of the company on her legal pad, and the woman showed her a practiced HR grin.

"Hi," Tony said, amiably.

"Hello, Tony, uh, Leung." She was reading Tony's name tag. "I'm Heather, and I work in HR for Global HemoSolutions. GHS for short."

"Nice to meet you. Here's a copy of my resume."

Heather read through it in less than thirty seconds, checking for key words, but when she looked up, she appeared interested.

"It says you did immunoassay R and D, and you have a med-tech license. Very impressive."

Tony didn't know about impressive, but it did show she was versatile. Performing routine testing and conducting research had radically different requirements.

"I like both types of lab work. For various reasons."

Heather said, "GHS is still in the R and D stage, but we would probably need clinical-lab people down the road." Heather handed Tony a glossy pamphlet.

She read, "Our vision is to make blood testing simple, painless, quick, and cost effective. All the things it is not, currently. We have and are developing patented proprietary technology so we can run hundreds of tests on just a couple drops of blood."

Whoa. *That* would be truly groundbreaking. Tony instantly decided she wanted to work for this company. To be part of creating something as advanced as what was described in the brochure was an amazing opportunity.

Tony formed her most earnest expression and spoke, holding Heather's gaze. "That idea fascinates me. I hope you'll interview me."

Heather nodded solemnly. "Based on your resume, it looks like you may be someone we'd like to interview. Our CEO, Erica Sanders, still prefers to do them, and she's very busy, but I am going to recommend she talk to you."

"That would be great." Tony shook hands with Heather. "Thanks for your time."

Tony visited other booths, but she was mostly going through the motions. She was pinning her hopes on Global HemoSolutions—and not just to get her out of the hospital lab.

Three years before, she had worked briefly for a biotech start-up, looking at cancer therapies. It went bust before it could begin clinical trials, but while she was there, it had been one of the most exhilarating experiences of her life. The hospital clinical-lab work appealed to her innate altruism, and the work was predictable. In a world of uncertainty, it was comforting to know if you performed steps in a certain order and in a specific way, you got an expected result. And if you did everything perfectly but didn't find the expected result, then you had to ferret out the reason, which appealed to Tony as well.

She'd inherited the curiosity and fix-it genes from her engineer dad, Joe. If something was amiss, then she would work on it until she had the answer. Research was similar but required even more patience, along with a sense of curiosity and imagination. Tony reminded herself that she could use all these qualities in the interview with GHS's CEO, if she could obtain one.

Tony sat across from Erica Sanders and attempted to make herself appear cool, competent, and in control. It was one level of nervousness to be interviewed for a job she'd convinced herself she had to have, and another when the interviewer was the company CEO and looked like Erica Sanders. Tony reproved herself for noticing the woman's looks, but they were hard to *not* notice. Even more compelling, though, was the way Erica talked.

After their introductions and the requisite small talk about how easy a time Tony had finding the company and what it was like to commute from San Francisco by train, Erica sat back, tented her fingers together, and said, "I have a vision where, no matter their age, their socioeconomic background, their gender, you name it, *anyone* should have access to information about their health. Some of that information can only come from blood tests. You work in a clinical laboratory, so you know how much doctors need and rely on results of such tests."

Tony nodded and decided to stay silent and hear Erica's spiel, which it certainly must be. Clearly, she sold her ideas as automatically as she breathed.

Erica paused and looked up at the ceiling. "Right now, what I described in our brochure doesn't exist. Two companies have monopolies over the blood-testing industry. They don't innovate. They overcharge the consumers and the insurance companies. And they have to take multiple tubes of blood from people, most of whom hate getting stuck with needles. My sister is one of those people. She practically faints when she has to give blood, and that's *before* they stick in the needle."

Erica stopped and made eye contact with Tony. "We are going to change that paradigm." Then she paused and let Tony absorb what she'd said.

She continued. "My engineers are working on a device no bigger than an ordinary CPU that can perform hundreds of blood tests on two drops of blood. The assay groups, one of which you'd work in, are readying the assays for our device to perform robotically."

Tony listened to all this information carefully, but she had no doubts. She knew where she wanted to be and what she wanted to do. "I want to help. I want to help you achieve your goals and think I can. I've got the sort of skills you're looking for, and I understand what you're trying to do."

Tony watched Erica's face. She'd looked serious, rather stern as she spoke, but when Tony responded, she slowly smiled and nodded. She wasn't just politely listening. Her profound expression said, "I see you get it. You hear what I'm saying." This felt less like a job interview and more like she was being evaluated for inclusion in a crusade. Did she have the right level of commitment? Did she grasp the significance of what Erica said? Tony hoped so.

"I think you can as well. I read your resume, and though you got your degree at Berkeley, I won't hold that against you." Erica looked mock-serious.

"Where did you go to school?" Tony grinned to show she got the joke.

"Stanford, naturally."

"Well, I won't hold that against *you*," Tony said playfully. Stanford University and the University of California, Berkeley famously rivaled each other in sports teams, outstanding students, prestigious research grants, you name it. Tony decided not to correct Erica for calling her alma mater Berkeley, instead of Cal, which was what the alumni called it, unlike the rest of the world. Unkind (or jealous) people called it Beserkley, due to its counter-culture past and lefty present. This name usually referred to the city of Berkeley, but the city and the university were sometimes merged into one. Cal was hard to get into. Maybe not as hard as Stanford, but it was still selective, and Tony was proud of where she'd received her bachelor's and master's degree.

Erica continued to scrutinize Tony as she fell silent. Tony waited and kept her eye contact.

"We need special people, Tony. We need the highest level of commitment you can give. There's no room for doubt. This is going to be hard."

Tony took a breath, then said, "I understand. I'm prepared to do whatever I have to do to help."

Erica smiled. "Now that we're clear about that, when can you start?"

"Excuse me?" Tony was taken aback. She wasn't sure she'd heard right. They hadn't not even talked salary, nor had Erica even offered an actual job with a title and a description.

"I want you to come work with me. You're exactly what I'm looking for. You'd be a perfect fit for the R and D group, and when we're ready to test patients, you could transfer to the clinical side if you wanted to."

"Um. Great. I accept. I need to give two weeks' notice at St Francis."

They shook hands and Tony left, floating on a pink cloud, not remembering until later, when she was on the Caltrain headed back to the City, that she'd forgotten to ask about salary. It didn't matter. It would probably be adequate. Money was definitely *not* the point of working for GHS. Changing the world was. Changing the world with Erica Sanders would be worth whatever salary she'd receive.

She called her dad, Joe, to tell him the good news.

"Congrats, honey. I'm proud of you. Your mother would be too, if she knew."

"Yeah. Thanks, Dad. I'm starting in two weeks. Talk to you later."

❖

Sheila Garrison had been a junior partner in her father Roy's venture capital investment firm for two and a half years. After finishing her MBA at Stanford, she went to work at a Wall Street investment bank as an analyst. Roy had wanted her to start working with him right away, but she needed some time on her own. She loved her dad, but he could be a little much to deal with.

"You'll be back," he'd predicted when she left for New York. And he was right. She did return to the Bay Area. Sheila loved spreadsheets and numbers, but she missed working with people. She returned to Menlo Park and joined her father's company, and he had the grace not to say "I told you so" explicitly, though his grin said it.

Sheila dove into screening CEO applicants to receive Pacific Partners funding. She had some early modest successes and only one real failure. One of her software companies had imploded, leaving Pacific Partners in the hole for a half a million bucks. Sheila was chagrined, but Roy took it in stride. "If you can't cope with failure, you're not going to make it in this business." Sheila moped for a few days, but she eventually accepted that some bad choices were inevitable. She had begun the study of Buddhism, which helped her cope with her disappointment as much as her dad's philosophical response to her judgment error had.

Sheila sat at her desk reviewing her calendar and her email, and she heard Roy say, "Knock-knock." She looked up, and he stood in the doorway of her office grinning.

He didn't wait for her response but strode in and flopped into one of her guest chairs. He was headed toward seventy-five in a few months, but his youthful enthusiasm made him look much younger.

He worked at keeping fit, and though she'd gotten him to stop dyeing his hair and let it go gray, he had the well-kept looks of a prosperous West Coast businessman, which was what he was.

"What's up?" Sheila asked, noting his demeanor. The Cheshire-cat grin and his leg draped over the arm of the chair and rocking said he was going to tell her something. He had a paper-bound document under his arm.

"Glad you asked. I was at a cocktail party last week and ran into Gary Frenzel. He told me about a new company."

Sheila nodded. Networking was the way it was done in Silicon Valley. Who you knew and who they knew.

"It's called Global HemoSolutions. I don't know what the heck that means, except they do blood testing and Gary's high on them. He talked to their CEO, and get this. She's a woman."

"Wow. That's something," Sheila said. "Did Gary invest?'

"Yup, he did, and he thinks we ought to get in, like now. They're starting series 2."

Roy meant that the company had done one round of investing and were looking for more money. Their firm, Pacific Partners, usually participated in Series 2 investments." Pacific Partners wouldn't invest at the beginning but would jump in a little further along in a company's growth arc. If you were an early investor and the start-up went bad, you were screwed, naturally. The CEO tended to know the first investors, who would be okay with losing their money.

Investors in later funding series, say Series 3 to Series 5, would further dilute the return on investment: ROI. They simply received a smaller piece of the profits because more people were involved. It was simple arithmetic: the later you joined the party, the lower the profits.

"What do you know about their business? What did Gary tell you?" Sheila asked.

Roy sighed. "I'm not sure I understand it, but Gary seemed to think it has enormous potential. He said, 'Erica looked me in the eye and told me this would revolutionize medicine, and gosh, I believed her.'"

Roy rolled his eyes and then became serious." I want you to read their prospectus and tell me what you think." He handed it to her, winked, and left her office.

Sheila understood that he wanted to move forward, at least with vetting this company and probably investing in it. Roy, an optimist, was always genuinely enthusiastic about their prospective companies, but he was also a realist. He'd had his share of success, but enough failures to make him humble and cautious, and she trusted his opinion. His track record of picking investments was strong, and since the late seventies he'd built Pacific Partners into a respected company. Their investors re-upped their contributions regularly and always wanted to know about the "next big thing." Sheila's experience as an analyst for an investment bank had allowed her father to hire her and make her a junior partner without any push-back from the other partners. He needed her expertise to evaluate the start-ups they considered funding.

Sheila brewed a cup of green tea and then took off her jacket and rolled up her shirt sleeves. She liked both the literal act itself and the symbolism of the act. *Get to work, girl.* Her study of Buddhism had taught her how to focus mindfully. Her jacket-doffing and sleeve-rolling signaled her to put her whole focus on the task at hand.

Global HemoSolutions' prospectus was a thick, handsome document featuring a glossy cover and bold, blue 36-point typeface for the title, as well as a graphic-designer color palette. Erica Sanders, the name of the CEO, was prominent on the second page under the introduction, and her photo looked professional.

The name of the company was rather grand, but start-up entrepreneurs had a license for grandiosity. They didn't get anywhere by thinking small, and being modest certainly didn't convince companies like her dad's to give them big bucks.

Sheila stared at Erica's photograph. She was very young, which was expected, but she was both female and pretty, which was not. Most of Pacific Partners' prospects were bright, talkative, scruffy young men. Ambitious nerds, as Sheila thought of them.

Global HemoSolutions intended to totally alter the nature of blood testing. This highly unusual start-up wasn't about unique software or a new platform to do an old thing in a new way; it was medical technology. Sheila needed to find out about the blood-testing market: who, how many companies were involved, and, of course, how much money they typically made. She wouldn't rely on the prospectus since she could verify those figures elsewhere.

Sheila looked at Erica's picture again. She had lots of black, glossy hair, and big dark-brown eyes. Not only was she young, only twenty-six, and female, but astoundingly attractive. But did she have the brains and the deep motivation to make something like she was proposing to do a success? Was she worth them dropping millions of dollars into her hands? Roy had given Sheila this question to answer. He took Gary's high estimation of Erica and the potential of her company seriously, but he expected Sheila to do an in-depth evaluation.

Sheila read the GHS prospectus once, then read it again, more slowly, focusing on market share, growth predictions, expenses versus capital, and cash flow. She also perused the list of current investors and the names of the management team. Early on, friends and family had contributed relatively small sums. Sheila read the detailed description of GHS technology and business, the most unusual aspect of the company. Her dad's firm and most of Silicon Valley focused on high-tech hardware and software. GHS was a biotech company, a whole other animal.

Erica's prospectus talked about a proprietary device. The word proprietary usually applied to software and must be similar when applied to a device. The device could run hundreds of tests from a couple drops of blood. Erica didn't say how it would work, but Sheila didn't have the background to understand such an explanation anyhow. The chair of Stanford University's biochemistry department served on the board, so they had access to some scientific expertise. Yet Erica's grandiose claims were just that: claims, though they all sounded terrific.

After Sheila finished reading the prospectus, she stood up and stretched, holding her long arms over her head as she looked out the window at the Santa Clara hills. She cleared her mind and did a short stint of prana breathing.

When she returned to her desk, she did some quick calculations. If GHS succeeded, Sheila's profit share would increase, maybe by a lot. She tried not to focus on money too much, but it was hard not to, since venture capitalism was, in the end, all about money. She wanted to invest in good companies that aimed to better humankind, and after reading the prospectus, she believed GHS was one of those companies. And, if she could believe the prospectus, the potential for profit was astronomical.

Sheila walked down the hall to Roy's office and knocked on the door frame of his open door.

"What's the verdict?"

"I say it's a 'go.' But I'll look a bit more deeply into the market."

He pumped his fist. "I had a feeling about this one. Sheila, if this works the way I think it will, you'll be a full partner, and I'm positive they'll approve you for a two percent share. I'm going to have you as point person for GHS."

She nodded and couldn't stop a triumphant smile.

"I'll call Erica Sanders."

The Global HemoSolutions facility was located in the Research Park area of Palo Alto. *She's in a good position, geographically at least.* Sheila noted the names of other companies like Google, Twitter, and Hewlett Packard along the way. It was the Valley way: people were big on aspiration, on location and look and gestalt. It was like you joined the group of winners, and then if you followed the rules, you'd be a winner too. Proximity to success bred success, or so people believed.

A security guard met Sheila at the door and gave her a visitor badge. High-tech people took security to almost ridiculous lengths. They had cube farms with lots of earnest-looking young people tapping away at their PCs or laptops. No one looking at them could possibly know what they were doing. Nonetheless, they liked to keep their visitors on short leashes to show how serious they were about everything.

The security guard stayed by Sheila's side as another guard left to notify Erica Sanders that the Pacific Partners rep had arrived. Roy made sure that all their clients knew that Sheila wasn't a gofer. She was junior partner. But Sheila was always aware that, though nepotism had perhaps gotten her in the door of Pacific Partners, she would last only if she was effective at what she did. She was scrupulously thorough and professional.

Sheila smiled at the guard and took a good look around. Ceiling-high windows surrounded the entryway to allow in as much light as possible. Behind the reception desk, the blue and white logo consisting of a large check mark, plus the company name, loomed. A few employees were sitting in a chair circle to her left, their heads bent together as they talked. These people could either be taking a break or having a real work meeting. It was impossible to say. The high-tech companies were notoriously casual about things like that.

The time drew out, and Sheila finally checked her watch. Over twenty minutes had passed. By habit, she was always precisely on time for her meetings. She'd picked that habit up from Roy, who always insisted on punctuality. He said it indicated two things: you meant business and you respected the person you were to meet with and his or her time. On the other hand, *her* time was not always respected. Sheila composed herself and quelled her impatience.

She picked a chair at random and sat down, crossed her legs, and looked at her email, composed and unruffled. Time delays could mean anything, but she hoped this one didn't mean the CEO was pulling a power trip right at the beginning of their potential relationship. That wouldn't bode well for the future. These entrepreneurs came to the VC as supplicants, and while they didn't have to be obsequious, they at least had to have manners. This was another item on the list of Roy's many criteria for judging prospective clients.

The side door opened, and the security guard walked through with a woman Sheila recognized as Erica Sanders. The guard walked a half-step behind her, like a bodyguard.

"Sheila Garrison?"

Sheila stood up and stuck her hand out. "You must be Erica."

Erica didn't smile, but she returned Sheila's eye contact unflinchingly and held it. Her handshake was just short of too firm, but Sheila wasn't easily intimidated or rattled.

"Nice to meet you. Roy's not with you?" Erica asked. It was clear she was disappointed.

"No. He asked me to take the first meeting with you."

"I see. Let me show you to my office." Her tone had lost its edge, as though Erica Sanders had made a lightning calculation about which approach, sugar or vinegar, was the best.

The guard trailed them as they moved through a hallway with large open-plan work rooms on either side. Sheila wanted to ask if she would be able to see the laboratory and other technical spaces, but she decided to let Erica direct their meeting.

They arrived at a large office next to a conference room. It was unadorned, with no pictures, no tchotchkes, no plants. This was a statement of sorts, Sheila speculated. *I have no life or any time for anything other than business.*

Sheila sat in one of the two spartan chairs in front of Erica's nearly empty desk that Erica indicated with a spare gesture. A laptop was placed precisely in front of the desk chair. That was it, other than a simple square of metal—a plaque of some sort, and Sheila couldn't read what it said.

Seated across from Erica, Sheila was able to observe her better, and she formed more impressions. The photograph in the prospectus didn't do justice to the way her eyes looked. They were large, so dark they were almost black, and took in Sheila without moving or even blinking. She was of medium height and slight stature. Sheila couldn't decide if her lack of motion was a zen-like stillness or something else. *Not zen.* Sheila had some experience, since she was a Zen Buddhist who attended services on Fridays, dharma talks twice a week, and sat *zazen,* meditated, at least a half hour a day. Erica Sanders, Sheila was convinced, was not a Buddhist. She didn't exude serenity in the least. She projected firm control and a veiled wariness. She didn't speak for several seconds, but Sheila was unfazed. She wasn't the least uncomfortable with silence. She treasured it for the rare commodity it was.

Erica at last said, "Thank you for coming, but I'm sorry it may be a wasted trip. In general, I prepare a presentation for prospective investors and conduct a tour. Without Roy present, I'll have to repeat it, and that's inefficient."

"Roy has delegated the vetting of you and your company to me. He perhaps didn't make it clear that I've been assigned to your account. I can have him call you. In the meantime, may we proceed? I'd love to see whatever you care to show me and whatever you feel may best inform me of your ideas, your plans for the company, your current operations. I'd like to make a thoroughly informed decision."

Sheila had plenty of experience working through negotiation snarls with clients. Like anything else involving more than one person, the venture-capital process worked best with the two parties cooperating instead of at odds. Erica, it was clear, was a control freak. She appeared to be unaware that it wasn't possible *or* desirable to control everything, such as when dealing with the person who wanted to give you a large amount of money with which you were expected to make even more.

Sheila watched Erica make more calculations. She seemed like the kind of person who would go along with what Sheila said and then call Roy later.

"All right. Let me dive right in then. We're around seven years old. I came up with the idea when I was a sophomore at Stanford and applied for a patent on a new way to do medical blood testing. My sister was deathly afraid of needles, and I thought there must be some way to perform blood testing that didn't take tubes and tubes of blood. Some tests can be done with a finger prick. I came up with a method to miniaturize multiple types of lab tests and fit them into a box just a little bigger than a computer CPU."

Erica leaned back in her chair and watched as Sheila absorbed what she'd just said.

"Quite impressive. How far are you from market?"

Erica grinned confidently. "Three years."

Without experience with this type of device, Sheila had no idea if this timeframe was realistic, but software developers routinely underestimated how long it would take to make their products consumer-ready, so she assumed Erica was as overoptimistic as all start-up CEOs.

"We have negotiated partnerships with the VA to place our devices in several medical centers, and several pharma companies plan to use our technology for clinical trials. The Graff Drugstores corporation wants to use our device to provide on-site testing in its stores. I can email you the details."

Sheila mirrored Erica's expression. "I would like to see all those agreements, and please tell me about your management team."

Erica launched into a rundown of all the great technical people she'd managed to hire. Curiously, she talked at length about her board members, even though she knew Sheila had read the prospectus. They were all well-known and well-regarded men and not just from the Valley. One was a former secretary of state for the second President Bush. That they were all male wasn't a huge surprise, but Sheila thought that Erica would have wanted at least one woman on her board. She'd perhaps probe her about that subject later, when they knew each other better.

"Are you ready for a tour?" Erica asked. Her brightness turned a bit brittle.

"I'd love to see your facility."

"Certainly. Please look this over and sign it." Erica slid a multipage document across her desk toward her. "I have to see if all's ready. Take your time and I'll be back." With that she stood up and left the office.

Sheila examined the non-disclosure agreement she'd been given. It was elaborate and ran for six pages. New companies were wary of competitors poaching their ideas, especially from their employees, but couldn't imagine how she, as an outsider on a show-and-tell tour, could possibly learn anything to disclose, let alone what this NDA was designed to cover. It was appropriate for an employee, especially a high-level manager. She shrugged, signed it, left it on the desk, and went to the door, thinking to use the bathroom, but the door was locked.

Surprised, she sat back down and waited. Erica Sanders took her concern for security to stratospheric levels. Their technology must be truly something special. Erica returned and sat down behind her desk. "I apologize, Sheila, but we'll have to reschedule. It might be for the best, since I'd very much like to have Roy come on the tour."

Stymied and a tad irritated, Sheila sighed but smiled briefly. "Of course. I understand. If you wouldn't mind, would you send me the names of some of your competitors? I'd like to know more about the business of medical testing. And please send any current agreements you may have with testing partners."

Erica nodded. Sheila took several deep breaths to calm herself, then shook Erica's hand and left.

Chapter Two

Back at her office, Sheila took a fifteen-minute break for meditation, and then she composed an email to her father with her thoughts better organized. In person, Erica was as compelling as her prospectus. She was mercurial and secretive, but those were practically built-in personality traits of start-up CEOs. GHS, from all available information, was a great investment prospect. Even if their income projections proved to be exaggerated, the business could still make a ton of money. Her email pinged with a message from Erica, containing the promised information on their industry partnerships and links to other blood-testing companies. She had sent nothing, however, from Graff Drugstores. Sheila made a note of that oversight. Erica or her assistant might have forgotten.

Sheila saved the documents to her desktop and began to read the material and make notes. A knock at her door startled her. It was Roy.

"Hi, sweetheart. How was the meeting with Erica?" Sheila wanted him not to use that term for her at work, but it was hard to persuade him to change.

"Good, mostly. Let me have another half hour, and I'll come talk to you."

She printed out all of Erica's material so he could read it in hard copy. He hated reading things on his computer. She'd been able to convince him that email was okay, but he was still dubious about everything else: text, chat, etc. He claimed he was just old-fashioned and liked phone calls and paper. She smiled as she neatly clipped everything together.

Roy was sitting with his feet up, tossing his nerf basketball into the net and missing when she entered his office. She put the stack of paper in front of him.

"So?" He grinned and raised his eyebrow. "We going to pull the trigger?"

"You've already decided, I think." Sheila laughed.

"No. I want to hear from you."

"Erica is persuasive, very persuasive. She's like an evangelist."

"If evangelists looked like supermodels." Roy gazed at the ceiling.

"I noticed." Sheila injected a note of dryness into her tone. She'd told herself that just because the woman was supernaturally beautiful, she wasn't necessarily trustworthy. On the other hand, she could be. Sheila didn't want to stereotype anyone.

"Well. All that aside, what do you think?" Roy asked.

Sheila took a breath. "The partnerships she's talking about could be worth a ton of money. Currently only two companies do blood testing, and it's a billion-dollar market. GHS would blow them away if they could do it faster and cheaper and with less blood. And no needles."

"Sounds great."

"Erica wouldn't give me a tour of the facility without you being there."

"I know. She called, and I told her you were the point person." Roy was working on his unconscious sexist language, and his effort was endearing. "But as you might imagine, she sweet-talked me into coming over there with you. I'd like to see it anyhow."

"Dad, I'm not sure if either you or I would even know what we were looking at and if it works. We don't know a thing about biotech labs. We're software people. Give me a new and trippy program for something that no one ever thought of or an online service thousands of people don't yet know they need, and I can judge those. I don't know anything about blood testing. That concerns me."

"Oh, I think Erica's smart enough to hire good technical help. We'll see what she shows us and who."

"Right. I'll set it up. Are we going to have dinner with Mom tonight?" Sheila's mother and dad were divorced, but they maintained a best-friend sort of relationship that Sheila was grateful for. She could spend time with both of them. Since she'd moved back to the Bay Area from, she hadn't had time to develop a social life. Her stint in New York had been short, and she'd been busy and not really done any dating there either. Here she was back in Silicon Valley, surrounded, theoretically, by a large population of smart, eligible women to choose from, and she'd had exactly two dates in a two-year-and-a-half span, neither of them worth a second look. *This has to change.*

❖

Roy and Sheila sat at the shiny conference room table at GHS and listened to Erica as she ran through a polished presentation about her company visualized in a detailed, glossy, PowerPoint slideshow. Unlike the prospectus, the slideshow delved more deeply into the process of blood testing and how GHS proposed to transform it. Erica projected pictures of what she called "microcaps"—tiny tubes where samples were captured—and then a picture of something called a Leonardo. It looked like an older, larger piece of computer hardware.

"We envision placing the Leonardo in people's homes. Think of the convenience and ease that will give a cancer patient, who can then perform her own blood tests in the comfort of her own home. The data is transmitted wirelessly wherever it needs to go—to doctors, anywhere."

When she wasn't focused on Erica, Sheila watched Roy. He never once took his eyes off Erica. Erica made eye contact with Roy at least twice as often as she did with Sheila, which left no doubt who Erica was really talking to. Sheila didn't mind, that much. She was a little surprised a female CEO would do that, though it was standard behavior for the male CEOs who pitched to them. But there were the savvy few who homed in on Sheila as much as they did on Roy during pitch meetings.

"Okay. We'll take a break, and then I'll give you a tour."

❖

Tony was called upstairs to the HR office to sign yet more papers and tried not to be annoyed. She was in her second week at GHS and working as hard and as fast as she could to absorb the details of her new job, so this was an unwelcome interruption.

Heather, the HR manager, as chirpy as ever, handed her a multipage document. "Non-disclosure agreement."

"I think I already signed this." Tony tried to keep her tone neutral.

"Yes, but this is a new version, and Erica wants me to use it. Sorry for making you sign twice."

Tony knew she ought to read it over thoroughly, but she wasn't in the mood, and she wanted to get back to the lab and back to work. She'd signed an NDA at the biotech company she used to work at and was familiar with them and what they said. It was common for companies to not want to let their technology out and to keep employees from talking about it in public or to competitors.

Tony riffled through the pages, noting a paragraph that read, "EMPLOYEE shall not mention the name of COMPANY on social media, including Facebook, Twitter, Instagram, and SnapChat, nor disclose to friends or family members that EMPLOYEE is working at COMPANY." *Huh?* That was strange. The level of security Erica imposed was higher than any she'd ever experienced, but she accepted that Erica had her reasons. She scrawled her signature on the last page and handed it to Heather.

Tony passed the ladies' room on her way to the stairs down to the laboratory area. For the sake of efficiency, she decided to stop in before she returned to the lab.

❖

Sheila left her security-guard shadow outside the door of the bathroom. If Erica was concerned with security, she might want to employ female guards, who could actually enter the women's restroom with their charges. Sheila could be whispering information into her phone while she was supposed to be urinating or fixing her hair. She stopped at the mirror to examine her hair, and it was fine. She kept it chin length, and it didn't need attention. It was a nice bronzy, dark red. Sheila ascribed to the maxim that lesbians needed above all to have good haircuts rather than elaborate hair styles.

Sheila wouldn't have had much to report or anyone to transmit secret information to if she did succeed in obtaining any. Leonardo resembled a blocky, silvery-gray box. Not the standard "black box" but its equivalent. Nor would Sheila have understood if she'd been shown its innards. Erica had led Sheila and Roy on a lightning walk-through of what she called the wet lab area. This meant the lab where chemistry was done with liquid reagents, hence "wet." Sheila knew nothing about laboratories and wouldn't know if they were building a smart bomb or curing cancer. The function of the engineering lab was clearer. The devices were under construction and undergoing testing there. Erica stood proudly in front of a real Leonardo and showed how blood samples in microcap tubes were taken and then fed into the device, and results were returned.

"We want people to put them in their homes." Erica patted Leonardo as though it were a beloved pet.

"Why Leonardo?" Sheila asked.

"Because, you know, da Vinci was a great painter but also an inventor."

Sheila trusted Erica's employees were up to the tasks she'd assigned them to. The technical resumes of the managers, listed in the prospectus, certainly looked impressive.

As she stood at the mirror, a dark-haired woman about her age emerged from one of the stalls, smiled at her, and went to the sink to wash her hands.

On impulse, Sheila said, "Excuse me. I see you work here?" Talking to someone was much better than trying to discern anything about GHS at random. Sheila was confined to knowing whatever

Erica thought was important to tell her. The front-line staff could be much more informative if asked specific questions. That is, if they *would* talk.

The woman looked at Sheila for a moment. "Yes. I do."

"What do you do, eh, Antoinette?" Sheila read the woman's name tag, which was clipped to the lapel of her white coat.

"Oh, sorry. Who are you?" Antoinette asked suspiciously.

This was interesting, but it jived with Erica's concern with secrecy. Sheila approved of that response.

"I'm Sheila Garrison, and we, my father and I, are thinking of investing in the company. I want to know if you like working here. I won't ask you to reveal details that will get you in trouble." Sheila formed what she hoped was an ingenuous expression.

Antoinette's guarded demeanor softened. "Oh, yeah. I mean, I just started a couple weeks ago, but sure. So far I love it."

"That's wonderful. I'm glad to hear it. That reassures me."

This was a tiny opinion sample, but it was still meaningful. Sheila had had enough practice in the past couple of years asking this question, and she could tell if the employee she questioned was lying. The element of surprise helped prompt a truthful response. Antoinette was looking closely at her, seeming curious and open to further conversation. She said, "I hope you've gotten a good impression of us."

Sheila laughed. "Oh my, absolutely. Your CEO is persuasive, to say the least, and she tells a compelling story."

"Oh, good. You probably know that companies like this need a lot of money to get going."

"Yes, I do. We're venture capitalists. That's our business," Sheila said, then laughed lightly.

Antoinette's eyebrows went up. "Wow. Great."

They stared at one another for a moment. Antoinette was cute and almost certainly a lesbian. She had short black hair, and under her lab coat she wore a black polo shirt and blue jeans, plus immaculate white sneakers. Then Sheila remembered she'd come in with a purpose, and she needed to get on with it before that security guard got antsy.

"Sorry. I must be going, but thanks for talking with me." Sheila ducked into a toilet stall and heard the bathroom door shut as Antoinette left. The afterimage of Antoinette stayed with her for the rest of the day, popping in and out of her mind.

❖

As Tony sat at her lab bench reviewing the protocol Abe had given her to execute, she had difficulty concentrating. She was picturing how the woman from the restroom looked—dark-red hair and sparkling, amused brown eyes, and she *looked* at Tony like she already knew everything about her. This was nuts because she rarely noticed a woman's appearance. She didn't consider herself that shallow, and she wasn't a flirt. In fact, she didn't think they'd *been* flirting. It was a pleasant, brief exchange but no more. She had work to do, and she had to get a grip.

To succeed at this research, she first had to demonstrate her proficiency at performing the tests as described. She was experienced, but Tony didn't like to take anything for granted. She wanted to be perfect.

Then she could dive into development. The vague directions she'd received from Abe were, "We're going to scale the immunoassay down, way down." He meant that they would perfect the test to work successfully on a much smaller volume. Tony was aware of the two-drop rule. Erica said that two drops of blood was all they would draw, and an unknown number of routine blood tests would be done on those two drops. A drop of fluid was approximately fifty microliters; hence, one hundred microliters would be their working volume. Since standard blood draws could go up to ten milliliters, about two teaspoons, this would be an interesting process. Tony was working on only one type of test, and doctors routinely ordered many others, depending upon what diagnoses they were considering. Hundreds, really. But Erica had been granted a patent for the Leonardo that would be able to perform these tests on the specified volume of blood sample.

"Good thing I like challenges," Tony said under her breath as she labeled the wells on her plate.

It was a simple enough assay, and Tony finished the setup and put the plate into the incubator. She had fifteen minutes to wait. At her desk, she reread the final steps: adding the enzyme and then reading the color change. Tony wondered if she'd ever see that woman from the restroom again. It wasn't likely, because it felt like a random encounter, but that was disappointing. Very disappointing. Tony's timer dinged, and she returned to her lab bench to finish her test.

❖

"The last thing I'd like to do is demonstrate how the device works," Erica said. "If you're willing, I'd like you to have your fingers pricked, and I'll have you tested for Vitamin D levels."

Sheila and Roy looked at each other, and Sheila nodded and said, "Sure. That would be great."

They'd seen the engineering department and a couple of prototypes of the Leonardo devices. An earnest engineer described how they fed blood samples into Leonardo and how precisely programmed, miniaturized robots inside it performed the same tests as humans did in laboratories, either commercial labs or hospital clinical labs. Then Leonardo returned a little printout with the numbers.

They weren't shown the interior of Leonardo, but Sheila reckoned she wouldn't know what the heck she was looking at anyhow. Erica said this was a working prototype of what they were in the process of developing.

Erica called in a technician, but she helped Roy and Sheila with their finger sticks herself and popped the microcaps in a slick-looking box that the technician whisked away, presumably downstairs to the lab or wherever the test would be run.

The three of them chatted while they waited, and twenty minutes later, the technician returned with their results. Sheila was impressed, though she didn't know what to make of her Vitamin D number.

"It's something to not have to endure that big needle stuck in my arm," she told Erica, who beamed.

"Isn't it? I don't know anyone who likes that, even if they don't faint like my sister does if she has to get her blood taken."

"What's the timeline before you can commercialize?"

"Sometime in the next eighteen months."

"I thought you said three years when we had our first meeting," Sheila said.

Erica didn't blink. "Oh, yes. I try to be conservative, but it's going to be much sooner. I've got teams of people working twelve hours a day."

"Don't mind Sheila. She likes to burrow into details," Roy said. "She's not trying to trip you up."

Sheila was mildly put off by her dad's comment, but she couldn't get into it with him. Not the time.

As he shook Erica's hand, Roy said, "You'll hear from us soon. It looks good. We have a few more inquiries to make."

In the car on their way back to the office, Sheila said, "Dad, we've talked before about you making comments about me to clients."

He was driving and didn't take his eyes off the road, but he frowned and looked abashed at the same time.

"I forgot. It wasn't important. Erica didn't mind."

"*I* mind, Dad."

"I'm sorry. I'll watch that. Don't get mad at me." Truly, sometimes Sheila felt like her dad was a little kid and she was the parent.

"Okay. I'm not mad. You think this is a go?"

This time, he turned to meet her gaze. "Yes. Don't you?"

"It looks super, but what do we really know about medical blood testing? Are those the inquiries you were going to make?"

Roy said, "Nah. I just made that up. We don't have to know everything. She said she's hired the best scientists and engineers she can find, and she trusts them. My gut says yes."

"Right. Your famous 'gut feeling.'" Sheila flashed on Antoinette. She was one of those scientists, obviously, based on her white lab coat. A nerd probably. Her slight awkwardness telegraphed that message, even if she didn't sport glasses and a bad haircut. Sheila berated herself for thinking in stereotypes. Antoinette had short, precisely cut black hair and dark, almost black eyes, a mellow voice, and a serious demeanor. Sheila generally liked the technical types, but one of her two dates had been with a software engineer, who, while attractive, had launched into a jargon-filled monologue over dinner. Nerdiness was good, up to a point. What would Antoinette be like in a social context? Sheila liked how serious she was, but at the same time, her eye contact was excellent, and her smile was genuine.

"What else do we want to know?" she asked.

"I've got all I need. What about you?" Roy grinned, seeming satisfied.

"It seems like you've made up your mind. I don't see any red flags, honestly, and even if the income projections are a little high, we'll see a monumental ROI within five years. Based on the market share they can steal away from Lab Corps and Quest Diagnostics, it'll be stratospheric."

"I know, dear. That's how I see it. Let's get together tomorrow and calculate the exact terms for our investment, send Erica a preliminary offer, and then go out for a drink."

Tony liked to be at work exactly at seven in the morning. This made for a long day since she had to catch Caltrain's bullet train by six fifteen a.m. She had no plans to move to Palo Alto, though, because finding apartments there was harder than finding them in San Francisco.

She sat at her desk and made a to-do list and read her email. She'd be ready to hit the lab in a half hour. This time of day was quiet in the cube farm because most of GHS didn't show up until later, and she liked it that way. So far, she also liked her coworkers. Abe, short for Ibrahim, her supervisor, was gentle and encouraging.

She was nearly ready to go into the lab when Abe appeared beside her.

"Hi, Tony. Good morning. Some of us are headed into town for coffee. Do you want to come?"

Tony hesitated, then decided to go. Why not? She wasn't the most gregarious person and tended to be shy around unfamiliar people, but she knew from experience that the only way to counteract that tendency was to get to know people. She'd had to learn that when she was in her twenties. Going out for coffee with her coworkers was a good idea. She bit back an automatic response of "No. I have to work."

"Okay. Sure."

They carpooled from the GHS campus into downtown Palo Alto. Tony liked the suburban vibe there, different from San Francisco's urban intensity. They arrived at Coupa Café, the "in" coffee joint of Silicon Valley, Tony was told on the ride over. Tony did like coffee, and though the brew at work was okay, better than the usual workplace fare because it was actually drinkable, she was always up for a good cup of café joe. Besides Abe, a member of the chemistry group who was working on different assays and an engineer were there. The GHS structure was odd. All the functional groups had leaders who reported to Erica. The company had no research director and very few people in middle management.

They waited in line and admired the cases of baked goods, chattering amiably. Tony had made her choice, upon the recommendation of Lara from the chemistry group, and happened to look back to the end of the ever-lengthening line. There, staring at her cell, was the woman she'd met in the upstairs bathroom last week. A shock of excitement rattled her, immediately followed by fear. She had a choice. She could do nothing but wait and see if the woman noticed her, or she could walk up to her and say hello. She turned to Lara. "I'll be right back. Save my place, please."

It didn't pay to think about this type of thing too hard because she could easily come up with reasons not to make a move. She felt as though an invisible hand were pushing her.

"Hi. Remember me?"

The woman raised her eyes, clearly startled, but as she apparently recognized Tony, she broke into a smile of pleasure. She wore another simple tailored pantsuit, black, this time, with a white shirt, and Tony swallowed, her throat tight with apprehension, though her unusual bravery thrilled her.

"My gosh, sure. You're Antoinette from GHS. We met last week, in the restroom." She laughed.

Tony decided not to correct her use of "Antoinette." Maybe later, if there *was* a later. *She remembers me. Wow.*

"Yeah. I wanted to say hello. I'm here with my coworkers." She gestured vaguely to the people farther along in line.

"Great. This is a terrific place. We have business meetings here sometimes. How's it going with your new job?

"Oh, it's going well. You know when you're new..." Now that Tony was there actually talking to the unknown woman, all her bravado drained away, and she was slipping into inarticulateness, not going to make a good impression.

"I do. I'm Sheila Garrison, by the way. I never introduced myself." She stuck out her hand and Tony took it. Her palm was smooth and dry, and Sheila didn't let go of her hand immediately, which further unnerved and pleased Tony.

"Good to meet you. Again. How is the, uh, investing?"

"Oh." Sheila laughed. Tony and her question seemed to amuse her. "It's fine. We made a preliminary offer to your boss and are talking to her later this week. I think everything will work out."

"Fabulous," Tony said, and she meant it. Then she saw that Lara was almost at the cash register.

"I have to go. Sorry."

"I understand. Perhaps I can call you sometime, or you can call me?"

Tony could only mutter, "Yeah, okay," as Sheila scribbled something on the back of a card.

"Here's my cell. Work number is fine as well. Enjoy your coffee."

"Thanks." Tony managed to make eye contact with Sheila before she turned and sprinted to the cash register just in time.

"I got you that almond croissant, right? Who was that you were talking to?" Lara asked as the group settled at a table.

"Oh. Her name's Sheila Garrison. She's a VC, and they're probably going to invest in us. I met her by accident last week up in carpet land." The technical people made a distinction between linoleum land, their domain, and the upstairs offices where the businesspeople resided: carpet land.

"Does Erica know you know her?" Gordon from engineering apparently had heard them talking and asked, with an edge to his question that Tony wondered about. Gordon was both older in age and in longevity with GHS than the others present. He was a bit gruff and standoffish, but he was kind and generous to his colleagues. Tony was surprised he'd even come along on an outing like this because he was far senior to everyone else, including Abe, who had been in his job for only six months.

"I don't *know* her. We just met for the second time. Why do you ask?"

Gordon paused, looked at Abe, and something nonverbal passed between them.

Gordon said, "Erica doesn't like for different parts of the operation to know the other parts very well. She likes to have all the information and us peons to have little or none."

"Sheila's not even part of the company. Why should it matter if we know each other?" Tony was mildly irked but intrigued. There was too much to learn when you were new to a company.

"It's probably fine. Erica is, well, eccentric, in case you haven't noticed." Gordon shrugged. Case closed.

"I don't know. Maybe she is eccentric, but that's not important." In reality, Tony was hugely enamored of Erica, though only in an intellectual sense. She was, after all, a young woman who'd started her own company. That was monumental. Gordon was likely still rather sexist. With some men, especially older ones, that attitude never seemed to go away.

Abe said, "We aren't at work, so let's talk about something else. I just saw the new *Iron Man* movie. Anyone want to know what I think?"

After a chorus of good-humored "noes," everyone laughed, and Lara said, "Go for it."

Tony had a choice, exactly the sort she hated to make. She could file Sheila's card away and forget about it or...she could call. She suspected she was being hit on, but she couldn't credit it. She wasn't the sort of girl that Sheila's sort of girl dated. Sheila was a pretty and polished business pro. They dated only their own kind, not Tony's kind—the plodding, awkward, lab-rat type. Yet here was the card with the phone numbers in her hand. Sheila had handed it to her with the admonition to call.

While Tony was no virgin, she had miniscule experience with women. She'd carried on with a few other coeds at Cal, but sex at college wasn't hard to come by. Since she'd left Cal, she'd been too involved with graduate work, studying for her license, then working long hours at the biotech start-up. GHS looked like it would be a similar situation—long work hours, intense concentration. Start-ups demanded mega amounts of time and energy. Sheila likely had leisure time to date, but Tony didn't. Still some sort of interest was there, probably friendship. That's what Tony's default pessimistic assessment said. But maybe not.

Yet, as she had been prompted at Coupa Café to walk up to Sheila, Tony called Sheila's cell and left a low-key message.

Great running into you at Coupa. Call me back when it's convenient.

Then she attempted to force her mind into work mode.

She left her phone on her desk and went to the lab, where Abe was ready to show her what he was up to.

He said, "Our objective is to scale down the assay so it works with two drops of blood, even if the blood has undergone some hemolysis and isn't super fresh. Erica's microcaps have preservatives, but she told me she wants to demonstrate the Leonardo to some investors before it is actually working so she wants to send the samples to us for testing."

"Oh. Hm. You mean like she'll take the samples and then put them in the cartridge and take them to the lab? Isn't that kind of underhanded?"

"Yeah, but don't you ever say that to anyone. Besides, it's just for show. Erica can wow all the outside people like investors. As soon as we perfect the assays and the engineers get it together, we'll be in business for real."

"Testing real patients," Tony said. She recalled how Erica's eyes had glowed as she described the parade of people coming into the drugstores.

"Righto. Okay, Tone. While we're working on this, we're the guinea pigs. Here are some lancets and some microcaps. Let's play vampire. I want your blood," he said, in a bad horror-movie accent.

Tony didn't mind Abe's shortening of her nickname, because it seemed like a sign of affection. They went to work with a number of assay kits and other reagents from different manufacturers to see what gave the best results with smaller quantities of reagents. The trial-and-error process would identify what they needed to change and by how much.

Science isn't glamorous. It's time-consuming and painstaking, and frequently an experiment doesn't work at all. But Tony didn't mind. She loved working to find a method that would yield the right result and was sure she and Abe would figure it out.

❖

Sheila watched Roy banter with Erica Sanders. She could swear he had a crush on her. She'd never seen him act like this with a client. As far as she knew, he didn't date, and hadn't since he and her mother had divorced when she was thirteen. Roy had devoted himself to taking care of her and was a wonderful father. He certainly deserved to have some romance in his life, but not with Erica, for tons of reasons.

As much as Roy teased and laughed and attempted to draw out Erica, she didn't seem interested. Her whole persona was detached, as though she lived on a different plane of existence than other humans. She came alive only when she talked about her company, her hopes for Leonardo and all the people who would be helped. All else seemed irrelevant to her, even money, unless it was for GHS. She even wore the same clothes she'd worn on the other two occasions they'd met: gray pantsuit, blue shirt.

Despite Sheila's misgivings, Roy had insisted on generous terms for the final funding agreement. Sheila had used the same framework for GHS they had for software companies with similar income projections, allowing the start-ups to exaggerate their projections to some extent. The prospective clients would show charts, which, in venture-capitalist jargon, were known as hockey-stick graphs: the company's income was expected to remain flat for three to five years and then suddenly shoot up in a nearly perpendicular angle. The goal for VCs ultimately was the "exit." Their client companies would either go public or they'd be bought, and either move would usher in a huge payout for all investors. Pacific Partners was the lead company for GHS Series 2, meaning they had the biggest stake of all the VC s who were participating: twenty-five percent. Roy had told Sheila that if all went well, she'd be awarded one percent. If Erica's projections were correct, Sheila could net well over a million dollars and could possibly receive a bonus as well.

Erica's confidence was infectious, and because of her talk of industry partnerships she'd signed, she'd received a valuation for GHS of three billion dollars. Roy had insisted to Sheila that their rate of return didn't have to be that high because GHS income would be enormous. Sheila went along finally because, essentially, Roy was her boss, and he was the final arbiter of the deal. They were going to pitch in thirty million dollars. Roy had talked it up with their partners, and they'd all agreed.

"She's a bona fide unicorn," Roy said, meaning GHS was a start-up already valued at one billion dollars or more. "This is going to be our greatest triumph."

With the GHS deal done, Sheila had more time to think about Tony and whether she'd call. She considered calling *her*, but Sheila always let romantic prospects call her, especially the intellectual types, who could be as skittish as feral cats. She'd run into a few software engineers and programming whizzes she'd been interested in, but for a variety of reasons, nothing had worked out with any of them. Tony seemed to be a bit more personable than the software people. She had, to her credit, made the move to talk to Sheila at Coupa Café.

She was in her office reading yet another prospectus for an online delivery service that the world didn't need. *Too late, you lose.* She threw the prospectus onto the "reject" pile. Her cell phone rang and showed a number she recognized as GHS, but the exchange wasn't Erica's or that of her finance director, whom Sheila had spent some time speaking with. She felt a spark of anticipation, realizing it could be Tony.

"This is Sheila." That was her customary crisp greeting.

"Hello?" The voice was tentative and low.

"Yes, hello, this is Sheila Garrison speaking. May I help you?" In spite of all her mindfulness practice, Sheila sometimes still succumbed to impatience.

"This is Tony Leung."

Sheila blanked, not recognizing the name.

"I'm sorry. Who is this?"

"You know me by Antoinette."

Sheila's spirit leaped. "Oh, yes. Antoinette. I know who you are. Is Tony your nickname?"

"Yes. That's usually what people call me. I don't want to be associated with Marie Antoinette."

"Ah, no. She wasn't a very popular queen."

"Nope."

After a longish pause when Tony didn't continue, Sheila asked, "How are you doing?"

"Oh, fine. Thanks. You?"

The conversation was quickly deteriorating, so Sheila decided to take over.

"I'm outstanding. Since you called, and I'm glad you did, why don't we do lunch sometime soon?"

"Yes. I was wondering if you wanted to get together," Tony said in a relieved tone. Sheila avoided laughing. That was why she'd given Tony her phone number.

"What about next week? I'm fine with Thursday."

"Sure. Thursday's good. You'll have to pick me up. I don't have a car. I take the train to work."

"No problem. What time?"

"Is noon okay?"

Sheila wanted to laugh again, but she simply said, "Right. I'll pick you up, and I'll choose the restaurant. Not Coupa Café. That's crazy-busy, and I don't want to see anyone I know."

"Why not?" Tony sounded alarmed.

"Oh, because I want us to have a calm, quiet lunch."

"Oh. Okay. I'll meet you out front, so you don't have to go through the whole security thing."

Hm. That fit with what Sheila knew about GHS and Erica's security concerns. She didn't want to have to sign another NDA just to go to lunch with Tony. Would Erica find something objectionable about *that*? It didn't matter, because it wouldn't deter Sheila. Once she was set on a path, nothing would stop her.

"Bye-bye. See you next week." Sheila keyed her phone off and smiled before she returned to her prospectus reviews.

CHAPTER THREE

To Tony's surprise, Sheila arrived to pick her up in a metallic-blue Volt. A Mercedes or BMW would have been more likely, given her profession.

Sheila drove well, navigating downtown Palo Alto's crowded streets calmly. She announced where they were going, then fell silent as she drove. But the absence of conversation didn't feel uncomfortable to Tony. It seemed normal.

Once they were seated at a table in Trefoil, an unpretentious place on Santa Clara Street, Tony took a closer look at Sheila. She was better looking than Tony had first thought. Her hair was precisely cut and somewhere between bronze and red, her eyes dark brown. Most striking was her air of serenity. Tony couldn't find any other way to put it. If she felt nervous about their meeting, she didn't show it. Sheila didn't fidget or have any other anxiety tells, like not making eye contact or playing with her hair. In contrast, Tony's psyche was permeated with social unease, but she'd worked hard over the years to hide it. She didn't think Sheila was hiding anything. She was as she appeared. After they were seated, Sheila put her menu aside and looked closely at Tony. "You don't like being called Antoinette?" she asked. "Other than the association you mentioned?"

Tony had a canned answer. "It's too pretentious and too long." Too girly as well, but she rarely said that. It was her mother's idea, and she objected to her mother's ideas on principle. Always.

"Yeah. The let-them-eat-cake and all."

Before she could stop herself, Tony said, "Cake isn't what cake means to us. Back in the eighteenth century, it meant the scum left on the pans they baked the bread in. Marie Antoinette said if the peasants didn't have bread, they could eat the scum from the bread-baking pans. Nice, huh?"

"Nasty. No wonder you don't want her name." Sheila appeared unfazed by Tony's pedantic digression.

"Nope. I like your name though. Is it Irish?"

"It sure is. Means heavenly." Sheila snorted.

"Oh, that's nice." Tony was horrified she'd used such a cliché, but it was too late. Sheila sipped her lemonade and smiled benignly.

They gave their orders to the waiter and then returned their attention to one another. Tony was almost beginning to relax, as though Sheila's calm was contagious. She'd certainly moved from nervous to neutral anyhow.

"What's it really like working at GHS?" Sheila asked.

Something about Sheila and the way she asked that question made Tony think she wanted to know for real and wasn't simply making conversation or satisfying a getting-to-know-you curiosity. Sheila didn't seem like a woman who asked trivial questions anyway.

"It's exciting, it's hard, it's sometimes confusing. And it's certainly challenging." Tony wasn't surprised when Sheila said, "Tell me more."

She wondered how forthcoming she ought to be. She had no idea if Sheila had a personal relationship with Erica—if it went beyond the investor-client connection. Tony didn't want what she said to Sheila to get back to Erica, whether it was positive or negative. In the few weeks since she started, she'd noticed Erica was clearly everyone's number-one topic. Even Abe, who was as mild and noncommittal as anyone, had an opinion, and it was clear that their CEO awed and frightened him. To answer Sheila's question, though, Tony concluded she ought to stick to her own experience and to spin it positively, which it was. Mostly.

"Oh, with a start-up, as you probably know, it can be chaotic. We're—the immunoassay group, I mean—are working on essentially miniaturizing the assay."

"What do you mean, immunoassay? You realize I'm ignorant when it comes to labs, though I can comprehend software as well as any non-tech person."

"Oh, yeah. Well, say you want to know if a person has a certain disease. Their blood will have certain molecules—proteins—and the immunoassay is designed that a reagent—an antibody to that protein—will react by binding to it. The reagent has another chemical attached—a fluorescent or light-producing chemical—which is measured by an instrument that detects that light. This can be done with radiation as well, but we prefer fluorescence. The amount of light measures the amount of the protein of interest in the person's blood, and that amount says whether the person is sick or not."

"Oh. Very clear. Thank you." Sheila beamed.

Tony changed the subject. "How did you ever end up being a venture capitalist?"

Sheila sketched her background for Tony. She was still a bit embarrassed that she worked for her father, though, in her heart, she didn't believe anything was wrong with it. Fathers had been bringing sons into their businesses since the beginning of time. She just had to be competent, and she was.

When she finished, Tony's expression was awed, but surprisingly she said, "You get to work with your dad? That is so cool."

Sheila blushed slightly, but Tony's reaction pleased her.

Tony added, "It would be super if I could work with mine. We aren't in the same type of work, though. But he's totally behind what I do. Your dad must really be happy to have you around."

"Oh, yes. He is, and it's great. He made me work my way up, however. He doesn't believe anyone shouldn't earn what they receive."

Tony grew somber. "Oh, that's the best way, I would think. What's your daily work life like?"

Sheila laughed. "You'd be surprised just how boring it is. I mostly go to back-to-back pitch meetings. One right after the other. It's extremely exhausting. I sometimes want to say, 'Yeah, okay, you can have the money, please. Just. stop. talking.' I have to struggle to stay focused. I either want to say yes to everyone—I have what my dad calls 'happy ears,' or if I'm out of sorts, I want them all to shut the fuck up."

It was Tony's turn to laugh. That description, along with the curse word, brought Sheila down from the pedestal Tony was dangerously close to putting her on. She was a mere human who sometimes was bored or frustrated or inattentive and was certainly irreverent. Along with her obvious love and admiration for her father, which was very like Tony's own, she now seemed more ordinary and at the same time infinitely more attractive than the more rarefied, yet superficial portrait of her that Tony's psyche had painted.

They moved on to more general topics, such has music and movies.

After they finished their entrées, they perused the dessert menus.

"I think this occasion warrants dessert, don't you?" Sheila asked, archly.

"I agree." Tony matched Sheila's tone. "If we can share."

"Of course. That seems like a good idea." Tony couldn't tell if Sheila was making fun of her or flirting.

When they received their strawberry ganache and its two forks, Sheila said, "I read about all the tests the GHS is offering. They want to use Erica's invention to do the tests. Is that what you're using?"

The intimate act of sharing a piece of cake, or so it seemed to Tony, was causing her to want to be open with Sheila. Or maybe it was the glass and a half of wine she'd drunk.

"Uh, no. We have to first make sure our immunoassay will work with super-tiny blood samples. *Then* the engineering group will design all the robotics and the servomechanisms to mimic what we do at the bench."

"Really? Erica gave me the impression that was already done, and you were perfecting it," Sheila said quietly, in an even tone, but Tony froze.

"Eh. We—my group—is. I think the engineers might have a prototype Leonardo that does a couple of tests. I honestly don't know for sure."

"Well, I'm certainly familiar with CEOs making extravagant promises about their products. I always try to listen to their pitches with a certain amount of skepticism," Sheila said. "I don't expect you to blab about all the technical details. I'm sure Erica wouldn't approve."

"Nope. She likes to keep discussion of details to a minimum. She focuses on the big picture." She was notably closed-mouthed with her own employees, who were then, in turn, oddly reticent with each other. It was unlike any other place Tony had worked. The typical biotech company environment was rife with gossip, speculation, all kinds of talk. But people had to work across groups and develop approaches that included everyone's input, and that wasn't done at GHS.

"Erica is always telling us we're going to change the world," Tony said, thinking that was a positive thing to say.

"She's told me the same thing," Sheila said and laughed. "I imagine that's what she says to everyone. When she talked about how Leonardo will revolutionize medical testing, I believed her."

"That's exactly why I wanted to work at GHS. I want to be part of that revolution."

"That's wonderful. Well. Here's to changing the world." Sheila fixed her gaze on Tony, who grinned back.

In her minimally decorated living room, Sheila knelt before her altar and lit a candle and a stick of light incense. She mirrored the beatific smile of the Buddha back to her statue of him. He was center stage on the altar, surrounded by the candle, a large quartz crystal, the incense stand, and the singing bowl. Sheila touched her Buddha and then her statue of Qin Yin, the goddess of wisdom and compassion. She rang the bowl three times. She routinely followed these steps to prepare herself for meditation.

She thought of Tony and what she wished for her and for them together, if that might be their fate. It was too soon to know. That Sheila was attracted to Tony's essence, to herself, was clear. She wanted to know all the answers to her questions immediately, but that wasn't the Buddhist way. She was taught to wait and be open, to be quiet and ready to receive. Her meditation practice helped her be patient, which wasn't her natural inclination.

Sheila took off her shoes, tucked her legs under her on the cushion, and, in the standard lotus pose, opened her palms upon her knees and breathed evenly. She sounded the singing bowl three times. She let the image of Tony's face fill her inner eye, then banished it. She set her timer for thirty minutes and began.

Her first meditation teacher had taught her to count to clear her mind. As long as she was counting, the unwanted thoughts came and went, if they came at all. She concentrated on her breathing and counting. The timer chimed gently, and Sheila opened her eyes. She was peaceful, her mind cleansed. She slept that night as she usually did, deeply, and woke the next morning full of gratitude.

"I have some news," Roy said a few weeks later. He stood at Sheila's doorway, leaning against the frame and looking as though he were about to burst.

"Well, come in, sit down, and tell me about it." Sheila thought again how young her father seemed. It was a good thing, she supposed, in balance. She didn't want him to be old before his time. His enthusiasm could shoot off in all sorts of directions, just like a teenager's. It was endearing, if exhausting. What now? What had captured his attention?

He folded himself into one of the armchairs facing Sheila's desk and crossed his leg, his foot bouncing up and down. He smirked for what seemed an overly long interval.

"What?" Sheila asked. "Don't keep me in suspense."

"Erica asked me to join the GHS board of directors. She's had a recent resignation."

"Why did she pick you?" Sheila was truly curious. Roy wasn't an obvious choice, other than he was a long-time Silicon Valley personage and knew a lot about the investment business. Just not a lot about GHS's business.

"Why not?" He appeared stung that Sheila would question this choice. She didn't mean it as a negative. Why was he being defensive?

"I didn't mean anything bad, Pops. I'm only curious. Did she say?"

"Nope. Only that she thought I'd be a good fit. That's flattering, considering the other members. Those guys are really solid. All of them. I'm in good company."

Roy was excited, and Sheila kept her thoughts to herself. Yes, the GHS board was solid all right—a solid slate of rich old white guys, all of them likely gaga over Erica and her shiny black hair and practiced sales spiel. Sheila didn't like to be cynical, but she was realistic. Buddhist practice thoroughly encouraged one to keep one's eyes open and assess the truth of people's words and then their actions.

It wasn't that Sheila disbelieved Erica. If she had, she wouldn't have recommended that they fund her. She only sensed an air of manipulation in the way she populated her company's board. Let's face it. An attractive young woman would be like catnip to men of a certain age. They might say, and it would be true, that Erica was intelligent and altruistic, and they were sure her company would be successful. But that didn't negate the almost-primal, unspoken sexual vibe she gave off that drew them in every bit as much as her abilities as a start-up CEO.

"Well, congratulations on your appointment. I'm sure it will be an…experience." Sheila stood up and hugged her dad. His momentary air of pique subsided, and he hugged her back.

"You're the best, little girl. You know it, right?" He didn't often say that to her after she'd turned twenty-one, but it was one of his old endearments, and it melted her.

"You're the best too, Daddy-o," she said.

He gave her the thumbs-up and exited her office, still grinning.

Sheila opened her calendar and looked up the date of her lunch with Tony. It had been exactly two weeks. She'd heard nothing from Tony since, and that bothered her. She wanted to know if Tony had ended that day feeling as optimistic and exhilarated as she had, but she didn't want to be pushy with someone who appeared to be reticent. On the other hand, if she didn't make a move, who would? She vacillated between email or phone call. Sheila liked email for its efficiency and clarity, but some situations called for phone contact. She called Tony and left a low-key message. *She'll know I'm interested if I bother to call.*

❖

Tony listened to Sheila's voice mail with a mixture of delight and alarm. She'd assumed their lunch was either a one-time or a friendly thing, not a date. She didn't want to get in touch with Sheila because she thought she'd come off as nerdy and awkward and unattractive. Sheila was impossibly smooth and sophisticated, and their proximity and interaction during lunch had merely highlighted the contrast between them. Lunch, Tony concluded, had been a dead end. But here was Sheila calling her—friendly and noncommittal, but still calling. What did it mean?

When it came to possibly romantic situations, Tony considered herself as abysmally nonromantic as anyone could be. She had been with women in college, but they weren't hard to snag. Then came grad school and then her first job and her second job, and Tony homed in on study and then on work. Her college hookups seemed insignificant, and she was uninterested to replicating those scenarios by going to bars and trying to meet women. She had ignored her loneliness and told herself she didn't have time to date. Truthfully, it had seemed intimidating and exhausting.

Tony replayed the voice mail and listened closely. Sheila's voice was marvelous. Low-pitched, not sexy per se, but not brisk or businesslike either, it was smooth and easy-going. She asked after Tony's health in a generic way and reiterated her enjoyment of their lunch date. She'd said the same thing when she dropped Tony off at GHS campus. This phone call appeared to be an invitation to call her that Sheila didn't express explicitly.

Tony's lab timer went off, interrupting her thought flow and making her jump. She slammed the "off" button in irritation, then high-tailed it down the hall to the laboratory. Timing was crucial. Incubation couldn't be overlong, or it would screw with the result. *Anything* could screw with the results, which was both the problem and the beauty of lab testing. With her coat on and her concentration focused, Tony stopped the reaction in her ninety-six well plates with a multichannel pipettor that allowed her to shoot the quenching reagent into all of the plate's wells in twelve swift movements. As always, she hoped the little tweaks to the reagent volumes would finally, at last, yield the right outcome. Abe would want to hear from her as soon as it was done. She threw the plate into the reader and waited anxiously for the results. She'd have to return to her conundrum with Sheila later.

Later turned out to be on the train ride home at seven thirty that night. Abe had had her repeat the assay with a new twist so he would have something to say first thing in the morning, after he met with Erica. Tony wasn't invited to Abe's meetings with Erica, and she wasn't certain if that was a good or a bad thing. It would make her feel more important if she was asked to sit in, but then again, sometimes Abe came back to the lab after a meeting with Erica looking a bit shell-shocked. From what little he shared with her, Tony knew he was under intense pressure. Time was not their friend, he said. This wasn't an unfamiliar situation for Tony. Abe told her all the functional assay groups were under orders to get their protocols perfected so engineering could design the robotics. He was too polite to speak negatively about Erica, but Tony inferred from the directions Abe gave her that Erica wanted better and faster from them. This was predictable: higher-ups didn't understand how long it took to troubleshoot and perfect assays. There weren't any shortcuts. An assay development took as long as it took, and that was always longer than you wanted it to.

Sheila. Tony wanted to *not* be ambivalent about Sheila. She'd wanted to talk to her the morning they met at Coupa Café, though she wasn't entirely clear why. She never walked up to someone. She was a strictly "I'll talk to you if you talk to me first" kind of girl. Sure, Sheila was attractive in an objective way. Her dark-red hair, her clear, pale complexion, her easy conversation were appealing. It was gratifying that Sheila had asked her to go out to lunch and Tony had agreed without quite knowing how it happened. It all seemed to fall under the category of too good to be true. Tony's self-esteem needed some work for sure.

Tony tapped the phone message, and Sheila picked up on the second ring.

"Hi there." Sheila's voice came through the phone bright and eager. "I'm thrilled you called me back."

"I wanted to," Tony said, and cut herself off before she could say "because it was the polite thing to do."

"I was wondering if you wanted to see more of Palo Alto, other than the Research Park area and the streets between GHS and Cal Train station." At lunch, Tony had mentioned her lack of familiarity with anything in Palo Alto but her company's campus and that one visit to Coupa Café. That Sheila had remembered her saying that blew Tony away. If nothing else, Sheila's attention to detail was admirable, and her attention in general was hugely flattering.

Tony's idea of what businesspeople were like was undergoing revision. She assumed someone like Sheila would be, if not exactly cold, then not super touchy-feely in an emotional way. Also, without any basis for her opinion, she envisioned Sheila as sexually assertive. While Sheila wasn't effusive or overtly sexual, she was amiable and projected an air of kindness and generosity, which was sexy without being sexy. Tony shivered and forced her attention back to what Sheila had just asked her.

"Oh. Yeah, sure. I guess so." Not a very enthusiastic response, but Tony was off balance again.

"Great. How do you feel about bike riding? Palo Alto is as flat as a pancake, so it's not hard to bike. We can take it easy."

Tony wasn't adept at bicycle riding, though she'd done a few rides in San Francisco in Golden Gate Park. She didn't want to expose her lack of experience to Sheila but...

"I don't have a bike."

"We'll rent you one, no sweat. Then we'll have lunch at the end, I promise."

"Um." Tony was annoyed at her wishy-washiness. She needed to stop being such a wimp. This was how people dated. It wasn't complicated like science was complicated.

"Come on. It'll be fun. I swear."

"Okay. Sure."

"Terrific. Next Saturday. Can you handle nine in the morning?"

Tony thought swiftly. She'd have to catch an eight am train, but it was doable.

"Yep. That's fine."

"Great. Text me about twenty minutes before the train will arrive, and I'll pick you up at the transit depot."

"Okay. Will do. Well. Bye."

"See ya soon."

Tony held her phone in her hand, more elated than nervous, but nervous was still there. *Grow up.* Sheila liked her and wanted to spend time with her. There was no downside to this and a considerable number of upsides.

❖

Before she could enjoy her date with Sheila, however, Tony was due to have Friday-night dinner with her dad.

She walked up the stairs to her family home, a modest brick house in the Richmond district, on a numbered street midway between Golden Gate Park and the Presidio.

She walked in the front door, shouting "Hello." Her dad came downstairs and hugged her.

"Hi, honey. I'm happy to see you."

"It's good to see you too, Dad."

He brewed tea for them. Tony had become a coffee person over the years, save for visits with her dad.

"How's work?" he asked.

"Oh, good, busy. Erica always wants results yesterday. How about you?"

"Still the same. Fine." He never said anything different. He was a mid-level mechanical engineer in a huge construction company.

Tony wasn't sure if Joe would admit it if things *weren't* fine. Joe would never say anything negative about anything. It wasn't his nature, which was part of the reason for their screwed-up family. He detested conflict and refused to participate in it ever. Period. Tony wanted him to have shut down his family passive-aggressively insulting her mom and her mom always saying critical things about Tony. But he'd done neither.

"I've met someone," Tony said abruptly. "She's in one of the companies that invested in GHS. She's a VC."

Joe raised his eyebrows. "Oh, really? How did that happen?"

Tony told him the story, and he listened without comment, as he usually did. He was a terrific listener, but he didn't often offer fatherly feedback. Tony loved that he was nonjudgmental about everything, including her, but still she sometimes wished he'd express an opinion or two.

He nodded with a vague smile. Tony waited, but she couldn't contain herself any longer.

"She comes from money, I think. But she's not, like, obvious about it." Tony hoped that would be a mark in Sheila's favor. His expression didn't change, and he didn't speak.

"Come on, Dad. Say something."

He took a sip from his teacup and looked at the ceiling. "What if the company doesn't work out? What happens then?"

"Dad, that's not going to happen. Why would you even think that?" This wasn't at all the response she'd expected.

"Well. Sometimes things don't. I read all the time about start-ups that go under. If she loses money on the deal, that could cause problems for the two of you, honey."

"We've just barely started dating. Sheesh. I really like her though. I can't imagine anything could go wrong." Thanks to her dad, though, Tony was suddenly apprehensive. She was taken aback that when Joe finally offered an opinion, it was negative.

"Besides, things are going fine," she said. "Venture-capital people take calculated risks. That's what they do. Sheila told me they believe they can make a lot of money."

"Just because they believe something doesn't make it true," Joe said and stood up. "I'm going to start dinner." At dinner, they stuck to small talk about the neighborhood and their family.

When Tony took the bus home, though, she had something new to worry about: her father's somewhat cryptic warning about Sheila and GHS.

❖

"We want a twenty-one speed," Sheila informed the clerk at the bicycle store firmly. "Peugeot or Specialized. And *not* a girl's bike."

When the man left to go look for a bicycle to meet Sheila's specifications, she turned to Tony and grinned. "I don't know why bike manufacturers persist with this nonsense of making men's and women's bikes, but they do. Even though no woman has ridden a bike in a skirt for a hundred years."

Tony, almost paralyzed with nerves both from being on a date with Sheila and anticipating this bike ride, could only nod and try to look cool.

It was another few minutes while Sheila supervised the adjustment of the bike seat to Tony's height. Tony, who was self-conscious about her short legs, found the attention excruciating, but watching Sheila in action directing the bike-store clerk was fun. Sheila's bicycle shorts revealed muscular thighs and calves. Tony was wearing a basic pair of shorts, which was all she had. She wasn't going to invest in any fancy equipment until she was sure she liked this new pastime and that she and Sheila were embarked upon a relationship and that it would be a regular thing. All of this was purely speculation.

At last they were ready. Sheila had insisted on paying for everything, including a new water bottle. Tony made a mild protest at the beginning but gave in as Sheila pointed out this was all her idea and for Tony to please allow her. Her certainty was sure sexy, and Tony suspected that control was her natural mode. Sheila was so unfailingly pleasant that her assertiveness wasn't hard to take, and Tony wasn't disposed to put up a fight anyhow. She had other things to worry about, such as keeping up with Sheila once they set off on their ride.

"Do you mind going to the Stanford campus? We can warm up a bit riding on the flats before we try a little hill climb up to the Dish. Then I want to show you the El Palo Alto."

Tony winced at the word hill, but she didn't want to admit any misgivings. At least not yet.

It turned out to not be too difficult once they got going. Unlike San Francisco's intimidating hills, Palo Alto's flat, wide streets let Tony get into a pedaling rhythm as she followed Sheila. The view from behind was quite nice. As promised, she set a moderate pace, and Tony began to relax and actually enjoy herself.

They stopped at a traffic light and pulled off to the side to drink water. The day was warming up, though it wasn't unpleasantly hot and wouldn't be, Sheila promised.

"I always check the weather before a ride. The climb up to the Dish is short."

Tony admired how Sheila's cheeks turned pink from exertion.

They rode to the entrance of the Dish.

"We can't go in, unfortunately. The trails don't allow bicycles. Only hiking."

"What is this thing?" Tony asked. "I can see it from GHS and always wondered what it was."

"It's a radio telescope. It tracks satellites. I don't actually know that much about it."

"How far have we ridden?" Tony asked.

"Oh, around three miles."

"Three miles!" Tony was astounded. She was mildly out of breath but not nearly as exhausted as she'd thought she'd be.

"Oh, sure. Bicycles are the most efficient form of transportation on the planet." Sheila grinned and took another pull on her water bottle. "Ready?"

They took off, and then they were at the El Palo Alto Park looking up at an immense redwood tree.

"What do you think?" Sheila asked brightly.

"I love it. I can't see the top of the tree," Tony said, and she meant it. More than anything else, she essentially liked how happy this outing seemed to make Sheila.

"How are you feeling? This wasn't too much for you, is it? We'll have to ride back downtown, of course."

"Oh, no. I'm good. I'm sweaty and might be sore tomorrow, but…"

Sheila put a smooth palm against Tony's back under her tee shirt, which had come untucked, rested it there for a moment, and then withdrew it.

"Yep. You're warm," Sheila said matter-of-factly, her face still. But Sheila's touch gave Tony a huge rush of arousal that came and went so quickly she barely had time to register it, but it was unmistakable.

"A bit, but I'm okay." Tony managed to keep her voice even. Their eyes met briefly.

At the restaurant Sheila chose, they ordered some cold drinks.

"Well, what did you think?" Sheila asked.

"About what?"

"About the bike ride, silly. What did you think I meant?" Sheila's dark eyes glittered in amusement.

"Nothing. I liked it very much."

"You had no trouble keeping up."

"Nope. Surprisingly enough."

"Next time, we'll try riding a little farther." Sheila paused and sipped her iced coffee. "How's our investment doing?"

"Our what?" Tony was confused.

Sheila laughed. "GHS. That place where you work. You know, the one I just sunk thirty million into a couple weeks ago."

Tony loved the way Sheila could just toss of that unbelievable figure so casually, but maybe her question wasn't as casual as it seemed.

"Okay, I guess. My perspective is pretty narrow. You ought to ask Erica."

"I will. I'm meeting with her next week, but I want to know what *you* think."

Tony sat back, drinking her tea as she bought herself some time to think. She was wondering about her NDA and how that applied to this situation. This was someone who had a genuine interest and was connected to GHS, even if she wasn't exactly part of it.

"Well. We're making progress with the immunoassay. I think we finally found the right balance with the reagents so we have accurate results on the small sample size."

"Excellent." Sheila beamed. "I think I get what you're talking about, but, mostly, if you're pleased, then I'm pleased."

"Quite a few other types of tests are in development, and I don't have anything to do with those. Also, there's Leonardo, and I don't know how that's going. I only know my tiny corner of the big picture."

"I understand. I'll hear the full story from Erica. You ready to go back to the bike store?"

"Yeah. Let's go."

After they returned the rental bike, Sheila drove Tony back to the transit center, and they sat in the car talking until it was time for Tony's train back to San Francisco.

"I hope you know how much I like you," Sheila said, her voice pitched low and gentle.

"Yes. I like you too." Tony's words sounded strangled. She thought she knew what was about to happen, and she equally wanted and feared it.

"Good then. Well, we ought to have lunch again soon."

"Yes. I'd like that."

Sheila looked at her, her expression a question mark.

Oh. She wants me to pick a time. Tony made a show of looking at her phone calendar. "Any day that works for you. I have to be cognizant of what I plan to do in the lab and schedule my lunch around it."

It was more that she had to structure her day around a lunch break that wouldn't disrupt any assays.

Sheila had pulled out her phone and was scrutinizing it as well. She looked up and directly at Tony.

"I see. How about Wednesday?" Sheila asked as she typed. "I'm free at noon and nothing till two."

"Sure. I'll plan on that." Tony was happy her voice wasn't shaking.

"I look forward to it," Sheila said as she put away her phone.

"Me too. My train leaves in a few minutes. I better go."

"Yes. I suppose you should. I had a great time. I'll see you Wednesday." With that, Sheila leaned toward her and kissed her gently on the mouth. Again, like Sheila's hand on her back during their bike ride, it was over so fast, Tony was unable to react, but she was frozen in place.

Sheila leaned back and grinned. "Don't miss your train."

"No. Thanks. Bye." Tony scrambled out of the car and forced herself to walk away slowly.

CHAPTER FOUR

It was both good and bad that the train ride between Palo Alto and San Francisco took an hour. Tony often used the time to think about work and whatever her current plans were. She could be on her phone, reading news or playing some stupid game to pass the time, and she did those things some of the time, but she'd read that people needed to take breaks from electronics, and she forced herself to stay off her phone for at least half of her commute, if not longer.

On this train ride, she wasn't even tempted to start a game of Angry Birds. She sat, gazing out the window, her mind filled with Sheila. Sheila cycling ahead of her during their bike ride, Sheila gesturing at the redwood tree, ordering coffee. Sheila sitting in the driver's seat of her electric car, smiling confidently.

It was time to accept that this extraordinary woman was interested in her. Tony wanted to deny it, push it away and ignore it, but that wasn't possible. It was real, and it was amazing and transcendent and exhilarating. Tony just hoped she'd be up to what she considered the challenge of forging a serious romantic connection with Sheila. She still wasn't positive that was what Sheila was after, but there was a good chance it was.

She'd never been in a relationship where she'd have to be honest and talk about her feelings and be vulnerable. It wasn't that she didn't *want* one, but she wasn't sure she was capable of being in a serious romantic partnership, if that was what this was turning into. She hoped it was, but things weren't clear. This could be something much less consequential, which would be okay, she supposed, but to her astonishment, she wanted it to be way more than merely a friendly hookup.

Tony had no idea what was going to happen and no way to predict how she'd behave or react to anything. For the first time in her life, she decided, she was going to have to be okay with that type of uncertainty and try not to overthink things too much. *Right.* She was the queen of overthinking.

Sheila hoped she hadn't scared Tony too much. The girl was like a shy forest critter who might bolt at any moment, even though she took such pains to appear otherwise, and that, in itself, was attractive. Sheila wasn't unused to taking charge. She enjoyed it, but she worried that she came off as over-confident. It wasn't as much cockiness but that she was comfortable with whatever transpired. That was the Buddhist way.

She figured a fast, not overly sexual kiss was the way to go the first time. Better kisses would come once Tony had settled down somewhat, and it looked like she would in time. If she was going to split, she would, Sheila reasoned. She'd say "no" to lunch and to anything else. Tony surely wasn't someone who would go along simply because it was another person's idea.

Before lunch with Tony, however, was a meeting with Erica. Roy had his own thing with the board, but Sheila wanted to be more involved in guiding Erica's decisions. In her experience, the young CEOs she worked with might initially resist her counsel, but they came around in time. The goal, after all, was to succeed and make money for everyone. The company founders with sense realized that Sheila, even at her relatively young age, had seen a lot and knew what would work and what wouldn't and had their best interests in mind, as well as her own. She struck a delicate balance between being too hands-on and not hands-on enough. It was all in the manner one employed when dispensing advice. Sheila liked to use examples of other companies and frame her advice as experiential or as "best practice." She tried to not be authoritarian, which tended to not work anyhow. People would just tune out.

Erica was late again, which could be a pattern. Once having secured monetary help, some people used time as a power play, as a way to assert their egos. *Your time is not as important as my time.* Requesting that Erica show up at her office could be interpreted as a power move, but Sheila was ready to address that possibility up front.

The assistant buzzed that Erica had arrived. *Okay. Twenty minutes is right on the edge of unacceptable.*

Sheila stood up, moved from behind her desk, and opened the door to her assistant Lily's polite knock.

"Erica. Good to see you. You want a coffee or tea or—?"

"Nothing. Thanks." Erica looked unfrazzled, but her clipped tone indicated she wasn't happy with being summoned.

"Very good. Thank you, Lily. Please have a seat." She indicated the couch at right angles to her desk. She took an armchair, leaving the coffee table between them.

"I'm grateful you were willing to come over here to meet," Sheila said. "Normally, I would come to you, but I understand your concerns with security and wanted to be sensitive."

"Thank you for your concern, but I'm perfectly fine with meeting you at Global. My office is secure enough."

Ah-hah. That was clear. Erica wished to maintain control subtly by setting their meeting on her turf.

"Why did you want to meet today?" Erica asked.

Sheila heard the low-level pique in Erica's tone, but she was savvy enough to not be openly hostile.

"I wanted to discuss with you the variety of assistance Pacific Partners can offer you now that we are officially in business."

Erica didn't respond and crossed her legs and her arms. *Uh-oh.* Defensive posture. Sheila had become adept at reading body language. It revealed a lot. Because of her Buddhist training, Sheila was irked but able to remain calm and non-confrontational.

She clasped her hands on her knee and took a short breath. "We like to ensure we do everything possible to help our partners achieve success. PP tends to invest in companies who are entering periods of growth. That can be challenging, as you will need more staff, possible website building, and other marketing tools. We have in-house consultants for all of those areas and can put them in play for your benefit."

Erica's expression didn't change from the superficially neutral one she wore. "I appreciate your offer, but we're fine."

She was polite enough, but it was a curious response. Why reject an offer of free help? In Sheila's experience, young companies welcomed the sort of structural help that they needn't pay for.

"If you're concerned about confidentiality, they'll work with that."

"No. I've got all the people necessary at the moment. If I need anyone else, though, I'll be sure to call you. Thanks for the offer."

"Certainly. It's always there." Of course, Sheila wouldn't tell her that the consultants she deployed often accrued some fascinating inside information. Employees, even discreet ones, would often let information slip. Erica could possibly know this already, or she could truly be well supplied with consultants already, or she merely didn't want anyone around her company who wasn't under her thumb.

"Is there anything else?" Erica asked. "If not, I'm busy, as you might imagine."

"No. Nothing else. I appreciate you taking the time to make the trek over from Paly." Pacific Partners' office was located in Menlo Park, the next town over from Palo Alto and the home of most of the VC firms in the Valley. There were others in San Francisco, but the VC companies tended to cluster close to where the action was, i.e. Silicon Valley and mostly in Research Park. Again, the idea that proximity to success would breed success was a sort of goofy idea, but who really knew?

They shook hands cordially enough, and Erica left. Sheila sat thinking about that encounter and decided that results over the next few months would tell the story. She would, of course, get reports on board meetings from Roy. Tony might tell her what she knew, but Tony was privy only to a tiny slice of the GHS business. Sheila liked lots of information. It was as crucial as money, perhaps more so.

Sheila switched her thinking of Erica off and onto lunch with Tony. That was more pleasurable than speculating about Erica and her somewhat pathological secrecy. Sheila was willing to let Erica's refusal of help go and see how matters progressed. That was how Buddhism counseled her to proceed, and this approach hadn't failed her yet. She was able to tell when to jump into some situations and when to sit back and wait.

❖

"You're leaving?" Tony asked Abe, stunned. "Why?"

"I got a better offer," he said, but he wouldn't look at her. That was a bad sign. "I couldn't pass it up."

"Where?"

"UC Santa Cruz. I decided to go back to academia. I'll get my own lab, teach undergrads, do a little research on the side."

"They pay more than GHS?" This didn't seem plausible.

"Nope. But it's closer to home and less stress." He was older than she, and Tony could sort of understand where he was coming from, but he wasn't *that* much older, and he'd seemed as gung-ho about the project as she was.

"What about your stock options?" This was a prime topic of conversation among the GHS staff. It was their incentive, aside from altruism and intellectual challenge, for working as hard as they did. If the company succeeded and went public or was sold, they would reap the benefits immediately, or they could hang on and exercise their options in the future for more money.

"What about them? I have to surrender them. I'm not vested yet."

"You do? That sucks."

Abe shrugged. "Can't be helped. You know, Tony, honestly, I shouldn't tell you this, but you deserve to know. Erica invited me to resign or she was going to fire me."

"What? Why?"

"She doesn't think I'm working hard enough or getting the results she wants or getting them fast enough. She's a major slave driver. I guess because she drives herself hard, she thinks the rest of us are superhuman too."

"Doesn't she know research like this takes a long time? Did you tell her?"

"I tried to, but she didn't want to hear it. She said the other functional assay groups are farther along, though I'm not sure I believe that. I don't see that they can work any faster than we can. She told me the engineering group needs a bunch of assays so they can work up a new prototype Leonardo device that she can use demonstrate to investors and other people when she makes sales pitches. I said I thought one assay would be enough for testing the Leonardo, and she looked at me like I was spouting heresy."

"Yikes." This was troubling news. It meant Erica wasn't being realistic about her expectations. Tony thought she and Abe were proceeding at a proper pace, maybe a little bit slow, but it was difficult and painstaking to modify established clinical assays to conform to Erica's requirements for two drops of blood. Surely, she understood that fact, but maybe she didn't. She was not, as Tony had heard, an actual trained science type. She'd dropped out of Stanford to found her company when she was a junior. She hadn't finished her degree. The talk was she wanted to fast-track her entrepreneurial dreams. Neither Steve Jobs nor Bill Gates was a college grad, so evidently Erica figured it wasn't a requirement.

"Well, best wishes to you, and good luck." She hugged him.

"Thanks. You too. You're going to need it."

Instead of going over to her dad's house on Friday, she called him. She was still at work at six in the evening. That meant she wouldn't be back to the City until after seven, and she wouldn't make it out to her family house in the Richmond District until almost eight.

"I'm working late because I'm trying to finish what my boss left for me and give the results to Erica. You know, the CEO I told you about is waiting for results."

"Okay. Well. You have to get those results to her." Tony knew he was disappointed, but he understood and approved her need to work hard.

❖

With one thing or another, Tony and Sheila weren't able to see each other until another three weeks had elapsed. This third date turned into another trip to the Stanford campus, again via bicycle. Because Stanford was Sheila's alma mater, Sheila wanted to take her on a tour. Tony didn't mind Sheila taking charge of the planning. It was restful for her to not have to think.

Tony said, "I have this image of Stanford and its students as nerds—Republican nerds."

Sheila laughed. "Well, you'll find enough of those types around, but you must be thinking of Herbert Hoover and the Hoover Institution. When I think of Berkeley, I think of protest. Surely, though, the Berkeley students do more studying than protesting?"

"We call it Cal," Tony said, automatically. "Yes, there are a lot of protests, but they involve a small fraction of the students. I, for one, wasn't into it. I'm not political. I used to avoid the tables and the pamphlet-waving people when I crossed Sproul Plaza."

"Well, so much for *my* stereotyping. As for me, I'm *not* a Republican." Sheila's eyes sparkled. "But I certainly am a football fan, and as you probably know, Stanford and Cal have a long-time rivalry."

"Uh, I may have heard something about that," Tony said lightly, but she truly had no interest in football, college or otherwise.

"You never went to the Big Game? Thanksgiving weekend? Stanford marching band?"

"Nope."

Sheila seemed disappointed and dismayed. "Well, this will never work."

"What will never work?" Tony thought she knew what Sheila meant, and she was alarmed.

"Us. You and me." Sheila appeared solemn.

Tony was speechless and crestfallen. She didn't know what she wanted exactly, but it seemed like Sheila thought they were an "us" that wasn't going anywhere.

"I'm kidding," Sheila said after looking at Tony's face. "I was joking."

"Oh. Good to know." Tony was relieved but made her voice sound neutral.

"You don't know when I'm teasing, do you? Sheila asked.

"No." Tony felt silly. "I guess I don't."

"Okay. I'll watch out for that," Sheila said, gently. "I can take you to a game this fall, if you want to go, that is." She was peering at Tony.

"Uh, yeah. Sure." Tony realized that she did want to go to a game with Sheila.

"Terrific. Come on. Let me show you the campus." She touched Tony's arm.

They'd dismounted their bikes near the entrance to the Stanford campus, just past the medical center, and Tony watched Sheila leap onto her bike and start pedaling away. Tony hastily climbed on her rental bicycle and followed her.

As they rode around, Tony couldn't help but compare Stanford to Cal. The Stanford campus, enormous and spread out, had a huge number of stucco buildings with red-tile roofs. Many people rode bicycles, which was clearly the most efficient way to get around, for there were far more bicycles than Tony remembered from Cal. Sheila stopped to point out her former dorm and the building that housed the economics department, where she'd spent a great deal of time as an undergrad, the student union, etc. Sheila's love of her alma mater charmed Tony more than the alma mater itself did.

For lunch, Sheila chose the Coffee House in the student union. Sheila directed her to leave her bike at the rack.

"Is it safe?"

"Yeah. For sure."

"I'd be worried about leaving my bike unlocked if I was in either the City or in Berkeley."

"I'm locking mine, but yours isn't that special."

"Right." Tony had to grin at Sheila's dismissal of her rental bicycle. Thousands of bicycles were sitting around, most of them unlocked.

The café carried a generic name, but the food was good. Tony couldn't recall a comparable place on the Cal campus. They ordered sandwiches and sat outside at picnic tables.

"I'm not one of those people who thinks their undergrad days were the best ever and nothing since has measured up. I just happen to like Stanford, especially the way it looks."

"I see that." Tony was more amused than anything else. Stanford was a grand university that thought very well of itself, but then again, Cal was also a famous university with its own institutional ego. It was just famous for different reasons.

Tony said, finally, "You know that Cal is one of the hardest public universities in the US to get into. All the UC campuses are."

Sheila smiled slightly. "Yes, I know that. Stanford is...unique."

"As you and I are different, not better or worse," Tony said with a touch of attitude.

Sheila's grin widened. "And we are getting to know each other."

Tony's slight pique dissipated, and she grinned back at Sheila.

After lunch they headed over to the Hoover Institution, and again, Sheila insisted on paying the admission. Tony thought it was sort of wacko that a university would charge admission to one of its own buildings, but she didn't say so.

In the lobby, Tony read about the building itself and the Hoover Institution, so she understood better what it was and how it came to be. It was part of Stanford but separate. Herbert Hoover, what little Tony knew of him, was a Republican who had been president when the Great Depression started and was forever associated with that time period. He had, however, an earlier career as a humanitarian who helped refugees. That made Tony think better of him.

"This is what I really wanted you to see," Sheila said in a suddenly shy manner. They had entered an elevator and were going up a few floors.

When the elevator door opened, they entered a deck that offered three hundred-and-sixty-five-degree views of the campus and, to the northeast, the City of San Francisco, shimmering in the haze beyond the San Mateo Bridge.

From above, Tony could see there was more variation to the architecture on the Stanford campus than she'd originally thought. But Sheila's face in profile was the best view. Her hair was a bit disheveled from the bike helmet, and she was slightly flushed, much as she might look when just getting out of bed after sex. Tony started to flush herself, thinking about that.

"It's nice up here," she said to Sheila to cover her unease, but she meant it.

"Really? You think so?" Sheila's uncertainty, a huge contrast to her usual aplomb, was amusingly unexpected.

"I do. Yeah." Tony looked out at the view and then back to Sheila again. Both of their expressions turned serious, and they fell quiet.

"I had my first kiss with a girl up here. It was at night after a party. We were both a little tipsy. The stars, the night, the view…you know." Her voice had taken on a dreamy quality as she recalled the occasion.

Sheila looked over Tony's shoulder behind her and then to their right, back toward the interior of the tower and the bells that gave the tower its name.

She took Tony's face in her hands and kissed her on the mouth, not hard but firmly and for a much longer time than she had before, and Tony closed her eyes and gave herself over to the experience. The sound of voices caused them to abruptly disengage. Tony was left with the impression of Sheila's lips, the smell of sunscreen on her cheeks, and a great many physical sensations in parts of her body she hadn't felt in a long time. Her stomach clenched, but in a pleasant fashion, and her crotch tingled. They turned as one and pretended to look at the view as the strangers who had emerged from the elevator milled around them.

"Have you seen enough? Ready to head back downstairs?" Sheila's voice wasn't obviously shaking, but Tony could detect a tiny tremor. It could be her imagination. She hoped not. She hoped Sheila had been gripped by similar feelings because of their kiss.

Tony realized that Sheila asked her questions all the time, not intrusive ones, but there were always at least two, and all aimed at taking Tony's emotional temperature. Sheila wanted to know how she was doing, how she was feeling. Did she need something to change? Tony had never experienced this level of concern, this sort of attentiveness. It was unnerving but flattering and could possibly become addicting.

She could only nod in response since her head was still woozy from their kiss.

Down at ground level, and back outside the Hoover Institution, they sat on a bench in a redwood grove, where they were shielded from the intense late-afternoon summer sun. After such a forward kiss, Sheila had retreated to a passive mien. It seemed to invite Tony to move forward, and she did, in a mild way, scooting over until their thighs touched.

"Thanks for showing me all this. I really like it, and I like that we aren't discussing GHS. I like to talk about work, but not all the time."

Sheila had been staring at the trees around them, which Tony didn't find unusual. The strong currents flowing between them had unnerved Tony and possibly Sheila too, so they had to take a short break, disengage somewhat.

She turned and looked directly at Tony and slowly smiled.

"I didn't want you to be bored. And I hoped you didn't mind the kiss. I wanted to do it in the bell tower because…it's one of my favorite places."

Tony said firmly, "I'm not bored, and yes, I liked the kiss. I like *you.*"

"Oh, good. I hope so. I have to say I wasn't clear whether you did. I kind of thought you did, but you're—"

"I'm reserved? Self-contained?"

"Yes to both. Not that anything's wrong with that. I like it, really."

"I'm glad you do because it doesn't mean I'm disinterested. Not at all."

"I know you aren't. You're not in a rush, and I'm willing to be patient because Buddha counsels patience above all. Especially if you don't want to go through life in a constant state of stress." Sheila looked closely at Tony, her meaning clear.

"I suppose that's true. I wish I was more patient," Tony said, thinking of their lab project and the emotional toll it took as she tried to meet Erica's expectations.

"You appear quite patient."

"That's how I like to appear. But I'm not. And patience is only one thing I like to project when I'm not feeling it."

"Oh?" Sheila turned to put her elbow on the back of the bench to prop her head on her hand and stare at Tony.

"Yes. I want to look like you don't intimidate me, when in fact, you do."

"Really? Why?" Two questions. As soon as she'd admitted her thoughts to Sheila, she wanted to retract them. Too late.

"You're...different. I don't know. I've, eh, never gone out with someone like you."

"What am I like? Am I scary? Too forward? Too controlling?"

"No. Not that." Oh boy, was she in trouble. If she wasn't honest, Sheila would know. If she said what she really thought, Sheila would likely be offended.

"You're...sophisticated, easy with people." Tony guessed that was a safe and true observation, though it wasn't the whole truth.

"And you? You're a science type—not overly social and kind of introverted. What's wrong with either?"

Sheila had her on that question. Tony's sense of inferiority had always made her view her personality as negative.

"Yes. I'm sort of shy and not very articulate."

"Ah, but you say a great deal more than you think. You don't take anything lightly or for granted. You're a deeply serious person. I think you don't expend your time frivolously on just anyone. I'm honored when you let me see you and spend time with you and get to know you."

"I'm glad," Tony said. "I like spending time with you."

Sheila grinned. "So, we're in agreement?"

"Well, yes."

"Fabulous. I'm going to do this again." Sheila kissed her. It felt wonderful, but Tony fought to tamp down her inclination to pull away. That instinct to withdraw came from having no physical contact for years. She could get back in practice, though, with Sheila.

"What now?" Sheila asked.

"Um, have I seen everything you want me to see?"

"Oh, you. Too funny. I don't think you've seen *everything*."

"No, I haven't." Tony was happy that sentence came out even and calm, though that wasn't how she felt. Sheila had packed that little word with hidden, provocative meaning.

"Well, then, shall I take you back to the train station?" Sheila's question sounded like that was the very last thing she wanted do.

"Yes, please. That would be nice."

As they sat in the car, Sheila was quiet and contemplative.

"Next time we see each other, I'd like to come to San Francisco and do something."

"Okay. What do you want to do?" Tony meant it.

"Oh, I'm up for almost anything. Pick whatever you'd like. It's San Francisco, so there must be zillions of choices."

"Right, sure. I can do that." This time Tony leaned forward to meet Sheila halfway, and Sheila's expression when they'd concluded their kiss was a mixture of satisfaction and triumph.

Tony tried as hard as she could to not feel like she'd been handed an arduous chore of choosing an outing in San Francisco, though it certainly felt that way. This ought not, as Sheila said, be a difficult thing. Tony could plan something fun for the two of them to do. It was a cinch that whatever it turned out to be, Sheila would like it. She was that sort of person, not demanding or particular, but relaxed and open to experience. Tony was attracted to that quality, but at the same time, it put pressure on *her* that she struggled not to be overwhelmed by. *It's not rocket science*. She grinned at the thought. *Dating is supposed to be enjoyable, not a problem to solve.*

CHAPTER FIVE

When Sheila told Roy that Erica had blown off her offer of business help, Roy shrugged, unconcerned.

"She feels like she's got it all covered, and you know how she wouldn't like any outsiders discovering any details about the product."

"Yes, Dad. I am well aware of that possibility. But even the cockiest software entrepreneur has agreed to use our services. Remember Grant Wilhelm? He had an ego the size of the SF Bay, but *he* told me the marketing consultant we sent him made a profound difference in his approach. And his company was one of our big successes. Huge IPO."

"I remember, but so? Erica's different. Don't worry about it. She must be doing something right. At the last board meeting, she told us she's going to sign a contract with the Veterans Administration to put Leonardo in all the VA hospitals in the country. Government contracts? Ca-ching." Roy imitated the sound of an old-fashioned cash register.

"Right. Did she give you the details of this deal or any of the other ones she's talked about? The agreements with the pharma companies, any of them?"

"She says the contracts are being reviewed by the lawyers. By the way, she's hired one of the biggest law firms in California. And she said the most famous advertising agency in the world is working on their marketing plan for the roll-out of Leonardo." Erica evidently always thought in superlatives. Sheila wondered about the psychology behind *that*. Overcompensation? Whatever.

"That's all terrific news. You're saying the board knows what she's up to, and it's all good."

"Hell, yeah. If it wasn't, I sure would say something, but we have to be diplomatic with Erica. Imagine how much doubt and nay-saying she has to put up with. You know, better than me, how sexist the Valley is. It still is. As a young woman she gets a lot of crap. I don't think anyone on the board wants to add to that."

Sheila smiled. Her dad as a feminist ally. How far he'd evolved. She suspected, though, that his new-found feminism and maybe that of the other board members was only skin deep. If Erica hadn't been beautiful, how much attention would the men of her dad's generation really pay? It was an imponderable question, and since Sheila wasn't going to ask him, it seemed pointless to speculate.

"Right, well, if you're satisfied, then I'm fine. By the way, did she ever snag someone with a medical background to join the board?"

"Yep. She has this senator. Finley, I think. He used to be an MD."

"Well, that's good." Sheila went on to discuss other investment prospects with Roy. GHS was moving forward, and Pacific Partners needed to get more business, which was mostly easy to do. The start-ups knocked on their door, and they could choose who to fund.

"I like this museum a lot," Tony said as they parked Sheila's Volt. "For one thing, the location is unbelievable, and their exhibits are eclectic but mostly European, and I like that."

"What's this?" Sheila asked as they walked from the parking lot toward the museum

"Holocaust Memorial." Tony said.

They stopped in front of the white figures behind barbed wire and looked quietly for a moment.

"I didn't know this was here," Sheila said.

"Yeah. I don't think it's well known. Come on. I want to show you something quick before we go to the museum."

"Yikes, it's chilly." Sheila complained, mildly. She pulled her cardigan sweater closed.

"I told you it would be. It's July," Tony said, reproving her gently. "But…look."

They had reached the road leading past the museum and could see the Golden Gate Bridge, a wreath of fog on its orange towers.

"This is the Lincoln Park Golf Course. It's got to have one of the best views of any golf course in the world."

"That it does." Sheila moved closer to Tony, seeking warmth. They stood for a moment looking at the bridge and the Marin hills.

"I'd have a hard time with being this cold in summer," Sheila said. "It's better in Palo Alto."

"I know. Down here is something pretty cool."

They approached a large block of polished granite with both English and Chinese writing. Beyond lay the Pacific Ocean.

"Shanghai is San Francisco's sister city," Tony said. "I love that. Considering how SF treated Chinese people in the nineteenth century, this is something."

"Oh? And how was that?" Sheila asked.

Tony was never surprised that Caucasians were ignorant of the history of Chinese people in California, but she was tolerant.

"Rank discrimination, naturally. They packed us into Chinatown and wouldn't let us have certain jobs. You know, the usual."

Sheila looked at her closely. "Nope. I didn't. You identify as Chinese?"

"Yep, I do, mostly."

Sheila smiled. "You'll have to tell me more about that."

"Uh-huh. Let's go to the museum. It'll be warmer inside."

They approached the entrance to the Palace of the Legion of Honor, an art museum as grandiose as its name. It had been named for the same museum in Paris.

"Look at this," Tony said, pointing to a figure on horseback at the entrance. "It's Joan of Arc."

"Ah. So it is. We claim her, don't we? Even if she wasn't a lesbian, she was a cross-dresser, yes?"

"Yeah. I think so." Tony laughed. She'd never thought of that.

"Okay. This a Rodin sculpture. The real thing," Tony said as they walked through the courtyard entrance.

"Wow," Sheila said.

"And over there, the Pacific Ocean." Tony waved her right arm toward it.

Sheila grinned. "Yes, it's all quite something."

It was enjoyable to watch Sheila's reactions as they wandered through the galleries. She'd suddenly stop in front of some Old Master painting, a Rembrandt or something, and grab Tony's arm.

"Oh, my God," she'd whisper. "Who the heck is this?" She meant who was the person in the painting. She'd read all the little explanations and stare at the painting. Then she'd say something like, "Why is his expression sad?" Or "What was she thinking while she was getting her portrait painted?" And Sheila would turn to Tony as though she had the answer. Tony would shake her head. Sheila's reactions to what they were seeing amused and touched her.

After they exhausted themselves looking at art, they bought some coffees and took them outside to enjoy the view some more. The sun came out but just barely.

"You don't have to talk about work if you don't want to, but I am curious, and I hope you don't mind if I ask you about it," Sheila said, somewhat hesitantly.

Tony was gratified that Sheila wasn't aggressive when it came to probing her for information about herself. Tony was out of practice at disclosing what she was thinking, or perhaps more accurately, she'd never been in practice, so she appreciated Sheila's giving her a choice in the matter. It was another thing at odds with Tony's preconceived notion of the kind of woman Sheila was. She expected Sheila to be hard-charging and sort of a don't-take-no-for-an-answer sort of person, but she wasn't.

"No. I don't mind. It's sort of in a holding pattern, since my manager left last week. I have stuff to do, but I haven't been given either a new boss or a new set of tasks and priorities. I don't like it."

"I'm not surprised. I bet you like to keep busy and engaged."

"Sure. But it's more than that. I have no idea of the bigger picture. I didn't even have that when Abe was still around. Well, I mean I know the big picture in the global sense. But I don't know what other people in the company are doing or how it all fits together.

Erica doesn't talk about it. We're all on separate networks. I can't even email someone in another group. Or message them."

Sheila frowned. "That seems odd. People usually need to communicate."

Tony nodded. "I thought so too, but I wasn't sure. Let's walk down the road a little way, admire the view some more, and then I think we need to go out to dinner on Clement Street, and given the neighborhood is my old stomping grounds, we have to do Pacific Rim cuisines. Whatever variety you like. I'm open."

"Oh, wow. In that case, I want Cambodian."

"Great idea. I know just the place."

At dinner, in answer to Sheila's question, Tony said, "I grew up about five blocks from here. It was good, I guess. It's a more suburban part of the City. My grade school was mixed Chinese and Caucasian. I went to Lowell High School, which has a lot of Asians. Since I'm not one hundred percent Chinese, I got kind of teased about that."

Sheila scrutinized her for a moment. "Did that hurt your feelings?"

Tony thought about the question. "Not exactly. I tried not to let it bother me, but I wasn't part of any of the cliques. I behaved like your typical high-achieving Chinese kid. I thought that would help make the other Chinese kids accept me, but it didn't. I had like one friend, who was Caucasian. I ended up mostly keeping to myself. I felt like I didn't fit in anywhere.

"Were you lonely?"

"Looking back, I was, but I tried to ignore it. I spent a lot of time with my dad. We built things."

"Lovely. I was close to my dad, Roy, too. Because we were tight, my mom felt left out. When they got a divorce, I said I wanted to live with my dad, and they said okay. What about your mother? What was she like?"

"If I could have just lived with my father, I would have been fine with that. My mom died when I was twenty, right after I came out." Tony paused to drink some wine. How much should she reveal? She wasn't a good discloser because baring herself made her uneasy. But Sheila was looking at her with a combination of tenderness and encouragement, so she kept talking, and to her surprise, she wanted Sheila to know about her.

"I was sorry when my mom died, but I think I was a little relieved. She wasn't comfortable with me, ever, in any way. I was always closer to my dad. Unlike most of the Chinese parents I know, he was totally cool with my sexuality. She wasn't. She was never comfortable with me in any way. I never knew why."

"Roy was great. It barely registered when I told him. We're similar in one way: daddy's girls." Sheila grinned.

"Yes, though that may be the only way." Tony grinned back.

Sheila rubbed the rim of her wineglass thoughtfully. "You ought to know this. My dad, Roy, is on the board of GHS. He joined right after we finalized the Series 2 funding."

"Oh. What's Series 2?"

"It's just the name for the second round of investment."

This time Tony paused. "How much money did you guys put in?"

Sheila looked at Tony levelly. "I'm not supposed to tell you. It's confidential, but it was thirty million from PP, and my dad put in five mil of his own money."

It took a couple of moments for Tony to absorb those numbers. She was truly looking at a woman who operated in another reality. Only Sheila's matter-of-fact statement of the exact figures involved kept Tony grounded. It was monumental that Sheila had let her know how much money was really at stake.

Sheila added, "There were other investors. I think the total may be close to one hundred and seventy-five mil total for Series 2."

"Million?" Tony whispered.

"Million." Sheila said, her face expressionless. She added, "Buddhist practice comes in handy when I'm dealing with those amounts of money."

Tony made a little joke to hide her dismay. "Well, that much money ought to keep the lights on in the lab and buy us a slew of ninety-six well plates."

"What are those?"

"Nothing. Just a lab gizmo I use a lot of."

"Right. Erica isn't specific about where the money goes and how much GHS spends each month. The burn rate, that is."

"Is that how much money GHS spends?"

"You got it. Usually reported as dollars per month."

"Huh. Isn't she kind of accountable to her board of directors?"

"You would think so, but they let her slide on a lot of details, my father tells me."

"Why would they let her skate on those details?"

"Erica seems to prefer older men." Sheila spoke straightforwardly but then waited for Tony's reaction.

"Oh. What do you think that means?" Tony asked. She wasn't sure, though it sounded vaguely bad. But her image of corporate life was exclusively populated by men, older or younger. That was what had made her want to work for Erica Sanders. She was one of a kind.

"I'm not sure, but she must have done a lot of serious networking to persuade them," Sheila said, then added, "They're all either Valley veterans like my dad or had big high-level government jobs like secretary of state for Bush II. That gives you an idea of the age range."

"Is it really as icky as it sounds? Older men, young woman?"

"I don't think it's overtly sexual, but it's unconscious."

"I have another question about the money part," Tony said.

"Sure."

"How much money will *you* make?"

Sheila's brown eyes glinted, her grin self-satisfied. "Good question. If Erica's income projections come true, GHS could be bringing in one billion in a couple years, depending on how fast you get to market."

"One billion for everybody? Her? The company?"

"Yeah, but just for us—our VC company—maybe a hundred and fifty million. I hope you have stock options, kiddo."

"Yep. I sure do." Tony tried to sound blasé, but the amounts of money Sheila described astounded her. Sheila truly existed in a whole other realm than she did.

"Then this ought to be an incentive for you work very, very hard."

Tony just stared at her, dumbfounded.

They shared another tender kiss before Sheila left to go home. Tony savored the memory of it and of the entire evening as she drifted off to sleep. *Okay. Maybe this dating thing is fun after all.*

❖

Erica called Tony into her office for a meeting but didn't say what it was about. Tony therefore didn't know if she ought to feel flattered or terrified. She sat still, hands on her knees. She'd brought a notepad just in case she needed to take notes.

Erica looked at the ceiling, then out the huge window behind her. It was tinted, and Tony wondered why. It faced the parking lot and was opaque from the outside. Tony had heard Erica's office windows were bulletproof. Over Erica's shoulder, Tony could see the Los Altos Hills in the distance. Erica finally turned her chair around to focus on Tony.

"Are you ready to step up?"

"Step up?" Tony echoed, taken off guard.

"We have limited time. I have made a commitment, and I want Leonardo in the hands of the folks at Graff with at least one test ready. For the pilot project. You're the one I'm counting on. Ibrahim said the immune assay was close to being ready. You're in the lab. What do you think?"

Tony's mind raced. The immunoassay was sort of close to release, but not quite. Ibrahim was a slow and exacting worker, and his estimate of time was appropriate, given their work, but she sometimes wondered if he was just a bit too plodding. It was the best practice to change only one assay parameter at a time, but, in some cases, Tony felt, it was better to move forward with something eighty-five to ninety percent sure to work, tweak the remaining parameters in question, and you could hit the target for your results faster. She'd suggested that approach a few times, but Abe always shut her down, and since he was the boss, she stopped asking. But he was likely fired because he wasn't making things happen fast enough.

"We're eighty-five percent there. I think we need to do a couple more trials and then can have the immunoassay ready to go." It was a bold promise, but Tony sensed Erica liked people to be bold because that was what she was.

As she spoke, Tony arranged her face in a somber and trustworthy expression.

Erica played with a lock of her black hair and regarded her without a word for what felt like an eon.

"Three days?" she asked, raising her eyebrows.

"Yes. I can have an answer for you in three days." Tony wasn't at all sure this was possible. It was better to under-promise and over-deliver instead of the converse, which was what she'd just done. But this was Erica, and she didn't want to say no or disappoint her. She was being offered a chance to prove something, perhaps prove her worth.

"Outstanding. That assay is crucial to our plans, and it *has* to work," Erica said passionately.

Tony was aware that the standard immunoassay was requested in almost eighty percent of blood-panel orders from doctors, and *that* was why Erica wanted it right away.

Erica, her eyes shining, stood up and shook Tony's hand. "I'm thrilled to hear you can do this. Let me know ASAP."

Tony returned to her desk and wrote up a plan of action. Her hand shook as she listed the experiments in order, noting which assay variables would change and by what degree. They'd been close when Abe left, and the experiments Tony had performed using the rest of his directions had pushed them closer. She'd been planning to talk to Erica in a few days anyhow, since she would need new marching orders as soon as they had the assay up to speed, and she wanted to ask if a new manager would be hired. Evidently, one wouldn't be. At least not right away.

She took her plan to the lab and began assembling items, preparing to get started. This was a huge opportunity, and she hoped she was up to the task. If Erica wanted results, that's what Tony intended to provide for her. Great results and delivered on deadline.

❖

A couple of days later, on Friday, Tony was close to completing her task when Erica came by the lab.

Tony said, "I've got just one more trial, and I can let you know by the end of the day."

Erica beamed and patted her on the shoulder. "Text me any time. I want to know as soon as you do."

Tony set up the assay and waited nervously through a forty-five-minute incubation for the results. But when she pulled the printout from the spectrophotometer, she knew even before she wrote all the calculations in her notebook that it was good. She'd successfully performed the immunoassay on only fifty microliters of fluid, which was the volume Erica had set for collection of blood samples in the microcaps.

She texted Erica, who phoned her right away and had her come to her office.

"You're sure?" she asked as Tony sat down.

"Yes. I'm sure. We can do it with the lower volume."

"Congratulations. I can't say how much this means to me and our ultimate goal. You're going to be the new group leader for the immunoassay group, and I'm assigning you to work with Gordo. He will incorporate this test into Leonardo, starting Monday. Take the rest of the day off." It was only three thirty in the afternoon. Erica never told anyone to take off early. She was a stone workaholic who never left before seven in the evening and expected everyone else to be there too.

Tony walked back to her desk. Her success with the assay overjoyed her, and her promotion stunned her. She hadn't worked with anyone else in GHS except Abe, and this meant she was moving to the next level. She was going to work with the one of the engineers and could see Leonardo actually perform the immunoassay. She wanted to call Sheila, but she ought to phone her dad first. He was always the one she called first with good news.

"Hey, honey. So good to hear your voice."

"Hi, Dad. I wanted to tell you right away. I was promoted. My manager left, and Erica gave me his job."

"Oh, wow, sweetie. That's fantastic. You deserve it."

"I hope so. I don't know much, except I'm going to start working with the engineering department to get the prototype going with our assay."

"That's wonderful. You be careful with those engineers, Tony, honey. You know how they are." He was joking about himself and engineers in general. They were stubborn, exacting, and opinionated—though Joe was so mild-mannered people didn't notice his flaws. Tony had inherited the same characteristics, which was good, because those characteristics came in handy with lab work too.

"I don't know if I can come over Friday." Truthfully, she thought she might be working late or seeing Sheila. Maybe both.

"Sure, sure, honey. Call me in a few days and tell me about your new job."

"I will. Love you, Dad."

After about twenty seconds of thought, Tony called Sheila and told her what had happened.

"Congrats. I knew you were a genius."

"I'm not a genius," Tony said, embarrassed but pleased as well.

"So, this is a big leap forward for GHS?"

"I don't know. Yeah. I guess it is. Say, do you want to get together? I've been let out of work early. It's unprecedented."

"Oh, shoot. No. I can't today. Back-to-back meetings and then a business dinner. But I'll miss you. I'm thinking of you."

Tony gulped. *Thinking of you.* Sheila sounded deeply regretful.

Sheila said, "We have to celebrate your success sometime soon. Let's talk tomorrow, okay?"

Tony and Gordon stood in the engineering lab in front of something that looked somewhat like Rube Goldberg had designed it. When she was ten years old, Tony's father had introduced her to what a Rube Goldberg device meant. He'd showed it to her as an example of how *not* to design something.

Leonardo 2.0 was about a third larger than a CPU but had arms coming out—robotic arms, Tony surmised—and a smaller auxiliary box clinging to one side. On the front panel of the main body was an LED and a couple of buttons.

"Wow," Tony said after giving the contraption the once-over.

"That's one word for it. A word that could mean either 'wow, great!' or 'wow, what a monstrosity,'" Gordon said, sounding glum, which surprised Tony. Engineers were usually quite proud of their handiwork.

"What do *you* think? You, after all, are the mastermind behind it, you and your team," Tony added.

"I'll keep my opinion to myself around here. That's safer."

Tony wanted to know more about what he meant, but she stayed silent. She recalled what Abe had told her before he left. Erica was impatient, to say the least.

"It's something that she let you actually work with us, face to face. I managed to get her to agree that if lab rats like you, Jack, and Martha could help me, it would go faster. That was the clincher." Gordon referred to two other assay group leaders, biochemists from R and D, like her. Tony had actually never met them. Having everyone report up to Erica was an odd way to manage. No R and D director. But, hey, she was the boss.

Tony laughed; she didn't mind being referred to as a lab rat. That was what she was. Did Gordon know he and his ilk were often called Mr. Robotos or enginerds behind their backs?

"Who are Jack and Martha?"

"Jack's the general chemistry guy, and Martha's an infectious-disease-testing expert."

"Oh, so this, uh, device will do all those tests?" That thought blew Tony away.

"That's the plan," Gordon said, but he didn't sound enthusiastic. More like dubious.

"It's not actually working yet, per se, but I can show you what the inside looks like," he said.

Gordon pried off the machine's outer casing, and he and Tony looked inside at a mishmash of electronics and metal channels. At the end of one of the robot arms, she recognized the unmistakable shape of a pipettor with a tip on the end, something she used every single day in the lab. But the tip was mashed, which couldn't be a good sign. A smashed pipette tip wouldn't deliver the precise volume required for accurate assay results.

Gordon said, "I tried to convince Erica we ought to try to achieve a working prototype for Leonardo and *then* miniaturize all the components, but she wouldn't hear of it. She's obsessed that it has to be the size someone could fit in his living room."

'That's a lot of functionality to pack into one little magic box. But she's the boss, I guess."

"Tell me about it. I got her to go with three assays to start with. That's complicated enough, and she wanted me to work on them with just the protocols from the lab folks. I told her, 'I'm not a lab person. I have to have all the lab people involved. She only caved because she realizes I don't know a thing about blood testing. She doesn't like to have any of us talking to anyone else, as you know. She wants to be the only one who knows everything. But she wants everything done, like, yesterday. And things just don't happen that way. You know the old contractor saying, right? You can have it fast, cheap, and marginal quality, or you can get it slow, expensive, and high quality."

Tony was apprehensive about her new role, but this process would be easier for her and Jack and Martha. They already knew precisely how assays were supposed to work. They had designed or modified the standard lab protocols to work with the smaller volumes. But Gordon had to do the hard work and replicate via mechanics how Tony, an actual highly trained human, performed an assay.

Tony stared at Leonardo and wondered how the heck it could do the same things an experienced lab person like her could. She didn't know much about robotics, but she'd heard they were amazing. The lab people were siloed from one another, and she'd never worked with either Jack or Martha. This would be an interesting situation.

CHAPTER SIX

R oy and Sheila went out to lunch after he'd attended the most recent GHS board meeting. Sheila was eager to hear about what was discussed and his impression of how the company was progressing. She and Tony had exchanged some phone calls, but they hadn't made any plans during the two weeks after Tony got her promotion because Tony was really busy. That was likely true, but it could also be true she'd gotten spooked. It was hard to tell. Sheila was prepared to wait. After their San Francisco date, the signs were good that they could move forward.

They were seated at one of the "good tables," Sheila noted. Her dad's long history in Silicon Valley still counted for something. He was still well known and well respected. She suspected some of the younger players thought he was old-fashioned and out of the loop, and that had fed into his enthusiasm for Global HemoSolutions. Everyone was always on the lookout for the next big thing. He wanted a truly big score, larger than he'd had in a long time. Their company was doing fine, profit-wise, but Roy hadn't been the toast of the Valley for one of "his" start-ups since before the dot-com bust in the early part of the century. His real fame dated from the nineteen eighties and early nineties—ancient history, relatively speaking. He wanted GHS to work for a lot of reasons, not just money.

"I'm hungry. How about you?" she asked him.

"Massively. Do you want a drink?"

Sheila was surprised to hear him ask. He knew she almost never drank at midday. He must want one, and that was unusual too, but he didn't like to drink alone.

"Nope. Thanks. You go ahead."

"Think I will. Just one."

When the waiter came over, Roy ordered a scotch.

"I'm interested to hear about the board meeting, Dad. Don't keep me in suspense any longer."

"It was fine. Erica's got it all under control. She wants to do another funding series. I want us to get in."

Another funding series? Already?

"*Dad.* More detail, please."

"Well. All right. She said she's going forward with the Graff partnership, and she expects to put Leonardo into forty stores on the West Coast by next year."

"What's their burn rate?" Sheila asked. "Did she say? Why do they need more money so soon?"

"Um, she didn't say."

Sheila asked, aghast, "She doesn't tell the board what the burn number is?"

"We can estimate that it's fairly high. You know how it goes with these folks. They *have* to spend a lot of money. And this is biotech, sweetie. Those labs *really* consume money fast."

He didn't sound at all concerned, which wasn't like him. Roy had become a successful VC by being hands-on and asking a lot of tough questions of the would-be entrepreneurs, which was what he'd taught her as well. It sure looked like Erica Sanders basically could do whatever she wanted.

"Doesn't anyone on the board ask questions of Erica—like what are the monthly expenses?"

Roy shrugged again. "She likes to talk about business deals and corporate partnerships and income projections. She doesn't like to be grilled about the details of running GHS."

"But Dad, I don't understand. Isn't oversight what boards are supposed to do?"

"Well, sure, but when you have a strong, competent CEO, oversight is a lot easier. Erica is a strong CEO, and I don't think you want the board to give the impression they don't think she can do the job because she's a woman."

Sheila sat back in her chair, staring at Roy. Tony had mentioned that her type of work, biotech, did take a lot of time and a lot of money, and maybe Erica's need for more investment was legitimate, but not her refusal to answer questions from her board of directors. That was just nuts.

"Dad, how much did you put in when you joined the board?" It was customary for board members to invest in the companies whose boards they were members of, usually in exchange for a discount price on shares.

He was quiet for a moment, and Sheila waited without saying anything.

"Five million," he said finally. He meant more of his own money; this was separate from the Pacific Partners stake. He'd invested a total of eight million dollars himself.

"Okay. You're all right with the level of detail Erica gives you guys?"

"Yeah, yeah. She tends to get irritated if someone asks too many questions, and then she clams up. She's really afraid something is going to get out in public, and that could be devastating."

This was all weird. Erica went way beyond the normal start-up CEO paranoia. The board of directors was comprised of professionals who understood confidentiality and wouldn't do anything to jeopardize a company's chance for success. That would be counter-productive and downright idiotic, considering the sums of money at stake.

Their food arrived, and they changed the subject to talk about trivia. Sheila pushed her mild concern aside. She truly trusted her father; his knowledge and experience were far beyond hers. She would rather think about Tony anyhow. Mostly she wondered what was up with her, and she decided to call her when she returned to her office after lunch.

"Hi, there," she said brightly when Tony picked up.

"Hi. How are you?"

Okay. She sounded pretty good.

"I miss seeing you." Sheila said, sincerely. "I was wondering what you were up to."

"Sorry I haven't called. It's the new job—in GHS," Tony said. "It's really keeping me busy, but I do want to see you."

That is good news.

"And I want to see you too. Lunch? Dinner?"

"How about breakfast instead?" Tony asked.

"I beg your pardon?" What was Tony proposing? Sheila thought that breakfast would follow, well, a sleepover. Was this what she meant? Sheila doubted that.

Tony laughed, sounding a little embarrassed. "I don't mean what you might think I mean. I always get to work early to organize myself. But these days I'm more likely to have to interact with others, and then we all tend to work late. Lunch and dinner breaks are iffy. I could meet you in the morning, right after I get off the train."

"Oh, I see. Sure, I'd love that. Just tell me when." Depending on how early was early, Sheila might have to reschedule her morning meditation, but she was willing.

"How about tomorrow?" Tony asked, further astounding her.

"Yes, of course."

"I'll text you when I know exactly when I'll be there. Probably sevenish. Is that okay?"

"It's perfect," Sheila said.

After she hung up, Tony sat for a moment staring at her screen saver—the old Apple fish. She *was* caught up with the project with Gordon, Jack, and Martha. It was all-consuming, and then there was the time pressure to get it done. Gordon said the Leonardo 2.0 had to be ready in six months. But when she wasn't involved with her work, she wondered about Sheila. That is, she pondered what to do with Sheila and when and if it was a good idea to pursue a relationship with her or break it off. It seemed easier and less fraught with uncertainty and complication if she broke it off, and a part of her wanted to stop, but most of the time when she wasn't thinking about work or at work, she fantasized about what it would be like if they were together.

"Stop being such a wimp," she whispered, but no one was around to hear her. She didn't know what would happen, so be it. In a funny way, her excitement about her work fed the part of her that craved a personal connection. She had never had those two vital parts of her life functioning properly and at the same time. To be clear, she'd hadn't had a relationship since her college hookups that had turned into friends or nothing.

That would be amazing: dating Sheila *and* working at GHS. Tony was, all of a sudden, happy and optimistic.

Tony slipped into the passenger seat of Sheila's Volt outside the Caltrain depot, favored her with a huge grin, and said, "Good morning" with far more verve than usual.

Sheila beamed back at her. "And a gracious good morning to you, Ms Leung. Why so animated? Not that I'm complaining."

Tony looked out the window. "I'm just in a good mood. I'm looking forward to going to work, but first I get to have breakfast with someone I like."

"Well, that *is* outstanding. Let's get to the Coupa Café and eat. I'm hungry. I hope you're okay with Coupa, since it's like right here."

"Oh, sure. We can be stereotypical Valleyites and discuss business over our lattes and organic eggs."

"That we can. Or we can talk about whatever you want." Sheila pulled into a parking place in the transit-center parking lot for convenience, since the café was around the corner.

They sat down and, after giving their orders, locked eyes across the small table.

"So?" Sheila said, her tone low and insinuating. "Tell me more about why you're cheerful today. It's not that you've been surly or anything. It's just noticeable."

"Erica has me working with the engineering lead and a couple of other chemists to really move Leonardo forward. She eventually wants it to be able to do hundreds of tests, but she'll settle for three for the moment. Gordon is the engineer, and he's the one that has to make it work. Two of the other lab people and I are advising him and making sure all the testing processes are where they have to be."

"That's terrific. No wonder you're so happy."

Their breakfasts arrived, and they both stopped talking for a bit.

Sheila swallowed a bite of toast and said in a confused tone, "I just thought of something. Roy and I got our blood tested months ago when we visited for a tour. On a Leonardo, I thought."

It was Tony's turn to be confused.

"Oh, no. That must have been the 1.0. We're working on the Leonardo 2.0. The thing has a zillion moving parts. Gordon had to design one piece of it at a time, starting with the cartridge where the blood tubes are situated. Another engineer was working on it at first, but he was let go, and Gordon had to basically start from scratch."

Sheila leaned back in her chair and said, as if she could read Tony's mind, "Huh. How did Leonardo do a blood test on Dad and me?"

To cover up her dismay, Tony ate some of her eggs and shook her head. "I don't know, but I could ask Gordon. He might know. Anyhow, we're all four working together, which is amazing, and we hope—we, meaning Jack and Martha and me—we can help Gordon get all the various parts of Leonardo up to speed so it can be used in clinical studies. I think that's what's next. Gordon sort of mentioned it. Pharma companies want to know how much of their drugs are in patients in their clinical trials. Erica says—"

"Well, look at you two. I wouldn't have predicted this." The voice speaking this sentence caused Tony to whip her head around just as Sheila did at exactly the same time.

Erica Sanders was standing next to their table, coffee go-cup in hand and staring from one to the other with a tight expression.

Sheila recovered the fastest. "Oh, hi, Erica. How nice to run into you." To Tony, she sounded unruffled and friendly. Tony's throat was tight, and she was feeling guilty and slightly terrified to have her CEO see her enjoying a cozy breakfast with one of the investors.

"It's nice to see you as well." Erica sounded like she viewed it as the opposite of nice. "Is this a business meeting I'm interrupting?"

"Oh, no. We're friends. I met Tony by accident when I was at GHS the first time." The look Sheila gave Erica wasn't surprised or dismayed, and she spoke evenly and firmly with not a hint of apology. Tony, on the other hand, felt incapable of articulating even one word, never mind a sentence.

"Well, this an interesting coincidence." Erica's tone held a note of hostility as well as curiosity. She looked first at Tony and then at Sheila, but neither of them spoke. Tony wanted to ask Erica *what* precisely was the coincidence? Her running into Sheila and Tony? Or Sheila and Tony having breakfast together? But she couldn't ask anything quite that forward and stayed quiet, a noncommittal smile plastered on her face.

It was borderline rude on Erica's part to continue to stand there interrupting their private conversation, and she must have realized it. After a long pause, she finally said, "Okay, then. Enjoy your breakfast. See you in the lab, Tony?"

"Oh, sure. I'll be in soon." To her ears, Tony thought she sounded like she was strangling.

"Excellent. Bye-bye Sheila. Good to run into you." And with that Erica left, and the two of them watched her walk out the door.

"Oops. I think I might be in trouble." Tony struggled to meet Sheila's serene gaze.

Sheila took a big gulp of coffee before she said, "No. I don't agree."

"What is Erica going to think? What will she do?" Tony had no idea why she was imbuing Sheila with the ability to see the future, which was ridiculous. But she needed *something*, probably reassurance.

Sheila reached across the table and put her hand over Tony's, her touch simultaneously calming and electrifying.

"Erica is your CEO, not your mom or your keeper. Whatever she thinks is whatever she thinks. You're an employee with a job to do."

Tony took a breath, and her disquiet lessened. Sheila's look and touch calmed her. Sheila gave her a small smile as she stroked her hand.

"Besides, in the Valley, if people policed everyone's dating and hookups, nothing would ever get done. You know the story: after money, sex is the big topic. Don't worry about it. You're not breaking any rules."

"Are we? Dating, I mean," Tony blurted. She knew the answer, but she wanted to hear Sheila say it aloud.

"Why, yes, we are." Sheila's grin was of a Cheshire-cat level of satisfaction. Tony turned her hand over and clasped Sheila's.

They sat quietly for another moment, and then Sheila said, "Let's get you to work. We want you to stay in Erica's good graces, and that's the best way."

In the car in front of the entrance to GHS, Tony couldn't help glancing nervously at the blank gray windows.

"Relax. Tony, you're good to go." Sheila patted Tony's shoulder.

"I hope so. Thanks." This time Tony leaned forward for their kiss. It was over too fast, but it was great and was steeped in promise. Sheila seemed to know always how far and how fast to go. She broke contact soon and gave Tony another encouraging smile.

When Tony stopped at her desk, her phone-message light was blinking, and she knew who it was. Tony hesitated, then decided that work came first. She'd get back to Erica later.

Tony, suited up in her lab coat, entered the engineering lab and found all her coworkers already there. They exchanged friendly greetings.

Gordon said, "I've made some adjustments at the intake port and with the pipette arm. Let's see if we can get complete or near-complete aspiration of sample volume. Jack, will you do the honors?" He meant for Jack to stick his finger with one of their disposable lancets. They had to provide their own blood samples for all the trial runs—and all four of them had sore, scarred fingers.

One of the first problems they were attempting to solve was ensuring that the entire blood sample could be used. The original volume was miniscule, and nothing could be wasted. Erica wouldn't hear of any increase, not even a doubling of what was essentially a drop of blood. The protocol called for two drops. Period. A finger stick would easily yield more, but they were limited to two squeezes of a pricked finger. This was supposed to be enough for all sorts of tests, which meant any loss had a big impact. Gordon was tweaking Leonardo's pipette mechanism so it would suck up the entire blood sample.

Leonardo's cover was removed, and they could see its innards. The robot pipette arm whirred as it went through its movements, exactly as though it was attached to the arm of a lab scientist working at a bench. They all watched its progress. The robot arm inserted the pipette tip into the microcap, and a pump aspirated the blood. Clearly a tiny amount was still left over. Tony and her lab cohorts knew that was inevitable. It wasn't possible to get to zero, but the trick was to get as much as possible. Tony estimated waste was no more than one microliter, one fiftieth of the original volume.

The pipette robot swiveled and attempted to expel the blood into the test chamber. It missed, and blood dripped all over the frame holding the test chamber.

"Oops," Gordon said. "I had that under control, but it must have drifted again when I was fiddling with the pump."

Tony shuddered. She caught the gazes of Jack and Martha, who mirrored her dismay. According to basic lab safety protocol, you couldn't have blood splashes all over the place. All human blood was treated as potentially infectious. Spills and contamination had to be cleaned up right away and basically couldn't happen inside Leonardo. The evidence of the frequency of blood spillage was visible everywhere. Tony took comfort in the fact that they used only their own blood, but still, her ingrained training made her freak out quietly every time this occurred. And it absolutely could not happen when they were testing patient samples whose infectious status was unknown. All that spilled blood would turn each Leonardo into a giant metal and plastic biohazard and expose whoever had to open it to fix it to pathogens like hepatitis and HIV. And these devices were to be sent to pharmaceutical companies and other places and put in the hands of customers.

As an engineer, Gordon knew nothing about blood safety. Tony thought about how to go about training him when the time came, because it surely would. Leonardo would require adjustment and calibration, and he'd be the one to have to perform those tasks.

"What do you think?" Gordon asked, meaning what did they think of the "dead" volume, as the leftover was called.

Martha said, echoing Tony's thoughts, "I think it's the best we can hope for."

"Dynamite. Let me get the aim problem back under control," Gordon said. "And then we can progress to the next step."

Tony and the other lab folks exchanged congratulations with Gordon, and they discussed which part of the system would be best to tackle next. Many components were involved. A centrifuge spun the blood and separated cells and plasma. A cytometer would count various types of white blood cells, and Tony's special concern was a photomultiplier tube that measured the amount of material that would bind to the antigens in their little sample wells and translate that into numbers. Each testing apparatus was a complex piece of equipment on its own, and if any one of them malfunctioned, the test results would be inaccurate. Commercial lab equipment was prone to fail, as all of them knew only too well. The Leonardo was a whole other level of unreliable.

This was going to a be long and painstaking process of trial and error and testing—not just of the assay itself, but of Leonardo. And Erica was waiting, metaphorically tapping her foot.

When Tony had a break and called her back, Erica summoned her to her office. Tony, remembering what Sheila had said, tamped her fear down. She didn't need to be defensive or offer explanations, Tony sternly told herself as she climbed the stairs to carpet land.

"Thanks for coming up," Erica said right away. "I really appreciate you taking the time to see me."

What was this? The boss calls, you go. That was basic employee behavior.

"Now, I don't want to dictate your private life, but I wanted to remind you of our need for discretion. If anything gets out about

Leonardo, some other company might find out about it, and we're sunk. We have to be very protective of all our trade secrets."

"Yes. I understand." Tony thought she detected an implied threat somewhere in that statement, but maybe she was the paranoid one. *Who's this "we"*? This was all Erica, it seemed. The royal "we."

"Oh, good. I just wanted to be sure you were okay." Again, her syrupy, faux-concerned tone put Tony off.

"Yep. Though I need to get back to work." Tony was sure Erica could relate to that.

As she walked downstairs back to the lab, it occurred to Tony that Erica's worries didn't even make sense. Tony, as an employee, and Sheila, as an investor, both had a profound interest in seeing GHS be successful. Neither of them had an incentive to blab company secrets to anyone. Tony wasn't sure why Erica would see their relationship as threatening. It was a puzzle she wouldn't likely solve, so she shoved it out of her head because she had to focus on a bigger problem Sheila and her father had had their blood tested on Leonardo 1.0, and Tony got the impression from Gordon that he was busy trying to make a working prototype.

She found him alone in the engineering lab, sitting by Leonardo with several of its pieces scattered around as he frowned at them.

"Hi, Gordo. How's it going?"

He turned and smiled sadly at her. "Oh, so very slowly. You know the drill."

"I sure do. You change one thing in a process, and then you have tweak something else. That's how it works in labs, and I'm guessing it's the same with robotics."

"Probably worse," he said.

"Hey, can I ask you a question?"

He put down the screwdriver he'd been fiddling with and focused on her.

"Yep. Fire away."

"Way before we started this project, Erica used to have Leonardo as a show-and-tell for investors and everybody, right?"

"Right." Gordon wasn't making eye contact with her and had stiffened.

"How did Erica use the old Leonardo to produce testing results, when it couldn't actually do anything yet?"

"Eamon would make it look like the blood was being tested by Leonardo, but the printout of the result was actually from a commercial blood analyzer." Eamon was the engineer Gordon had replaced.

"Oh. Isn't that a little bit of a fake-out?" Tony asked. "And what commercial blood analyzer? Do we have one?"

"Yeah. Erica wanted to show off to people like the president of Graff Drugs and other big investors. Yes, we have an Advia. You've never seen it because it's behind a locked door that you don't have card-key access to. Eamon had to turn over his stuff to me when he was canned."

"Right. I see." This was becoming stranger and stranger, but Tony could see the utility of having an Advia. It was one of the standard commercial blood analyzers hospital clinical labs used. GHS could compare the results of Leonardo to those rendered by the Advia to see how close they were. The twist was the Advia analyzer required a whole lot more blood.

"How did that work?" Tony asked, "Advias need a five-cc blood sample."

"Eamon and his team modified the Advia to work with smaller volumes."

"But…"

"We have a diluter, and we can use the Advia in case we can't get Leonardo working so we can generate data."

"But…?" Tony was thoroughly confused.

Gordon's long face was a blank. "We have to have backup. In case, you know, Leonardo 2.0 craps out, but we're going to get Leonardo working."

"But that means the test results that Erica got for show-and-tell were from another device altogether."

Gordon became visibly tense. "Yeah, so?"

"Well, people got the actual results of blood tests that were supposedly done in Leonardo. How could that be?"

"You're a smart chick. Can I say chick?"

"Not really, but I'll ignore it this time." He was clearly stalling. "Come *on*. What's the story?"

"As a smart *woman*, you would know that sometimes it pays to not ask too many questions around here."

Well, that was ridiculous. Research people like them were paid to ask a lot of questions and to provide answers to them.

"I'm just curious. It's kind of weird."

"Okay," he said, swiveling on his stool. "You could find out from someone else. It's not that big of a deal. Just don't go around talking about it."

"I promise," Tony said, sincerely.

"Erica needed to have something to show, as you said. What Eamon did was make it *look* like the Leonardo did the test, but he programmed it with the result, and that's what was shown on the printout. It all looked impressive, and the investors oohed and ahhed, and Erica was able to raise money."

"I see." Tony was uneasy. That sure sounded underhanded and deceitful.

"Yeah. That was the way it went. Eamon couldn't actually make Leonardo work, but Erica needed *something*."

"Right. Well. Thanks for the information. I can tell you don't like to talk about it."

"Not only that, Tony, but we truly *can't* talk about it. If anything gets back to Erica, she pitches a huge fit and then fires the guy who talks. I know you're a trustworthy person, so I wanted to answer your question, but I'm telling you, be careful."

"I will. Guess we better step up our game. We want Erica to *really* have something to show the outside investors."

"Yeah. Better get cracking," he said, morosely.

Tony left the engineering lab and decided to have lunch at her desk instead of in the cafeteria. She felt burdened by the secret Gordon had shared with her, along with gratified by his trust. She wanted to believe that Erica must have her reasons for doing what she did. Money must be it. They *had* to have money to keep the company in business. Research, testing, and perfecting a complex technology took time and scads of people and piles of money, and there were no shortcuts. Nor were there any guarantees that any of it would ultimately work, as Tony had discovered when she'd worked for the now-defunct biotech company.

But that company, as far as she could tell, had never misled anyone. She didn't know for sure, but she thought their investors must have a good idea of what was going on. Then she thought about the amounts of money involved. The investment figure Sheila had told her, along with the what might be the potential future worth of the company, staggered her. She felt nauseated. What if Leonardo didn't work?

It wasn't until she'd almost finished her tuna sandwich that she realized that Gordon's secret tale was one she ought *not* to share with Sheila. She was under an NDA, a non-disclosure agreement, and she wasn't supposed to talk about anything to do with GHS. She wasn't even allowed to put the *name* of the company where she worked in her LinkedIn profile. But Sheila had asked her a question, and something told her that Sheila would remember and ask her again.

Tony and her dad were having their usual Friday chat, except it was by phone, and it was nine thirty at night. Tony had just gotten home and was exhausted.

She had stayed at work for twelve hours every day, including Friday. She'd finally concluded it wasn't worthwhile to show up at seven a.m. only to have to wait for other people and then stay late into the evening. She started later, and that helped, a little bit. Not only was Tony not able to make her regular Friday visit with her dad, but worse, she had to keep putting Sheila off. Sheila was sad, but by some miracle she was tolerant of Tony's insane work hours. Sheila had been traveling part of the time as well.

She only said, "We'll get together when you can. I'm not going anywhere."

Tony was reassured and hoped the opportunity for another date would come soon.

"Sorry this is so late, Dad."

"Sure honey. How's work?" he asked.

How was work? Tony wasn't sure how to answer that question. It was hard, for sure. Did she like it? Yes. But it was interfering with the progress of her relationship with Sheila. And Tony was eager to make progress, even as she feared the unknown future. She also thought about the secret she carried. Trying to decide whether to tell Sheila about Gordon's little tidbit about Leonardo wasn't helpful to her psyche.

"It's fine. How about you?"

"I'm good." He talked about trivia from his workplace.

Listening to him actually soothed Tony, and she began to doze off. "Dad, I have to get off the phone and get some sleep."

"Sure, sure, sweetie. Talk to you soon."

CHAPTER SEVEN

They'd not made any plans after the breakfast date that Erica Sanders had interrupted because work at the lab continued at its ruthless pace. Tony wanted very much not to lose her momentum with Sheila, and she feared Sheila would lose interest, but that didn't appear to be happening.

Whenever they talked, Sheila was sympathetic to Tony's plight, and all she said was, "I can wait." Tony and Sheila began a routine of texting back and forth when Tony was commuting, and they shared a phone call every few days.

Between the mental and temporal demands of her work and her anxieties about the Leonardo and whether to tell Sheila her secret, Tony was able to justify her avoidance of making plans. But at the same time, she wanted to see Sheila and, if she could manage, sleep with her. They were headed down that path, but the toxic brain cloud of her secret complicated matters. Tony wanted to come clean before they had sex, but at the same time, if she did, it might not happen at all. In any case, she wasn't yet able to be in the same actual space as Sheila, so neither sex nor spilling a secret was going to happen.

When she walked into the lab on Friday morning, Erica was there, lab coat on, leaning against the table while she talked with the development group, as they'd been named. Before this moment, Gordon was the only one seeing and interacting with Erica.

"How nice you could join us, Tony," Erica said with an edge to her voice. Tony's cohorts all wore shell-shocked expressions, and her own shoulders tensed immediately. She couldn't be *that* late because it was only nine fifteen.

Explanations about her whereabouts were out of the question, and she nodded briefly, waiting to hear what was going on.

"We have to step up the pace with Leonardo," Erica said. "Gordon thinks you can get one of the tests to work—the immunoassay. I'm going to Europe next week, and I want to show the Swiss something that is actually real. I need this done by next Tuesday. Tony, this is your baby. Can you do it?"

Tony froze. She'd have to oversee every moment that Gordon spent working on Leonardo to make sure it would produce real results. They were, at that moment, not even close to having the Leonardo perform *any* of the assays properly.

"Okay." She spoke with far more confidence than she felt.

"Dynamite," Erica said. "I knew I could depend on you. I'll check in later." With that, she strode out of the lab without a single backward look.

Gordon was pale, but Jack and Martha looked relieved. Their tests were not chosen. Tony wondered why Erica had picked her assay. Was this some sort of trial by fire?

Jack said, "Look, whatever we can do to help. We'll hang in with you."

"Thanks." But Tony didn't say they really couldn't do anything. It was all going to be up to her and Gordon.

Luckily, Gordon had managed to make the robot arm functional, and the group was about to go forward with reagent-fluid handling. The last step of Tony's assay was the spectrophotometer reading that rendered the actual numbers. She hoped that piece of the Leonardo operations would be straightforward. Gordon had managed to install a small but functional spec after he'd torn apart a full-size spec and rebuilt it in miniature. But nothing about R and D was ever easy *or* straightforward. Neither Gordon nor Tony was an expert on the technology of specs. Tony treated it as she treated all lab equipment—as a means to an end. She couldn't even troubleshoot the spec if it malfunctioned.

Tony supposed the paring down of Erica's expectations from three assays to just one was good, but then she had drastically shortened the deadline.

Gordon grinned without humor and said, "Alrighty then, Tony. Please write up the protocol, and we can get this monster programmed."

Tony had already worked out the volumes of the reagents. She hoped that Gordon could get the Leonardo's robots to execute the fluid transfers properly.

At seven p.m., Tony said, "You know, if I don't get something to eat soon, I'm going to faint, and that's that."

Gordon looked at her. "We don't have time to go out to dinner. Let me call Erica."

He got off the phone and said, "She says not to worry. She'll have some Mexican catered in. Half an hour."

"Fine," Tony said. "I'll be back in fifteen." She'd barely gone to the bathroom in the last five hours. She didn't know if Sheila had ever called back. She was certain she was going to miss the last train back to SF at this rate, and she didn't relish spending the night in her desk chair. She knew if she asked, Sheila would come pick her up and take her home. What happened after that, she wasn't sure.

Tony went to her desk, and her phone said Sheila had called. She found a pack of Keebler crackers in her desk and munched on them while she formed what she wanted to say to Sheila.

Hearing Sheila's mellow, friendly tone on her voice mail made her feel a bit more grounded, and excited in spite of how tired she was.

"Hi there. It's Tony."

Sheila laughed and said archly, "Hi, this is Sheila, and I know it's you. What's happening?"

"I'm working late. Erica wants this thing done for next Tuesday. I don't know when I'm getting out of here, but the last train to the City is in an hour, and I'm not going to make it. Can I—?"

"You ought to stay with me," Sheila said instantly. "Text me when you're ready, and I'll pick you up. I have a guest room and an extra toothbrush. Don't worry."

"Really? That would be fabulous." Tony thought, *Guest room? Yes, that makes the most sense, but is that what I want?* Sheila seemed to have been waiting for her call. Or maybe she was always prepared to have women stay the night with her with no warning. Tony dismissed the implications of *that* thought. Sheila would be the kind of person who planned ahead and prepared for whatever might transpire, whatever circumstances. Sheila's question about the Leonardo and its problematical answer floated into Tony's head and then out again.

After their hasty dinner, Tony and Gordon returned to the engineering lab. Tony made a couple of adjustments to the procedure, and Gordon changed the Leonardo's program. It still couldn't render the right result according the to the quantity of analyte that Tony had spiked the samples with, but it was getting closer.

Gordon was gray-faced, and at nine o'clock he said, "That's *it.* I'm done for the day. My brain refuses to work. It's off the clock for me. We can pick up where we left off tomorrow morning. Do you need a ride or anything?"

Tony felt the way he looked, but when she said, "Nope. I've got a friend picking me up," a lovely little rush of anticipation overrode her fatigue.

Sheila strode through her condo doing a quick inspection. It was guest-ready, thanks to the efforts of her cleaning service. Tony was coming over, but was it for romantic purposes? Sheila thought not. She'd likely be exhausted and merely want to go to sleep. But a tiny spark of arousal lit her mind and body anyhow. It was possible they could… Though it would be just like them to spend their first night together platonically. *Never mind.* Whatever would happen, would happen. It was times like these that Sheila was most grateful for Buddhist training. She needed to keep her emotions under control and be there for Tony.

She turned on the hot tub and chilled some wine, just in case Tony wanted a drink. She pulled out some snacks: fruit and nuts and cheese. She wanted to be sure that if Tony wanted something, she was ready to provide it, no matter what it was.

Sheila sat down on the couch and concentrated on breathing and calming herself. The ping of the text from Tony saying she was ready startled her, but she grinned and texted that she was leaving. It was convenient that she lived twenty minutes from the GHS facility.

As she pulled up to the GHS front door, she noticed a couple of cars in the lot. Some people were working late. Erica must be a either a slave driver or uncommonly able to inspire loyalty and hard work.

Tony opened the car door and said, "Whew, am I ever glad to see you."

"I would like to think that's always true." Sheila liked to tease Tony sometimes, but she was also trying to cover her uncertainty.

"And it is, but especially tonight." Sheila decided the prudent interpretation of that comment was that Tony was tired from working a long day.

On the way to Sheila's home, Tony gave her a short rundown of why she was working late and again thanked her for the offer of a place to crash.

"I'll have to go back to GHS tomorrow morning, but I hope I can go home tomorrow night and sleep in my own bed and change clothes. We—Gordon and I, that is—think we can finish the final run-throughs Monday."

Sheila steered through the quiet streets of Palo Alto and then its next-door neighbor, Menlo Park. Tony appeared to be feeling okay, but her manner gave no clue of what she expected the night to be like.

"Is Erica still at work?" Sheila asked.

"Oh, yes. She famously never leaves before ten and often stays until midnight. Then she comes back at five or six in the morning. She claims to need only four hours of sleep a night."

"That seems a bit unhinged and maybe unhealthy," Sheila said. "But I guess if you're going to make your staff work until late at night, you ought to set a good example."

"She's inspiring, amazing, really. We all want to please her." Tony looked out her window, talking half to herself. Sheila wondered what Tony was actually thinking but decided not to ask. She'd find out eventually.

"That's good to hear. Start-ups need loyal people because it's way hard to make something like this a success. Well. Here we are."

It was a dumb thing to say, but in spite of all her Buddhist training, Sheila's nervousness flared as she pulled into her parking space in the garage under her building, turned the car off, and plugged it into its charger. She moved through her familiar homecoming motions automatically, while her unusually busy brain flew ahead.

Tony exited the passenger seat and favored her with an enigmatic glance, then repeated vaguely, "Here we are."

❖

Tony was certain Sheila's home would be ultramodern, sleek and spare, much like her. She would surely have new, up-to-date furniture and the latest in kitchen gadgets, and everything would shine. It wasn't exactly like that.

Though her living room wasn't cluttered, and the sofa and chairs were clearly not old, they looked soft and comfy. The lighting was low, and some kind of soft, New Agey music was playing. The biggest surprise was what Tony assumed was an altar that dominated the living room. It sported candles, a big statue of the Buddha, and lots of other things Tony didn't quite recognize.

"Huh," she muttered involuntarily as she examined it.

Sheila had dead-bolted her front door and taken her jacket off, and she walked over to stand next to Tony in front of the Buddha.

"This is a little much, yes?" she asked in a self-deprecating manner.

"Oh, no. I've only seen something like this in a temple. I went to the Zen center in SF for some reason once." Tony touched the singing bowl and looked over the candles and prayer symbols thoughtfully.

"You're a serious Buddhist?" She turned to look at Sheila, who was standing behind her. Sheila's expression was unreadable, but she seemed to be watching for Tony's reaction.

"I don't know about that, but I try to live my life in a way that follows Buddhist principles."

"I'd like to know more about that, but maybe some other time," Tony said.

"Of course. You must be tired. Do you want something to drink? Do you want to sit in the hot tub for a bit?"

"I don't want anything alcoholic. It would probably send me right to sleep. The hot tub sounds good, but I don't have a bathing suit." Tony realized, as soon as she spoke the last sentence, how stupid it sounded. Bathing suits in hot tubs were not expected. Tony had visited the Kabuki Hot Springs in Japantown in San Francisco on women's nights and gotten naked with strangers. Sheila *wasn't* a stranger, which was likely the problem

"I don't want to make you feel uncomfortable," Sheila said. "Whatever you want to do is fine."

Her mind racing, Tony continued to mindlessly finger the objects on the altar, including the crystal. Because of her silly remark about bathing suits, the air around them had taken on a sexual charge. Was that where this was going? Tony had been laser-focused on work; she'd pushed all those sorts of thoughts of sex out of her mind, but they had suddenly leaped to the fore. Sheila surely felt the change in energy because she had practically whispered her last two statements. Tony was being presented with a challenge to propel their connection forward, and she realized she wanted to take it. Her mental and physical fatigue receded, replaced by the prospect of making love with Sheila.

Sheila was standing near her, not touching her, but Tony was hyperaware of their proximity. She stopped fiddling with the objects on the Buddha altar and turned to face Sheila. Her face, partly shadowed, was still, and she looked attentive.

"Yeah. Hot tub sounds good. I could use some relaxation."

"Absolutely. It always helps me sleep better." Sheila had recovered her aplomb. "I'll go collect some towels and drinking water for us. If you'd like, you can go ahead and get in. It's out on the deck, through this door. I'll just be a moment or two."

Sheila then turned and walked away. Tony was astounded at how sensitive she was, almost as though Sheila could read her mind.

Tony went out on the deck and turned the hot-tub cover back. She undressed, looking up at the sky. A few stars were winking, but the lights of Silicon Valley dimmed most of them. It was a mild, late-September night—not cold, not warm, the epitome of Bay Area's excellent weather.

She lowered herself into the water, the sensation fantastic. Hot tubs could be too hot or not hot enough, but this one hit the sweet spot. She found the button for the jets and turned them on. Sunk up to her neck in swirling warm water, Tony realized how tense she was as she began to relax.

Sheila emerged from the living room onto the deck, wearing a bathrobe and burdened by towels, plastic tumblers of water, and another bathrobe. She set everything down on a deck chair and took off her robe. Tony struggled to stay casual and not stare but found it impossible. Sheila climbed into the hot tub and took a seat on the bench across from Tony and grinned at her.

"How is it?" she asked, gently. Tony had absorbed a quick impression of Sheila's body before she looked away. She had mid-sized breasts and hips, flat stomach, and long legs. And, surprisingly, a pierced navel.

"Feels great. Working for twelve hours straight did a number on me, but I wasn't conscious of it until I got in the hot tub and it's like ah, time to chill, at last." She tilted her head back against the rim of the tub.

Sheila laughed lightly and fluttered the water with her fingers. "Isn't that the truth? You never know how hyper you are until you're not. We tense our entire bodies as though we're bracing for an attack. We forget to breathe deeply, which makes us even *more* keyed up. Anxiety plus adrenaline. It's not good for us."

"No. I suppose not. How do you stop it?"

Sheila took a deep breath. "I meditate, and I try to always check in with my mind and my body and ask, 'What state am I in?'"

"I don't think of anything else but what I'm doing in the lab."

"Focusing on the task before you is mindfulness as well, but it's not good if your mind and body are in a state of tension like a stretched rubber band. Where do you carry all your tension? Shoulders? Neck?"

"Both, I guess."

"Do you want me to give you a neck massage?"

"Uh, sure." The sexual energy that was at a low-level hum notched up in volume as Sheila moved over and sat next to her on her bench. They were naked and extremely close together.

Tony turned slightly to let Sheila have access to her neck, and her butt made contact with Sheila's thigh. As long as they'd been sitting opposite one another, submerged up to their armpits, Tony could pretend nothing was going on. Some dim lights were hanging on the corners of the deck to provide light for safety, but after that one glimpse, Tony couldn't see Sheila as she sat in the dark water. Sheila put her hands on Tony's shoulders and squeezed.

"Relax," she whispered into Tony's ear. She kneaded Tony's tight shoulders and stiff neck. Her touch was heavenly, and she kept it up for a while as she found the points of tightness in Tony's muscles and worked on loosening them.

Tony didn't exactly fall asleep, but she slid into a sort of semi-consciousness, where she remained aware of multiple sensations: Sheila's hands on her neck, the light brush of her nipples against her back, warm water.

"Better?" Sheila asked softly.

"Yes." Tony was barely able to form the word.

"Good." Sheila kissed her neck, just under her left ear. Tony hadn't known how sensitive a spot that was until she felt Sheila's lips.

"Is that okay?" Sheila asked.

Tony was reduced to a nod. Complicated feelings swirled in her: sexual arousal, apprehension of a different sort than she had been experiencing—the anticipation type. And it was leavened by calm and Tony's sense of the inevitable.

Sheila turned Tony around and deftly lifted her onto her lap and embraced her. The full body contact made Tony gasp. Their kiss was far more urgent than any of their others. Their tongues met as their mouths opened. Dreamlike, Tony's mind split into two, one half experiencing the touches she and Sheila were sharing and the other half observing their actions.

"Come with me," Sheila said, taking Tony's hand as she stood up and had Tony step out of the hot tub. The abrupt withdrawal of Sheila's body and the blast of cool night air jarred her. Sheila wrapped her in a towel, then put on her bathrobe. She led her through the living room and into the large bedroom in the back of the condo.

I know what's going to happen. It's what I want.

Tony wasn't tired anymore. She was wide-awake and alert.

They stood by the bed, and Sheila rubbed Tony with the towel as she kissed her. She threw off her robe and let the towel fall away.

"Aren't we going to get the sheets wet?" Tony muttered, knowing this was probably a pointless question.

Sheila kept kissing her but snickered against her neck, "Oh, such a practical girl you are. It's fine. Here. We can dry off some more."

She yanked the covers aside and lay down, pulling Tony on top of her, then swiftly rolling her over so she was on the bottom. Tony tried to still her perpetually active mind. *Not the time for talk. Just feel.* Sheila was stronger than Tony imagined, and she was, in effect, pinned as firmly as one of the dead beetles she'd studied in entomology class. This thought caused her to giggle.

Sheila raised her head. "What? Am I tickling you?"

Tony put her palm on the back of Sheila's neck and shook her head. "No. Sorry. I'll tell you later."

The lighting in Sheila's bedroom was subtle enough to see some details but not overbearing—in other words, perfect for seduction. The next thought that floated through Tony's mind was of how many other women had been where she was. *Stop. Thinking.*

Sheila was evidently not overthinking anything. She was on a mission, but it didn't strike Tony that she was in any way anxious. She wasn't urgent. She was tender, her movements slow, almost meditative. But effective. Tony was growing more aroused by the second. When Sheila kissed her way down her body, pausing for a moment at her breasts and navel, Tony's active mind at last emptied, and she let pure sensation take over.

Sheila pushed her legs apart and knelt between them, her hands gently resting on Tony's hips. She took a deep breath, opened her eyes, and looked into Tony's. At this point, Tony wanted more than anything for her to continue. She was ready.

Sheila slowly thrust one finger in, then a second. She moved all the way out, then back in, murmuring approvingly as Tony rose to meet her. She kept it up until Tony moaned. "You're killing me."

"No. I'm not. You'll be fine." Sheila withdrew her fingers slowly, slid down the bed, and replaced her fingers with her tongue. Tony let out a tiny scream. It was almost unbearable how good that felt. Sheila licked her clitoris slowly once, then again, but faster. She pressed Tony's thighs back and fully opened her. Tony could move only enough to tense and relax her legs. Their lovemaking was still somehow meditative. Sheila was methodical, stopping and starting in response to Tony's movements. Tony came suddenly in a series of long contractions. Sheila hung on until Tony couldn't take it anymore and screamed, "Enough!" She slapped Sheila's head harder than she meant to.

Sheila simply said "Okay," stopped, and returned to her side to scoop her into a warm hug as Tony caught her breath, astounded, grateful.

Tony began to touch Sheila, dragging her fingertips across her chest and stomach.

"Your fingers have an interesting rough feel," Sheila said.

"Oh, it's my finger-prick scars," Tony said. "Am I hurting you?"

"Not at all. Please continue." Tony's fingers were sore, but she noted that fact in a distant fashion. She wanted only to be as good to and for Sheila as Sheila had been for her.

CHAPTER EIGHT

Sheila woke up early, as always. It was the same no matter how much or how little sleep she'd had. She didn't mind because it meant she could get certain things done in the early morning. She smiled fondly at Tony, who was still soundly asleep. She was such a dear and so earnest and a surprisingly good lover. Sheila tried to not have high expectations when it came to sex because they were such a trap. Buddhist principles counseled against having expectations anyhow. But it was a natural inclination.

Sheila slipped out of bed, put her robe and slippers on, and went to the living room. She recalled one of her dates, a handsome software-marketing expert who was intelligent and a smooth talker, befitting her profession, but she was lousy in bed. Not a drop of sensitivity or awareness.

Tony's serious demeanor had struck Sheila immediately. This was a woman who would surely pay the utmost attention to her. And she was right. Tony was ardent but a bit tentative at first, in a good way. Her style was perfect. Sheila liked control, but she really liked giving it up as well. Buddhists described that as balance.

At her living-room altar, she lit a candle, said a little prayer of gratitude, then meditated for fifteen minutes. As she stood up, she touched her Qin Yin statue with a kiss from her fingers to Qin Yin's head and a whispered a thanks. Then she went and made coffee and woke Tony up with a fresh cup.

"Oh, wow. This is wonderful," Tony said. "It's all wonderful. I can't believe I'm here with you."

Sheila kissed her hair and her cheek. "It's quite real, and if you didn't have to go back to work right away, I'd give you another dose of reality."

Tony looked so woebegone, Sheila had to laugh.

"Don't worry, sweetie. There's always later. And that reminds me. What were you snickering about last night as we were, ahem, getting started?"

Tony reddened, but she said, "I was thinking you had me pinned like a dead bug."

"Oh, very romantic. You know how to charm your girlfriends."

"Well, I meant it as a positive thing," Tony said, sounding sad.

"Don't worry. It's cute. I can think of you as a dead beetle."

"Right." Tony gulped a big mouthful of coffee, then grinned.

Tony didn't want to stop kissing Sheila as they sat in her Volt in the GHS parking lot. Tony thought she might simply dissolve into a puddle of despair if they ceased to be in physically close. It was time to go to work though.

"What are you going to do today?" Tony asked between kisses.

Sheila responded the same way. "Pick up dry cleaning, go for a bike ride, then to meditation at four."

Tony stopped and moved her head back to see Sheila's face. "Wait a second. I thought you meditated at home at your altar."

"I do. Every day. But I like to go to the meditation center to be in a group too. It's a different experience to meditate surrounded by other folks who are doing the same. It's over at five thirty. Want me to pick you up, and we can, you know, eat dinner?" She raised her eyebrows and stroked the top of Tony's hand with her finger, and Tony had a rush of sex memory in her crotch.

"As lovely as that sounds, I have to go home and take care of my own chores. I made Gordon promise that we'd take Sunday off, and I'd work as long as I needed to the other days."

"I understand. Well. This was an astonishing, transcendent night, and I hate to leave you, but that's the way it goes."

"I'll call you, I promise, and thank you. For everything."

Sheila kissed her one more time. "No. Thank *you*. Now go help Ms Sanders change the world."

Tony grinned, nodded, and jumped out of the Volt. As she walked to the front door, she remembered she still owed Sheila an answer to her question. They'd been too distracted by sex, but Tony was sure that Sheila would remember the question she asked sometime very soon. What was done was done.

Tony went to her desk and put her bag down and her lab coat on, squaring her shoulders as she buttoned it. She took a swig of water and, by force of will, altered her thought process from focusing on Sheila and delicious sex to thinking of work. She walked to the lab, where Gordon was already buried in the Leonardo with his ever-present screwdriver and penlight.

❖

At four thirty on Saturday afternoon, Gordon and Tony once more stood shoulder to shoulder in front of Leonardo.

"Here goes," he said, and flipped the switch. They watched as the robot withdrew the blood sample, dispensed it into the reaction chamber, and then added the reagents. It was an excruciating four minutes as the reaction occurred and then the fluid made its way into the spectrophotometer for its analysis. They both watched as the little printer to the side finally spit out its result.

It looked right. The number was close. Not exactly the amount Tony had spiked the sample with, but nothing is ever exact in lab tests. She showed the printout to Gordon and said, "Eureka. You got it to work, man. You're a genius." They high-fived.

"We're done. I'll tell Erica first thing Monday. No. I'll call her. She gave me her cell number."

"Wait," Tony said. Gordon stared at her, obviously puzzled.

"Let me into the Tiki room so I can run this sample on the Advia. You guys revamped it to test the correct sample size, yes?"

"Well. Yes, but—"

"We can at least tell if the results agree, you see?"

"No. Not really."

"I should see almost exactly the same result from Leonardo as we get from the Advia, assuming the Advia is correct, which I'm not a hundred percent sure it is since I haven't run QC on it or even used it, but we can at least assume that it's more or less up to speed and can tell us if Leonardo is close. Get it?"

"Oh, sure. Yes."

"On Monday, we can run Leonardo a bunch more times and determine if the result is repeatable. If it is, that's great. If not, then you'll have to tinker some more."

"Oh, crap. I hope not. I've about exhausted all my ideas. I'm hoping that since we've established the basic movements, I can modify Leonardo as needed for the Jack and Martha assays."

"Terrific. Poke your finger, Gordo, and get me some blood. All my fingers are done for. I think I'm permanently scarred. I need a blank sample for the Advia."

"You got it, Doctor Leung." Tony didn't have a PhD, but that was Gordon's affectionate nickname for her. Tony wanted her fingers to heal from all the blood pricks. She thought of touching Sheila and not having it be painful.

While she was waiting for incubations, first on the Leonardo, then on the Advia, Tony was grateful for the downtime to relive the night she'd spent with Sheila. During her workday, she had been surprised and gratified that, in spite of hardly any sleep, her mind was clear, all her synapses firing. Maybe sex was truly the boon to human existence she'd heard it was.

A half hour later, Tony and Gordon looked at the two printouts side by side as Tony made a quick calculation. They found a two-percent difference.

"That's acceptable variation," she said. "We're golden. Call Erica."

When he clicked his phone off, he said, "She's ecstatic and said we ought to go home and get some rest."

"Wow. She must really be happy."

Gordon rolled his eyes. "Don't question what she said. Let's meet back here Monday morning and do your whatchacallit tests."

"Repeatablility."

"That's the one."

As Tony gathered her possessions in the office, she hesitated and then called Sheila but got her voice mail. She left a message, recalling that Sheila said she'd be finished meditating at five thirty. She sat at her desk and closed her eyes, glad for some downtime. In between dozing off and waking up, she thought about her night with Sheila. Her cell ringing jolted her.

"Hello there, you." Sheila's voice sounded exactly as it had the night before when they were in bed, which made Tony shiver.

"Hi. We're done. For the moment. Until Monday. I ought to go home but…"

"I have an idea. We can eat dinner, and I'll take you home."

"You'll drive me…" Tony wasn't sure she understood.

"Yeah. I'll drive you home just for the pleasure of your company, and maybe, oh, you might invite me to stay over at your house? Maybe?"

"That sounds great." Tony was surprised at how fast her libido overrode her practical nature. At that moment, nothing was going to interfere with her seeing and touching Sheila.

When Tony and Sheila reluctantly parted Sunday evening, and Sheila went home to prepare for her work week, it was like Tony's arm was being torn off. Everything between them was perfect. Tony didn't believe in perfection, but she was ready to say that she had achieved it with Sheila. Their physical compatibility was stunning, but so were their other interactions.

In the past, Tony could possibly have good sex but not especially scintillating conversation, or conversely, she'd made friends but had no sexual chemistry with someone, though she'd tried that route a couple of times. She seemed to have achieved both with Sheila. Sheila was so…easy. Not in the manner Tony had heard that word applied, which implied promiscuity. She was easy in that she never even appeared irritated or bored or distracted. Whatever they did, Sheila took pleasure in it and clearly in Tony's company.

She hadn't brought up her question about Leonardo, likely because she was simply patiently waiting for Tony to provide an answer. Tony doubted very much that she'd forgotten. Sheila didn't forget things. She already knew how Tony liked her coffee and her parents' names and backgrounds and a dozen other things. She simply had incredible focus and memory.

Tony had no idea what she was going to say. The truth would be best, but that could cause Sheila consternation. It had given Tony pause, for sure. She tried and failed to make up some excuse for Erica's choice to mislead Sheila and her father. Lying was contrary to Tony's code of ethics, and she was certain it would be to Sheila's as well. Could Sheila rescind their investment? That was likely out of the question. This was going to make her nuts if she didn't do something about it soon. It was a matter of trust, Tony concluded. Sheila had been forthcoming with her about the Pacific Partners' stake in the company.

"I want to congratulate you both and thank you for your hard work. This is going to be an extraordinary help when I meet with Lycee day after tomorrow," Erica said on Monday morning.

Gordon and Tony looked at each other. Tony felt it was up to her as the lab scientist to make clear to the boss that they were far from finished.

"Erica?"

Erica said nothing, but her almost-black eyes turned to laser on Tony, and that gaze unnerved her, but she steeled herself to speak. "We have to do some more runs to show that Leonardo will behave consistently. You know. Give the same result every time."

"I understand, sure. You will need to do that, but right at the moment, I've got to have the shipping department prepare the Leonardo for me to take on the plane to France. I'll bring it back, and you can continue your work. Gordon, please start modifying all the rest of our Leonardos." Gordon paled. A number of prototype models were sitting around in Disneyworld—their nickname for the engineering lab.

"Um, okay," Gordon said, glancing at Tony to gauge her reaction.

"All right. If that's what you need to do," Tony said, tightly.

"Wonderful, again. Thanks so much to both of you."

They stood up and left Erica's office.

"What do you think?" Tony asked Gordon when they returned to Disneyworld.

"I think…that Erica is impatient. She needs to get more investors and more money, and hire more people. We need resources. If this is the way she wants to roll, well, she's the boss. I know you don't approve. Neither do I. We have our personal ways of working and what we think is right, but…"

"The fakery bothers me. And her doing things with Leonardo before we're finished with development. Doesn't it bother you? She doesn't listen to what we say or respect our suggestions."

"Of course, it bothers me," Gordon said angrily. "But you know what would happen if we objected? We'd be out on our asses in a nanosecond."

"Right." Tony knew this was true. She'd heard about some people who had said no in one way or another to Erica. They were gone.

"So, we just need to keep on keepin' on and let her be the CEO, who pays us to do what we do. She doesn't need us to argue with her."

"You're right," Tony said. "I know you are." But did she really believe it? For the time being, she'd go along with that view.

Tony called Sheila late Monday afternoon. "I have to work late."

"Looks like that's going to be a standard thing. Not that I mind. To me, with people like you and Gordon going balls-out all the time, that's more evidence that GHS is going to be successful. I'm sure Erica needs you two to do what you do."

"Yep," Tony said. It was all she could manage. She was a mass of confusion and dread. Her memory, which had been erased it seemed by making love for the first time with Sheila, came flooding back. She still had that question from Sheila to answer.

All day Monday, she and Gordon had spent hours and hours rerunning tests and had had to beg other staff to donate blood because their fingers were shot.

Tony was disappointed and frustrated Leonardo couldn't render a single result in any consistent way. It was not reproducible, not even for the immunoassay. They had two more tests to perfect, but they ultimately had to develop hundreds. That's what Erica had said. Leonardo had to be able to do all the standard medical blood assays as well or better than any commercial laboratory.

Worse than that, Tony didn't know what she could or should say to Sheila about any of this. She didn't want to create a bad or erroneous impression about the state of GHS to a major investor whom she happened to be sleeping with and could potentially fall in love with. Someone who deserved her honesty.

She had no idea what to do. Sheila was still talking, and Tony had lost track.

"I'm sorry. I'm so tired, I kind of spaced out there. What was the last thing you said?"

"I said, you need a hot tub and a neck massage, and then you need a couple or three orgasms, and you'll feel *much* better."

That was probably true, and it all sounded wonderful. But… none of that was going to soothe Tony's troubled psyche.

"Are you still there, Tony?" Sheila asked after a moment.

"Yeah. Yeah, sure. Sorry I spaced out again." Tony felt guiltier than ever.

"Do you want me to come pick you up? Can you leave in a little while?"

"Um. No. I have to stay. And I want to go home tonight. Rain check?"

"Of course. You do whatever you need to. I'll talk to you soon." Sheila rang off.

Tony caught the Caltrain home, which, as usual, afforded her far too much time to think. The more she thought, the worse she felt and the less sure of what she ought to do. Sheila noticed everything, and she had certainly picked up when they were talking on the phone that something was awry. Tony had been as talkative as a magpie on their weekend together, and today she was the opposite.

She was going to have to say something to Sheila and risk ending a relationship that had barely begun. She couldn't abide dishonesty: her own and/or anyone else's. And that brought up Erica's behavior and what to make of it.

Tony thought about the phrase "the end justifies the means." She'd never believed it was true. People always have to make moral choices. On the other hand, she wasn't certain she possessed all the pertinent information. She had only her own impressions. Gordon appeared to be making some sort of peace with the status quo. Perhaps things weren't as bad as they seemed. Maybe her moral code was a bit too rigid and ought not to be applied equally to everything and everybody the same way every time.

She wanted to talk to her dad, but something stopped her: his odd warning of a couple months before about Sheila. She decided to go ahead with her plan to talk to Sheila and tell her the truth.

After the phone call with Tony, Sheila hung up and sat for a moment, assessing her mental and physical state. She was unbalanced because of Tony's abrupt change of behavior. Something was wrong, but Tony wasn't ready to discuss it and obviously needed some mental and physical space. Sheila was fairly sure whatever it was had nothing to do with her or with them, but she'd just have to wait. In the meantime, she had more pitch meetings to schedule and other companies to keep an eye on. In Buddhist practice, if something troubled one, one needed to look within oneself for the reason for the disturbance and await more information.

Sheila was rewarded when Tony called her late in the week and said, "Things have settled down at work, and I hope you have some time to see me."

"Oh, my dear, I have time, and I would love to see you. Will you come for the weekend?"

Again, she heard a pause, short but perceptible. "I'd like that."

"Friday at...?" Sheila wanted Tony to establish the time of their meeting.

"Five will be fine."

When Tony stepped into her car, Sheila leaned forward, and the kiss they shared was suffused with memory and redolent of desire and encouraged her optimism. Tony, though, broke the kiss and backed off with a sad and strange half smile.

"How are you?" Sheila asked.

"I'm hanging in there. You?"

"Very well. Are you hungry, or should we go directly to bed and eat later? First things first and all?" It was a trial shot. Sheila hadn't any idea of how Tony would react, and it was good she was prepared, because Tony flinched slightly.

"Sorry. Could we get something to eat and just talk for a while?"

"Absolutely. Mexican okay?"

"Sure."

They were seated at a table in La Casa and had already given their orders before Tony took a deep breath and said, "I'm sorry for being incommunicado. It's borderline rude after we had such a great time together last weekend."

"No need to apologize. I didn't experience your actions as anything other than you needed some space to deal with something I'm not privy to and would find out about if you choose to share it with me."

"Wow. Most people would flip out if I was so distant with them after the, er, experience we had. They'd think I was the worst bitch in the world." Tony paused, then said, "Or that I had a screw loose."

Sheila smiled slightly. "That's not how I roll. Torqueing myself into a mass of nerves because you didn't behave how I expected you to behave wouldn't help either of us."

Tony was astonished, though she ought not to be, at Sheila's equanimity. She hoped it would last through what she was planning to say.

"You are someone unique and unprecedented, at least in my experience." Tony didn't bother to hide her awe.

Sheila grinned and raised her water in toast.

They paused as their dinners arrived.

Tony was starting to discover that Sheila's dearth of words was the essence of her leaving space for Tony to open up. She had concluded that she could do only one thing, and that was to tell Sheila the truth. Sheila had once asked her about what it was like to work at GHS, and she'd answered in one way. The answer to that question had changed. Tony didn't know very much about romantic relationships, but she was sure she couldn't be physically close to a woman and not emotionally close. She had to speak her mind, tell the truth. Sheila would respond however she was going to respond, and Tony would have to deal with the consequences.

Tony told her in a fair amount of detail what had transpired with Sheila and Roy's introduction to the wonders of Leonardo and what Erica had recently done with the demo for the Swiss pharmaceutical firm, Lycee LTD.

Like she always did, Sheila listened intently and said nothing until Tony stopped talking. She took another sip of water and smiled in a rueful manner. "Have you ever heard the phrase, 'Fake it till you make it'?"

"No, and it doesn't sound like a good idea."

Sheila laughed and then said, "It may not be the best idea in most circumstances, but it's a common MO in the Valley. Sometimes we rely far too much on appearances and perception versus substance and reality."

"I see what Erica did as dishonest."

"That it is, in an objective way. She misrepresented her company's product."

"She has misled people on at least two occasions. People who she wants to do business with like you and your dad."

"Yes, she did, and this bears watching, but it's not going to make us, my dad and me, get cold feet."

"It won't? Doesn't it make you worry that you're not going to recoup your investment? Or worse, that it's how Erica operates?"

"Tony, my dear, first of all, do you think we've never lost money on a company?"

"I don't know."

"We have before, and we will again. Do *you* believe GHS is going to be successful?"

"I hope so, but we have a way to go. Erica's idea is really something. Did you know she holds five patents? She thinks we can make it work, and I believe her. But it's going to take time for us to iron out all the bugs. A lot of time."

"Yes. I know about the patents. Of course, I don't know about biotech or medical devices, but some software companies didn't have all the bugs exterminated from their programs when they released them, and they made millions anyhow."

"We can't release something that doesn't work because lives are at stake. This isn't some dopey app to get your take-out food delivered faster," Tony said angrily.

Sheila grabbed her hand and squeezed it gently. "No, it's not, and you are the kind of person who will do whatever it takes to create a perfect product. You *are* staying at GHS?" Sheila raised her eyebrows.

"So, you're not upset?" Tony's brief flash of ire subsided, and she was relieved. And, when she thought about it, not all that surprised. Sheila was *not* like most people. She responded in due time to whatever was said to her. She didn't react or, worse, overreact. It must be the Zen Buddhism, Tony reasoned.

"Not at all."

"You won't talk to Erica about this?"

"Oh, no. That wouldn't be wise. Information is always helpful, though it is to be shared judiciously. She would know where the info came from, and I have a feeling that would rebound on you in a bad way. I'm taking it in and keeping it quiet."

"You still want to see me? And yes, I'm staying at GHS. I still believe, though I wasn't happy with what I told you."

"Yes, I want to see you. More than ever. Now finish your quesadilla, my dear. We have places to go and things to do." Sheila squeezed her hand again, intertwined their fingers, and her eyes sparkled.

The place was, of course, Sheila's condo, and the "things" were a lot of sex and a lot of hot tub and more sex *in* the hot tub.

They were lying in bed, resting, and Tony said, "I think I'm pretty naive. I went to work for GHS believing Erica was the most wonderful woman I'd ever met and the most inspiring CEO possible and that she wanted us to do well by doing good. I didn't reckon on deceit being involved. I'm not used to that."

She was wrapped up in Sheila's arms and feeling peaceful and secure as well as sleepy.

Sheila kissed the top of her head and squeezed her tighter. "I love that about you. I knew the first time we talked that you were honest and loyal. Please don't ever lose that attitude. It's priceless. As for Erica, I've seen her type before. The CEOs I talk to, they're single-minded to an extreme. They will not let anything stand in the way of their goals. That's a good thing, because they couldn't do what they do otherwise. They will always bend rules. The trick is they can't bend them until they break them. We'll see what happens with GHS. I hope you'll continue to give me the lowdown on the happenings in the lab. I promise I will never break your confidence, not even with my dad, and certainly not to Erica."

Tony took a deep breath. "Oh my God. Thanks. That's great. I ought not to have told you about the blood-test demos. I would get fired for sure if Erica found out."

"Since Erica demands NDAs from *visitors*, I'm certain she wouldn't be happy with you telling me what you did. But I'm glad you did. It will stay between us."

They gazed at each other a moment and then shared a deep kiss.

Tony not only had her fears allayed about telling Sheila the truth, but she was going back to work Monday with renewed optimism and determination. If Erica was working on creating a good impression of GHS so that she could attract more investment, it was up to Tony, Gordon, and all the rest of the staff to back up Erica's efforts with reality.

❖

On Sunday afternoon, Sheila took an hour off to go to a dharma talk.

"I'm fine here. It'll be nice to rest for a while. Read or watch TV," Tony said.

"Thanks. We'll go out to dinner when I come home, and I'll take you back to the City."

"You can take me to the train station. It's fine. You don't have to drive all the way to San Francisco and then have to come all the way back. Seriously."

"We'll argue about it later, sweetie," Sheila said, grinning tenderly.

While Sheila was gone, Tony didn't spend a lot of time on any of the pastimes she had mentioned; she looked around Sheila's condo.

Sheila had a desk in her bedroom and a bookcase holding, among other things, a fair amount of what Tony figured was Buddhist literature. Over the desk hung two posters. Well, they were fancier than posters, they were more like art works. The words were written in calligraphy, with birds and Chinese characters surrounding the print. One was the Four Noble Truths. The other was the Eightfold Way.

Right understanding (*Samma ditthi*)
Right thought (*Samma sankappa*)
Right speech (*Samma vaca*)
Right action (*Samma kammanta*)
Right livelihood (*Samma ajiva*)
Right effort (*Samma vayama*)
Right mindfulness (*Samma sati*)
Right concentration (*Samma samadh*

The Four Noble Truths
The truth of suffering (Dukkha)
The truth of the origin of suffering (*Samudāya*)
The truth of the cessation of suffering (*Nirodha*)
The truth of the path to the cessation of suffering (*Magga*)

Tony stared at the two posters for some minutes. The Eightfold Path made sense. She recalled Sheila using the word mindfulness that first night they were together and Sheila was giving her a massage. So much was going on then, she'd forgotten to ask what Sheila had meant. Tony knew about Buddhism, but she'd never given it much thought. Her parents were Methodists and took her to church every Sunday when she was a kid. Her mother naturally made disparaging comments about Buddhism. "New Age claptrap" was the term her mom had used, though even Tony knew Buddhism was thousands of years old.

Here was Sheila, though, apparently a serious practitioner, if the presence of an altar and all these books meant anything. Tony looked over the altar again as well. She picked up each object as though it contained some sort of secret meaning about Sheila that she could absorb by touch. While they ate dinner later at a vegetarian restaurant, Tony asked, "How long have you been a Buddhist?"

"Since I moved back to the Bay area, about three years."

"How did you start?"

"One of the CEOs who pitched us talked about Buddhism. I was surprised and asked him a lot of questions about it. I realized as I learned more about it that I was missing spirituality in my life."

"A venture capitalist as a Buddhist. It doesn't seem to match."

Sheila laughed. "I've heard that before, but Buddhism is about a way of life and has a special emphasis on ethics that truly helps me make good decisions. It helps me with all areas of my life. With you, for instance."

"With me? How?" Tony didn't know if this news was flattering or alarming.

"Buddhism counsels patience and compassion toward everyone. I could tell you weren't at all sure if I was for real and if you wanted to get involved with me. I liked you so much, my inclination was to race forward at top speed to win you, but that wouldn't have been a good idea. I had to wait for you make up your own mind. And you did." Sheila saluted her with her teacup. They were eschewing alcohol for the evening.

Sheila had said, "Buddhism doesn't explicitly forbid alcohol, but I don't drink very often. I prefer to not have my consciousness altered in that fashion, but I like to be sociable on occasion."

Tony said, "I've never met anyone as calm and serene as you. Most people are masses of angst and always trying to control everything. You're different."

"Yes. Buddhism helps with those tendencies. I still have them, but they're not as bad as they used to be. I can slow down and let go when I need to. And in the world of Silicon Valley, slowing down and letting go of expectations is a real challenge, but it's possible."

"What about the crystals? I don't picture you as a crystal kind of person."

"Oh? What kind of person is a crystal kind of person?" Sheila asked, her tone humorous.

Tony was on the spot again. "Um, someone who dresses in tie-dye and has about a thousand pieces of jewelry and talks about 'aura' and 'chakra' and 'vibrations.' Not someone like you."

"I get it. Well, all I know is the touch and presence of that quartz crystal on my altar alters my consciousness in a subtle way. Like my practice of meditation."

"Well, here's to your altered consciousness, whatever that may mean. It certainly seems to work for you," Tony said, and they clicked teacups again.

Later that evening after Sheila had driven her home despite her protests, Tony thought about what Sheila had told her. It was true that Sheila had won her trust by not pursuing her. She let Tony come to her and, in doing so, gave Tony the emotional space to open up her psyche. And thanks to Sheila's astute reading of her personality, Tony realized she had jumped off the cliff she was teetering on and was in love with Sheila.

CHAPTER NINE

Sheila always looked forward to the annual conference for Silicon Valley women. It was a huge networking event that drew all sorts of people, not just women from all corners of the tech industry in the Bay Area. When she opened up the Evite, she wasn't surprised to see that the keynote speaker was Erica Sanders.

Sheila took her seat amongst the four hundred women and a scattering of men. The pace of change was glacial in Silicon Valley, at least in regard to women and their representation. Erica and GHS certainly represented a leap forward. She and her company's success could likely accelerate progress farther and faster. That, to Sheila, was at least as important as the vast quantity of money Pacific Partners would accrue if GHS succeeded.

Erica nodded her thanks to the conference chair and stood at the podium. For a long moment she didn't speak, but stared over the crowd as though trying to make eye contact with each and every person.

"Change is hard. Change is necessary. Change is unstoppable. You all have heard the old saying, 'Lead, follow, or get out of the way.'" Erica listened to the scattered murmurs and laughter without expression.

"I intend to lead." The room erupted in cheers and yells. Erica's satisfaction at the response she evoked was clear. She went on to offer a few more generalized statements on women in the workplace, with asides regarding the Valley in particular. All of it was well received.

But the gist of her talk was heavily skewed toward GHS and its innovation and its rosy future. It was a sales talk, in other words, and to Sheila, it was no longer inspirational. The crowd appeared to adore it, but Sheila was put off. This wasn't an occasion to hype a product or one's own company

Afterward, Erica was mobbed by admirers, and Sheila wasn't moved to wait in line to offer her personal congratulations. She went to the lobby and out the front door to breathe in some fresh air and absorb some natural light before returning to the convention hall. She had pulled out her phone and looked at her incoming calls. She wanted to call Tony right away but had a number of business calls that were more pressing. But before she could even choose a message to return, she felt a tap on her shoulder and turned. It was Erica.

"Oh, hello. How are you? Great speech."

"Hi, thanks. I saw you sitting in the audience, and I thought I might take a moment to speak with you."

"Of course." That was a mighty short acknowledgement of Sheila's praise. Well, Erica didn't have to be overly gracious with compliments she received. No one would expect a man to be.

"I'm sure you know how things can look one way and be something else altogether."

Sheila's antennae went up. What was Erica referring to? She wasn't glowing with happiness about her successful speech as she ought to have been. She seemed keyed up.

"I think I might know what you mean, but please be explicit."

"Good. Because I think you know why I need to get something cleared up with you." It was her discovering Sheila and Tony having breakfast. That had to be it. *She doesn't like it, but she can't do anything about it.*

"I can't dictate the personal relationships of my staff."

Oh, but you'd like to, wouldn't you, Sheila appended, silently offering Erica a noncommittal smile.

"But I do require they exercise the utmost discretion regarding their work at GHS. If any proprietary information would leak, it could be devastating to our bottom line."

"Oh, certainly." To call out Erica or not call her on her agenda, that was the dilemma. *Say as little as possible. She can't afford to offend me. Not in any way.*

"I trust your judgment, Sheila. You, after all, showed good judgment in choosing to fund us." *Ah-ha.* Trying to leaven things with flattery and a little humor. Good choice.

"I believe that demonstrated our commitment to your future success," Sheila said in an even tone.

"Yes, it did, and I'm grateful, but I can't leave anything to chance." As if Erica was able to bend the entire universe to her will.

"I appreciate that. You can rely on me. Please be assured."

"Okay. Thanks much. See you soon." With that Erica walked away and was met by yet another starry-eyed admirer.

Sheila watched her for a moment, then picked up her phone and made her calls.

"I don't think she's about to fire you. But I believe she wouldn't hesitate to if she even suspected you had leaked something," Sheila told Tony later that day.

"Oh, I know. There's a lot of gossip around at work about who she's fired and why."

"I recommend you be careful. Very, very careful, especially about who you talk to and what you talk about."

"I plan on it."

About a month after Tony spent her first night with Sheila, an email notice went out to the entire company distribution list, notifying them of an "all-hands" meeting later in the afternoon in the cafeteria.

Tony wasn't concerned about disruption of her work. It was on hold currently because Gordon was busy trying to modify the spectrophotometer to perform accurately every time. They'd decided that the spec was the source of their inconsistent results. Tony didn't have much to do but wait until he was ready for another run. She had more time to obsess about Sheila and when and if she should make her big announcement of love. It seemed like she'd fallen in love too fast, and she was leery of telling Sheila.

She wasn't optimistic that Gordon could solve the spectrophotometer problem any time soon, if at all. Specs were notoriously sensitive, and the one in Leonardo had been, like all the analytical components, reverse-engineered to make it fit in the available space. Gordon had created it by tearing apart a normal-size spectrophotometer and then recreating it, except on a much smaller scale. Tony had nothing but admiration for Gordon's abilities, but she doubted even he could manage to create a miniature spec that was as good as the original.

It could go wrong innumerable ways. Since Tony had no electronics or mechanical aptitude to speak of, she was interested only in what a given instrument could do. The most important thing was it had been able to perform reliably. Could she and Gordon possibly convince Erica to make Leonardo any bigger?

Gordon had tried, but Erica was determined that it had to be consumer friendly, i.e., small and simple to use. This was her mantra, and nothing could change her view. In spite of the evidence, and even with modifications, it wasn't simple or straightforward for the proverbial person on the street to use. But once a thought was established in Erica's brain, it was extremely hard to dislodge it.

To test the Leonardo's consumer friendliness, Gordon had taken an early version of the Leonardo 2.0 to a software company in the City, where one of his friends worked. The employees allowed themselves to be guinea pigs. They could manage to prick their fingers, but then they had to collect the blood drops using a gizmo called a transfer pen and get the blood into the microcaps and then into the Leonardo. In other words, lay people had to undertake a lab process. None of them were able to do it right the first time, or even the second and third time.

When Tony heard this, she wasn't surprised. Even handling one's own blood gave a lot of people pause. But Gordon's test subjects were able to do it eventually. It was probably better that Erica's current vision was for patients to go to Graff Drugstores, where a drugstore employee took their blood and then operated the Leonardo. Gordon noted that it had taken a lot of convincing for Erica to back off her "Leonardo in every living room" idea. But it was a good sign that she, at last, listened to reason and permitted a modification of her original vision.

Tony joined the rest of the GHS staff as they sat in the big light-filled room, chattering among themselves about the reason for the all-hands meeting and drinking the free sodas provided. Someone had told Tony that Erica wanted the cafeteria to be totally free because she didn't want GHS people to go out for lunch but to stay on campus all day, every day, and work more. And at least one wit had added, "And not be able to talk to anyone besides other GHS employees."

At fifteen after four, Erica walked in accompanied by a short, dark man. She was very good at making an entrance. Whenever she called a meeting, she was between ten and twenty minutes late to make sure all eyes turned to her when she entered the room. Tony considered Erica disrespectful of her employees to use this trick, but like most things about Erica, it worked for her, and she kept right on doing it.

The assembled employees applauded as Erica and her mystery guest took spots in the front of the cafeteria, which had been designed with large meetings in mind. It even had a small stage.

Erica waved and grinned, acknowledging the applause. The strange man did an even stranger thing: he waved as though everyone knew him. Tony pegged him as Indian or Pakistani. A head shorter than Erica, he wore blue jeans and a white shirt.

The noise finally died down, and Erica, as was her custom, scanned the room silently for a good thirty seconds. The man with her grew solemn and turned his focus to her.

"It's good to see everyone. Welcome to another day of changing the world." Everyone laughed and cheered. Erica liked to spout motivational quotes and sayings.

When the noise died down, Erica said, "This is a very special occasion and this"—she turned to look at the man next to her—"is a very special person I'd like to introduce to you. Hakim Alvi. He likes to be called Huey. He is GlobalHemoSolutions' new executive vice chairman and chief operating officer."

Huey? Sounds like a cartoon character.

Erica continued. "I've had to spend more time traveling and working on business deals, so I needed someone to look after the day-to-day operations. That's going to be Huey. He comes from the software world, where he made a lot of money in the first dot-com boom. He doesn't need to work, but he agreed to help us out. Please welcome Huey to GHS."

More cheers and shouts erupted. Erica had made it clear early on that when they had a big meeting, she expected a lot of enthusiasm, and people delivered.

This might be a really good development. Erica was obviously busy. An executive who was around all the time and accessible to the employees could surely be helpful to their day-to-day work.

Huey made a nice generic speech about how much he was looking forward to working with everyone, and that was that. After the meeting broke up, Tony sought out Gordon, intending to ask him about the next step for Leonardo.

He was standing next to Ricardo, the supply-chain manager who always knew more company gossip than anyone. Though Ricardo was an affable and good-natured fellow, Tony didn't like gossip, so she avoided talking to him.

Ricardo rubbed his chin as he watched Huey go around shaking everyone's hands. To Gordon he said, "I know this dude."

"You do?"

"Yeah. One time, Erica got a little tipsy at a party, and he came to pick her up."

"I don't remember that," Gordon said, sounding dubious.

"Yeah. Only a couple of people noticed. He's an odd sort of guy, don't you think? Maybe stuck in a seventies time warp? Those designer jeans?" Ricardo shook his head.

Gordon laughed and so did Tony, in spite of herself.

"Well, he's our boss now," Tony pointed out. "So we have to get used to him."

"Right," Gordon said. "Got to get work. See ya, man," he said to Ricardo as he turned to walk away, and Tony followed him, waving to Ricardo as they left the cafeteria.

"What's next with Leonardo tests?" Tony asked.

"Nothing," Gordon said. "I'm getting some help, and we need to come up with a new box."

"What?" This abrupt change of direction astounded her.

"Well, the good news is Erica is okay with this new Leonardo being bigger. I can take most of the Leonardo innards and transfer them into something that fits better."

"What am I going to do in the meantime?"

"Don't know. You might ask Huey." Gordon grinned evilly.

Tony had come to realize that staying over at Sheila's house saved her a huge amount of commute time. Sheila would drive her to work to make certain she'd arrive at seven as usual, without her having to get up at five. She and Sheila woke up about five forty-five, lolled in bed for a half hour or so, had breakfast, showered, and voila. She was at her desk. It was easy. Part of Tony's mind told her it was way too easy.

She was able at least to voice this concern to Sheila and have a serious conversation about it, another first for Tony. She had become accustomed to keeping mum about what was bothering her after several bad reactions from her mother when she'd disclosed things about herself as a teenager. She deduced that when people were dating, they talked over things. They spent time together and talked. With Sheila, she was on the hook for being honest about what she was thinking. Their interaction over the fake Leonardo blood-test results showed Tony that she *could* be forthcoming, and Sheila was fine; she didn't freak out or lose her temper. Tony wasn't even sure she'd *ever* get angry. At least Tony had yet to see it happen. She had not, however, stated the current primary thing on her mind.

"What about staying with me bothers you?" Sheila asked, reasonably.

"I'm imposing."

"That's definitely not true. I want you around. I like you being with me. I like sleeping with you. It must be something else."

"I don't know," Tony said reluctantly, though she *did* know. She was afraid she was becoming far too dependent. She was used to being on her own, going her own way. But all she said was she thought she was staying with Sheila too often.

"Well, when you know, you can tell me. Meanwhile, what do you want for dinner?" They were trying to eat out less. This meant Sheila would cook, which she did very well. But of course, it was another example, in Tony's view, of how intertwined they'd become in an extremely brief time. It had been only a couple of months since the fateful hot-tub night.

"Quinoa and beans and salad?"

"Sure."

It was over dinner that Tony finally blurted out, "Are we doing that lesbian thing and moving way too close, way too fast?"

Sheila didn't answer right away. She wrinkled her nose and grinned to herself, for she wasn't looking at Tony.

"Is that what you think is happening? I know it's annoying for me to answer a question with a question."

"Yeah. I do think that," Tony admitted. "And yes, it is a little annoying when you answer a question with a question."

"Well, I'll watch out for that thing. As to what you asked, I like to let things unfold organically. I don't like a lot of process, I like to allow matters to progress naturally, but I do, however, not want you to be uncomfortable. Although…" Sheila raised her eyebrows.

"What?"

"Lack of comfort isn't a bad thing all the time."

"Right," Tony said. "I'm not used to any of this, and it feels weird."

"May I suggest that you may not always recognize happiness for what it is."

Tony sat back in her chair and looked back at Sheila, who was smiling gently. *I'm crazy about this woman.* And, amazingly, she's crazy about me. *That's probably why I feel unsettled. Too many good vibes and not enough angst. I'm used to angst or...nothing. Why can't I tell her how I feel?*

"I'm a dope." Tony put her head in her hands.

Sheila stood up and came around the table, then made Tony stand up and hug her.

"You're not a dope. Just a slightly nervous human. It will pass." They kissed and Tony relaxed.

Tony backed up a bit so she could meet Sheila's eyes. "I'm pretty sure I'm in love with you."

Sheila tilted her head. "Oh? Pretty sure?"

Tony was suddenly uncertain. "Yes. I think so."

"Well, I hope you're sure, because I'm *sure* I'm in love with you."

"Okay." And the rest of Tony's response was another kiss.

It took six months for Sheila to bring up the idea that they move in together. Tony did agree that she was occupying the world's most expensive mailbox, i.e. the apartment she rented in the City, but she had misgivings and wouldn't say definitively either way.

"I've never lived with anyone before. I don't think I'd be very good at it," she said.

"Well, you've been doing it for the past six months in reality, though we don't call it that."

"Well. Yes. But I could always go back to my apartment if this doesn't work—back-up plan."

"True, but do you know what that sounds like? Like you don't think this is going to work. Is that what you think?"

"Er. No. I don't." She was shading the truth. She *wanted* Sheila and her to work. She just wasn't sure they would.

Sheila had an answer for everything. Nothing about their relationship, either in a practical or emotional sense, was problematical. Tony couldn't think of a time she'd felt more secure; Sheila was an outstanding girlfriend. And Tony no longer had to endure an hour-and-a-half commute on the Muni and Caltrain to get to work. She was working longer hours than ever, and Sheila was picking her up at work to take her back to the condo, where their relaxation in the hot tub and shared dinner infinitely soothed her. She could find no real reason not to move in with Sheila.

Except the differential in the levels of their income. That was jarring. One of the few things Tony remembered her mother saying that she agreed with was that Tony had to be able to take care of herself.

"And..." Sheila said. "Once GHS goes public or gets sold, I'm going to be a full partner, and I'll make a couple million." Another huge shock for Tony, but she didn't say anything. Again, Sheila's attitude toward money was light years away from hers.

Sheila said, "Get in there and work your butt off so GHS will go forward." Tony knew Sheila was teasing, but the admonition still gave her pause.

Sheila added, "When that happens, we'll take a trip somewhere—wherever you want to go. Africa? China? France?" She laughed and hugged Tony, who hugged her back and kept her misgivings to herself. They seemed trivial and unrealistic. It was, Tony decided, just her fear of the unknown and perceived lack of control. She and Sheila talked about that frequently. Tony had been open with her finally about how much she didn't trust herself when dealing with new things.

The pace of change at GHS was speeding up. Because of her background, Tony had been transferred to the new clinical department. Huey Alvi had given her this news. She wanted to ask him about Gordon but was afraid to. The week before she was transferred, Huey had fired Gordon. One day he was there, and the next day he was gone. He didn't even say good-bye to Tony.

In desperation, Tony sought out Ricardo down on the loading dock for possible explanations.

Ricardo affected a blasé attitude as he sat with his feet on his desk and supervised the incoming deliveries and tracked the orders made.

"Hi, Ricardo."

"Hey, Tony. You looking for something?"

"Nope. I'm not looking for a delivery. I want to know what happened to Gordon."

"Oh, boy. What a shit show. I heard from Albert—he's one of the product managers—Gordo got the boot because Erica wants a better box than Leonardo. She's made some wild promise to the Graff people, the drugstore folks, that there's going to be a GHS device in every one of their chains by next year. And they're planning to start with a pilot project of forty in Nevada. Huey found out Gordo was emailing with some other ex-GHS people and talking smack about the company. That's the real reason. If Erica likes you, she'll keep you around and find you something else to do if you're somehow not making it happen in your current job. If she doesn't like you or you piss her off..." He mimed someone being kicked.

"Are they reading our emails?" Tony couldn't believe what she was hearing.

"You better believe they are, and you better be careful. IT monitors everything. All our emails. You know the chat functions are turned off. We aren't encouraged to talk to other people in the company. Huey even has HR looking at people's Facebook pages to see if people are posting negative crap about GHS."

"Big Brother is watching," Tony said, trying to be funny. She didn't find any of it funny. She was suddenly scared, though she had no plans to say anything negative about GHS to anyone by email or on Facebook. She wasn't even on Facebook. The only person she confided in was Sheila. She rarely said anything to her dad.

"Holy *1984*, Batman," Ricardo said, but he wasn't smiling.

"How come you know all this?" Tony asked.

"Because *everyone* comes down here one way or another. Except Huey. It's beneath him. He doesn't care about me and my boys. We're just peripheral. I like it that way. It's a safe space, and I'm like a shrink." Ricardo grinned, modestly. "Everyone tells me stuff."

❖

All of this was in Tony's mind when she went to see Huey after he summoned her. In his office was a strange man whom he introduced as Sanjay.

"Antoinette, we need you on the clinical side. There's going to be a lot of lab testing. Sanjay is the new director of the lab, and you'll be reporting to him."

Because Tony knew a director of a clinical laboratory had to be an MD and a board-certified pathologist, it made sense. She couldn't take such a position; she didn't have the credentials.

Huey didn't say any more about her new job. She assumed this Sanjay fellow would make those explanations. Huey sat down and started staring at his laptop, so they were evidently dismissed. Tony wondered if Huey really was Erica's boyfriend. If so, yuck, in about fifty different ways. He was older and, well, ugly.

As they walked out, Sanjay said, "It's nice to meet you. We have a lot to do."

Tony smiled weakly. It was a puzzle as to what they were going to exactly do, since they didn't have any GHS-built instruments that could do patient testing. That's what Gordo had been working on before he was fired.

They had the Advia and the Siemens commercial blood analyzers that had been refitted to work on smaller sample volumes. What were they going to do and how were they going to run an actual clinical lab to test patients' blood on the faulty Leonardos? Where did the drug-store plan fit in? She, fortunately, was not paid to come up with the answers to those questions. Sanjay was her new boss, and she presumed she'd be clued in when the time came.

When Roy came back from the GHS board meeting, Sheila wanted to ask him for an update, but she thought he ought to be volunteering to talk about what was going on with GHS. Tony told her some bits and pieces, but they mostly had to do with her frustrations in the lab, which were many. Tony, however, always put a good face on whatever craziness was going on, telling Sheila glitches were the nature of product development in the biotech world. She was upbeat, loyal, and relentlessly hardworking. Tony did mention that the employee turnover rate at GHS was astronomical, far higher than in her past experience. That was one of the things Sheila wanted to see if Roy and, by extension, the whole board was aware of and if Erica had offered any explanations. What Roy had told her seemed to indicate that Erica didn't talk about anything that might be negative, like a high-turnover rate. And no one asked.

When they were able to spend time together, Sheila often had to struggle to cajole Tony to relax. She was wound tight almost all the time and struggled to let go of work when she wasn't actually at the lab.

They went out for bike rides most weekends, and Sheila thought it was time for Tony to have her own bicycle and not have to use crummy rental bikes anymore. It was going to take some finesse, though, because Tony didn't like Sheila to buy things for her. She wasn't comfortable with what she considered a high level of dependence, but that's exactly what Sheila planned to do.

She was looking online at various bicycles and sources for them when she heard her father's voice in the hall. She walked to her door and called, "Hi, Dad."

He was speaking to one of their research assistants and seemed quite animated. After a moment, he strolled into her office and sat down.

"You look happy," Sheila said, and he smirked.

"We found out today that *Time* is going to interview Erica for a cover story and profile."

"Wowee. That's cool."

"She's going to do it next week. She's getting a stylist, the whole deal."

"What else came up at the board meeting?"

"Oh, not much. The Graff project is to start in six months."

"So, did you ever see the actual agreements she's signed? Do you know the scope of the project and how much money? That reminds me. Whatever happened to the VA project?" Sheila had asked Tony if she'd ever heard of that, and she'd said no.

"She said the VA project fell through. Lawyers are still reviewing the Graff agreement. You know how long that takes." He rolled his eyes.

"Did anyone on the board see it?'

"Well, no, but she has, you know, lawyers—pretty pricey and famous ones, I hear."

"Uh-huh." Sheila was perplexed. What exactly did this board of directors actually do? They were strangely hands-off. It was a matter of confidentiality, but she hoped Roy would be somewhat more forthcoming with her since he was, well, her dad as well as her boss. But no, he didn't say much and that made her even more curious.

Chapter Ten

Tony and Sheila were in bed on a Saturday morning in June, having slept in. It was, in fact, nine a.m., and Tony didn't even want to move. She'd worked until nine o'clock the night before. Sanjay had told her they had to have three new tests ready in less than three months. They had the new assay designs from R and D and would have to finesse them into standard functional clinical lab assays, using, as always, a tiny amount of fluid.

Tony would have to do all the work because she was the only one in the lab. What would happen if these lab tests didn't work on Leonardo? Or even on either of the two commercial machines? Or whatever the new machine someone was supposedly designing?

These questions flowed constantly through Tony's brain, but she merely had to do her job and hope for the best. She was at that moment thinking about going back to sleep, but Sheila was slowly stroking her, and that was waking her up.

She turned over, pulled Sheila into a hug, and squeezed her hard, bike-rider's butt. Tony was developing one as well, which she was proud of.

One of Sheila's more amusing quirks was that she giggled during sex, an action wholly out of step with her usual measured demeanor.

"Do that again," Sheila said, snickering, and Tony obeyed, thinking it wasn't too onerous a task.

"I could do this all morning. Your ass is really something."

"Thanks, but I'd like you to touch other parts of me as well."

"Which parts?"

"Which ones do you think, Brainiac?"

"Right."

Tony rolled them over, took the top position, and ground their bodies together. She could feel moisture on her thigh.

"What have you been doing while I was still asleep?"

Sheila kissed her. "Nothing. Just thinking of you."

"Ah. That's nice."

Sheila thrust hard against her leg, which was a signal she wanted Tony to do more. She was no longer giggling. Tony stuck her hand between them and teased Sheila's labia apart with her index finger. She was slippery. Sheila came once, but Tony hung on because Sheila was multi-orgasmic. They rolled over to let Sheila recover.

"I don't think I'm in the mood," Tony said. "Yesterday was endless. I didn't think we'd ever stop. I have to go back in this afternoon. I told Sanjay, though, that half a day was all I could do, and I needed Sunday off. I don't want to get burned out."

Sheila rubbed Tony's stomach gently. "That's fine. I can make it up to you later. Do you want to talk about anything?"

"Nope. Don't think so. It's the same old, same old. We've got a mysterious deadline. Sanjay doesn't tell me details, just 'we have to finish this, and it has to be right away.' I presume he gets his marching orders from Huey."

"Yep. That *is* a funny name. Like you said, a cartoon character."

Tony laughed and agreed. Only it turned out Huey wasn't anything like a cartoon character but more like a horror-movie villain. She'd heard enough from Ricardo to not want to have any personal interaction with him but couldn't avoid him completely. He would come into the lab and harass Sanjay.

Sheila hugged Tony and kissed her cheek and her forehead, then stroked her hair. Tony loved how well she comforted her without being sexual or even verbal.

Tony relaxed in Sheila's arms for a few more minutes, then forced herself to get out of bed and prepare to go back to work.

❖

In spite of Sheila's counsel to let it go, Tony continued to puzzle over Erica's odd management of GHS.

For one thing, the lack of communication among different functional areas bothered her greatly. In her old job at the biotech company, to get anything accomplished, everyone had to know the goals and the timelines. It could be chaotic, with endless meetings where everyone fought and argued, but they eventually reached consensus, and the projects went forward. Also, there was no regulatory group. Those types of person could be royal pains, but anyone who wanted government approval, usually from the Food and Drug Administration, the FDA, had to have in-house regulatory gurus. Tony thought the FDA would surely have to approve Leonardo, but she saw no indication they were working toward that goal. Tony was experienced with clinical lab regulations, but no regulatory expert was looking over her shoulder and checking up on her. It was a relief, but it was super weird and unsettling

Finally, they didn't have an occupational health and safety expert to make sure they didn't harm or infect themselves while they were working with human blood and other hazards. No one seemed to care, Tony noted. Safety in the lab was, in the end, basically Sanjay's problem. Tony would police her own activities and protect herself.

Other folks were around when Tony arrived. Sanjay was already there as well, standing by the lab bench with one of the new engineers. Tony thought his name was Hung but wasn't sure. Behind them was a Leonardo.

Tony put on her lab coat and, after she was introduced, asked Hung in a friendly manner, "How's this thing doing? Is it ready for prime time?"

Hung shrugged. "Erica said she wanted for us to improve the design so she could get a bunch made to send out to those drugstore people."

Tony was curious. Leonardo was, well, in her experience, a piece of crap. When she was in the R and D group, they hadn't been given time to make it work, and then Gordo was fired. Then Tony was transferred to the clinical group.

Sanjay said, "Research has developed a brand-new potassium test and herpes test for the Leonardos they want to send to Graff stores. We have to do all the testing and the QC. Then they can start testing patient samples asap."

This was even worse news. They weren't in any manner ready to test patients. The lab wasn't fully set up, and the device wasn't vetted. Tony knew how to assay for herpes and potassium levels on commercial analyzers, but even the ones they were using were rendering flaky results because of the diluted sample volumes. This new directive was, to put it mildly, questionable, and Tony considered it demented, but she clamped down on her tendency to voice her objections. Mostly.

When Hung left, Tony said flatly to Sanjay, "What's going on? We've used this thing before, and it doesn't work. How can we test patient samples on it?"

Sanjay, an older fellow, in his fifties maybe, laid-back to a fault, shrugged. "Erica asked if we could be ready to go in four months. I said yes."

Tony was coming to suspect that Sanjay really had no idea how a clinical lab had to be run. He was just the name on the CLIA license with MD after it. Worse, she suspected he was a yes-man. Erica adored the people who would promise to fulfill her wishes no matter how absurd. Ricardo had told her so on more than one occasion. And he always assured her that those who asked too many questions were given the heave-ho.

Sanjay said, "We'll be fine. I've gotten permission to hire another tech. You're going to be my line supervisor."

"I'm not sure about this." Tony said to Sheila. "I'm not that practiced a cyclist. This is way too fancy a bike for me." She harbored misgivings about allowing Sheila to gift her with such an expensive present. It made her feel uneasy.

"You'll come to like it very much, I predict, because it's much better than the rental bikes. I promise it'll be more fun for you. We can go on more ambitious rides."

"Right." Tony climbed on the Specialized racer and took a spin around the parking lot of the condo complex. It felt effortless to ride, like she was riding on air, and she barely had to exert herself to push the pedals. She changed gears smoothly.

Tony glided back to where Sheila stood waiting by her own bike and beaming at her.

"Okay," she said. "You're right. It's much better."

"Yay! We'll do the Alpine Portola route. Not too challenging. I want you to get really used to your new bike before we try anything harder."

They'd done the ride before, and on her new bike, Tony had less trouble keeping up with Sheila, who pushed the pace faster. When they climbed the slight hill that led them back to Sheila's condo, Tony definitely noticed the difference both in the way the bike behaved and her lessened exhaustion.

She told Sheila, "Wow. This is amazingly different. I'm tired but, you know, not completely done in. I love this bike. Thank you so much."

"So, you're going to keep it and not make me send it back?" Sheila arched her eyebrow playfully.

"Nope. I'm sold."

"Wonderful. Since you say you're not very tired, I've got something in mind."

"Oh? Are you going to tell me?"

"No. I'm not, and you're just going to have to deal." Sheila mock-glared at her. "Surprises can be delightful."

"Right."

They locked their bikes in the garage and went around the corner to the back door of their building. Sheila wasn't positive Tony would go along with her intended scenario. While Tony had loosened up a bit over the six-months-plus length of their relationship, she still tended to answer no automatically to something outside her experience. Sheila had been planning this surprise for the right time.

They drank some cold water from the refrigerator to rehydrate.

"Are you hungry?" Sheila asked.

"Not really. I'll wait till we eat dinner."

"Good." Sheila caught Tony's eye and gave her the little grin—the corners of her mouth rose only a touch—that was their signal. *I want to make love.* She reinforced it by crossing the kitchen and putting her arms around Tony and pulling her into a slow but emphatic kiss. Tony responded with a murmured "umm" of pleasure. Then she said, "I ought to take a shower first."

Sheila stepped back but kept her hands on Tony's shoulders. "How about skipping the shower? You took one this morning, and so did I. That wasn't a long ride. We're not disgusting. I'm not afraid of a little good, clean sweat."

Tony stared at her quizzically. "Really?"

Sheila kissed her neck. "Really." Then she patted and squeezed her ass.

"Besides, as far as getting off, I'm halfway there. I find the bicycle seat, well, stimulating. If you know what I mean." Sheila raised her eyebrows

This time, Tony grinned back. "I thought I was the only one."

"No. Not at all. You game?" Sheila kept kissing her and rubbing her back and her butt. Tony yielded, and she knew she would achieve her objective.

Faintly, Tony said, "Yes."

"Let's go." Sheila took her hand and led her to the bedroom.

She took off Tony's cycling jersey, then her sports bra. She repeated the actions on herself so they could embrace skin on skin. Tony's neck had a film of sweat, and Sheila licked some of it. It was true that neither of them would be as fresh as if they'd just showered, but that was the turn-on. To Sheila, Tony smelled great. She exuded the essence of herself, tangy and warm, like a savory pastry. Sheila sat down on the bed and kissed Tony's stomach and peeled down her tight bicycling shorts.

Yes, she was already aroused, and the scent of her arousal swirled into Sheila's nostrils. Sheila buried her face in Tony's stomach as Tony grabbed her hair.

"You good?" Sheila raised her face and looked into Tony's eyes.

"Yes," he said, her voice ragged.

Sheila pushed Tony backward onto the bed, took her bike shorts all the way off, and kissed the insides of Tony's thighs. Tony moaned.

"I can't wait," Sheila said hoarsely, opened her labia, and dove in tongue first.

Tony screamed, "Oh, God," as she came, hard, after three licks. It was the stimulation of their bike ride.

Sheila wouldn't let her go until she collapsed on her back, panting.

When Tony regained her breath, she whispered, "Basically, I can't say 'no' to you."

Sheila hugged her tight. "Good. I don't ever want to make you have to say no. Only 'yes.'"

They stayed still, both panting for a few moments, until Tony said, "You want some too, I bet."

"Well, yeah." Sheila's tone was mock-indignant.

"Righto." Tony rolled over and pinned Sheila down to the mattress with a thigh between her legs. "Here we go."

Sheila sat at her desk reading yet more prospecti from companies seeking mega-bucks for their revolutionary, at least in their opinion, ideas. She was pleasantly reliving their post-bicycling sexual encounter from the day before, instead of concentrating on her reading. Not proper mindfulness. But hey. Who's perfect?

Her cell phone rang, and it was her dad's number. Odd. He didn't usually call her. He would merely stick his head in the door of her office if he wanted to talk to her.

"Sheila, honey?" He sounded oddly muffled, as though struggling to get his words out.

"Dad, what's wrong?" She was alarmed. What he said next terrified her.

"My face is numb. My arm is numb. What's going…" He couldn't finish the sentence. Sheila's memory kicked into gear. *He's having a stroke. Oh, no.*

When Roy turned seventy-five, Sheila had cajoled him into giving her powers of attorney—medical, financial, and legal—for him. The whole shebang. He was in relatively good health, but he had high blood pressure and an allergy to exercise and a penchant for eating rare steaks and chocolate cake far more often than Sheila considered wise, but she didn't want to get into nagging.

She'd said, "You're at risk for something happening, Dad, and we have to plan for that."

She'd read up on potentially catastrophic health events.

"Dad, you're having a stroke. Call 911. Right. Now. I'll meet you at the Santa Clara Valley Medical Center."

"Okay." He sounded like he was talking from the bottom of a well.

Sheila stopped at the front desk and told her receptionist that Roy was having a medical emergency and she'd call later with an update. Rina would know what to say to people, and she'd take messages.

In her Volt, driving to the hospital, Sheila called Tony in her cell phone's hands-free mode. She had to leave a message because, without a doubt, Tony was in the lab and mostly didn't answer her phone when she was there because, she said, it wrecked her concentration. She'd call back as soon as she could.

It took only a ten-minute ride up the 280 freeway to the hospital. Sheila hoped the ambulance was as fast. She went directly to the ER and was told he'd only just arrived and was being evaluated. The nurse asked her to wait until the doctor called her.

Sheila sat in the crummy plastic waiting-room chair and performed breathing exercises to calm herself, then closed her eyes and meditated until she felt a hand on her shoulder. She opened her eyes to see a young, attractive, female doctor peering at her.

"Ms Garrison. I'm Doctor Wen. I want to update you on your dad, Roy Garrison. Correct?"

That's correct. Nice to meet you, Doctor."

"Certainly. He's suffered a mild stroke. He's stable at the moment. We're admitting him."

"Okay, good. Anything I need to do right now?"

"Are you the only next of kin?"

"He and my mother are divorced. I'm his medical power of attorney. May I see him?"

"Yes. Shortly."

Sheila tried to call Tony again, but she still didn't pick up. Feeling adrift, Sheila tried to clear her mind and remain calm. She decided she ought to call one of the Pacific Partners investors, Gary Frenzel. He had known Roy the longest.

It was while informing Gary about what had happened that Sheila slowly realized this event would have a major impact on their business. Among other things, someone else would have to attend GHS board meetings in Roy's place. Sheila decided immediately it would be her. Other partners could pick up the rest of Roy's board commitments. She told Gary, and he agreed. They'd meet in a couple of days, after Sheila had a chance to learn more medical details, especially Roy's prognosis.

She stood at his bedside and held his hand. In his stroke-damaged voice, Roy tried to apologize.

"It's okay, Dad. Take it easy, please. Don't worry. Everything's all right. I talked to Gary, and we've got it covered."

He managed to choke out the words, "Tell Erica Sanders."

She patted his hand. "I will, Dad, ASAP."

Back in her office, Sheila called Erica Sanders first. It wasn't as though GHS was the most important company they had a stake in, though their commitment was big. Other firms had progressed farther down the road to solvency. It was unique in that Roy had taken the unusual step of throwing millions of his personal fortune into GHS. That made his interest in their success greater. He obviously had a great affection and admiration for Erica Sanders personally.

Erica called back right away since Sheila had left a message stating that Roy had suffered a medical emergency.

"Thanks for letting me know. What happened?"

Sheila described the situation.

"Do you know when he'll be back to work?"

This struck Sheila as an insensitive question, but she tamped down her irritation.

"No, I don't. The doctor advised me it could be anywhere from three months to a year to never. It depends on his recovery."

Erica was silent.

"But," Sheila said, "I'll be taking his place until he's recovered."

"That's not necessary. We can make quorum for the meeting. He can take a leave of absence." Erica said it nicely, but Sheila detected an undercurrent of…something. Anger? Distrust?

"Oh, I'm sure you can appreciate our position. Roy asked me to take this on since I'm the principal on your account." He hadn't in fact asked her to sit on the board in his absence, but she knew he would, and *she* considered it vital they keep a close eye on GHS.

"Very good," Erica said with clear reluctance. "I'll send you an invite to the next board meeting, which is next week." Sheila could almost hear the wheels turning in Erica's mind.

"Thanks, and please send any relevant recent documents."

"Certainly."

It was clear Erica didn't especially want Sheila to be on her board of directors, but why?

❖

They brought some Italian takeout back to Sheila's condo. Tony had, as usual, stayed at work until after seven. She would have stayed longer, but when she heard about Roy, she wanted and needed to be there for Sheila.

"I suppose I ought not to be surprised," Sheila said, sadly. "He used to be a terrible smoker. He stopped years ago, but I don't think that helps in the long term. He loves scotch and rare steaks, too. His blood pressure was astronomical, and he probably wasn't consistently taking his meds. He was a stroke or heart attack waiting to happen."

She was devouring a cannoli as she talked. Tony figured she was stress-eating, because it was unusual for her to be voracious. Such behavior made her smile, but she decided not to mention it to Sheila. Even the perpetually chill Buddhist had her limits and her right to not be perfect.

"You can run the company while he's getting better."

"Well, yeah, the senior partners and I can carry on. I hope they don't veer off in any odd directions without talking to me. I don't think they will."

"But you *are* going to take his place on the board of GHS?"

"Yep. I don't think Erica wants me there but too bad."

"Why wouldn't she? That's nuts."

"I don't know, but I'll probably find out in due time."

Tony walked around to Sheila's side of the table and hugged and kissed her.

"I need you," Sheila whispered.

"I know. I'm here," Tony replied, hoping she was up to the challenge.

❖

"Tony, I would like you to meet Tan." Sanjay indicated the young guy standing next to him with a deer-in-headlights stare.

"Hi, Tan. Nice to meet you."

Tony had her hands full with ordering supplies and trying without success to coax consistent results out of the commercial analyzers. Without explaining why, Sanjay had ordered her to get them up to speed for testing diluted samples. But Tony grimly congratulated herself on being right. They going to use commercial analyzers until Leonardo was ready. If it was ever ready. Tony tamped down her thoughts on the implications of *that*.

"Get Tan oriented," Sanjay said and, without another word, left the lab.

Tony showed Tan around and asked him a few questions, but he was not extremely forthcoming. She judged he wasn't confident of his English skills. She'd worked around this before. All she cared about was if his lab skills were up to par. She left him to read some of the protocols she'd written up. Sanjay had asked her to to write them because that was how you worked in a clinical lab. People had to have the recipes to follow. She was still modifying her protocols for the Advia analyzer. She didn't know what was going to happen with Leonardo. It was back with the engineering group, and she wasn't in the loop to know what or how they were doing.

Shit. This place is a train wreck. And Tony wondered again why she was enduring this monstrous amount of uncertainty and lack of real information from management. The answer, of course, because of Erica's vision. She thought of the greater good, the big picture, the mountain they were all going to scale. She silently recited these clichés in hopes their message would keep her steady.

Tony decided to visit Ricardo down at the loading dock. He was always at least good for a laugh of the black-humored variety, and a lot of the GHS staff visited with him because he was a fount of gossip, rumor, and, often, hard information. Tony had lost her disdain for gossip and hearsay because it was becoming clear that any misstep, the wrong question to the wrong person, could result in being fired. She decided she needn't blindly believe everything Ric said, but she ought not to dismiss him either.

The loading dock was a safe space for employees. Huey didn't like to go there because he might get a smudge on his stupid, out-of-fashion, designer jeans. He tended to stalk the offices and lab areas, trying to see who was there and who might be slacking off. On the loading dock, there was only one security camera. It faced the driveway and was, unlike all the other security cameras, actually dedicated to protecting GHS from outside threats instead of spying on the employees.

"Hey, Ricardo. How are you?" They bumped fists a la Michelle and Barak Obama.

"Oh, Tony, you have no idea." He rolled his eyes. "But I'm hanging in there."

She sat down in his guest chair. "Do you know anything about Sanjay Vishnu? Like what's the deal with him?"

"He's Erica's new golden boy, and he's tight with Huey. That's all I know."

"He's the weirdest, most hands-off lab director I've ever worked for. Is anything else going on?"

Ricardo spun his chair three hundred sixty degrees and touched his finger pads thoughtfully but didn't answer.

"So, here's the million-dollar question, Ric. I was in product development for a couple months, then I got thrown into clinical, and

Sanjay doesn't say anything to me, but he hired a new guy, Tan, and we're stocking up with everything. What's going on?"

"It's Graff. You're going to do patient testing."

"With Leonardo?" Tony was flummoxed. Exactly one test was functional, and it was barely working. It hadn't even been properly QC'd according to the clinical lab protocols Tony was versed in. And the old Leonardo was supposedly being replaced with an updated version that who knew how long it would take to arrive

Tony put all the various stands together and ended up saying what was in her head to Ricardo, though she probably shouldn't have. But he nodded sagely as she spoke.

"They are manufacturing Leonardos to put into the Graff stores, but they're not ready to go. First, they'll ship the patient samples back here to us for the tests. But we have only a few that can be run on Leonardo, and even then, they haven't been thoroughly QC'd. How are they going to do all those different tests?" Tony stopped talking, and it hit her.

"We're going to run them on the Advia. That's not really kosher. It's not been QC'd either, and the manufacturer's specs are for much larger volumes of blood. We're not supposed to use them except according to the manufacturer's specs. Except Gordon said they've solved that problem by diluting the samples. But..." She looked at Ricardo, and he was clearly following what she said. He nodded.

"Senorita, I think you understand. We're doing it GHS style." He spun around in his chair again and added, "You think it's nuts, I know, but it's all about what her majesty wants, her majesty gets, full stop." He meant Erica.

"Do you think Graff knows what the story is?" Tony asked.

"Oh, I think they've been told a story for sure."

Tony was quiet for a moment and then asked Ricardo, "What makes you think this is what's going to happen? With Graff, I mean?"

"Well, two things. I've been receiving a buttload of shipments of what I know are parts for Leonardo. And the enginerds are always down here the second there's a delivery. They won't say, but I think they're ramping up production. And I'm pretty sure it's for the Graff's deal. Todd, the product-liaison dude, let that slip the other day.

They're going to put Leonardos into a bunch of drugstores around the Bay Area."

"To do what?"

"What else, dude? Run tests on site."

"But they don't work," Tony said, astonished.

"Since when has that ever been an issue?" Ricardo asked, acidly. "I think there's a deal that the stores are going to ship the patient samples over here, and then you guys will test them and send results back via Wi-Fi."

"How do you know that?" Tony was astonished at Ricardo's statement.

"Simple. Huey told me in his usual gentle, sweet manner: 'Get a contract with DHL, and make sure they know we'll get twenty percent discount, and don't tell them it's for human samples because they'll want more paperwork.'" Ricardo imitated Huey's brusque, accented growl.

"So, we're going to test using the Advias?" Tony said more to herself than to Ricardo.

"Yep. Oh, and I know what else you ought to know. Watch out. I heard from Ari in Security that Huey comes by his office every morning and demands the previous day's proxy-card-reader data."

"What for?"

"He can tell who's badging in and out and when."

"Oh." Tony absorbed this tidbit.

"What else do you know about Huey?" Tony asked Ricardo.

"I'm glad you asked. This is a good one. I was having a couple beers with Warren from HR the other day. You know, Heather's lackey? I don't think he's going to be around much longer though." Ricardo chuckled. "He's too irreverent. 'Not a team player' is how he says Heather sees him. But she won't fire anyone unless she's told to. And she always plays along with management. Some HR person she is—"

"Ric, what else about Huey?"

He leaned close, their knees almost touching. "He reads Glassdoor every week to see if anyone's posted a bad review of Global. Then he starts snooping around to try to figure out who it was."

GlassDoor was an online employee forum where people could post anonymously. Tony read it occasionally, and after Ricardo's statement, she resolved to start visiting the site more often.

"But get this. Warren says Heather made him write a glowing review of GHS to counter the bad reviews, and Huey made her make him do it."

"Wow."

Ricardo leaned back, flipping a pencil back and forth and smirking at her.

"You got to watch your back around here. I'm telling you."

"Thanks for the info, Ric. You're a good guy." Tony meant that, and she tossed him a fond look.

He blushed. "Tony girl, you say the sweetest things." He was using what he obviously considered a "queeny" voice. But Tony wasn't going to reprove him, this time. She would be back to see Ricardo for more information. *Not* gossip. She remembered what Sheila had said about information and how key it was. And she wondered how much of this she ought to tell Sheila.

❖

"We're lucky we're both morning people," Tony told Sheila.

"Yes. If you weren't a morning person, that would be a deal breaker for me. I knew you were a good catch when you first told me you took Caltrain in the City to make it to work by seven. Holy shit, I thought. This one's a keeper." She kissed Tony for emphasis.

Tony's work hours were such that she could just manage to eat dinner and fall into bed when she came home. Or she took Caltrain back to the City, and they had only a brief phone conversation.

The mornings of the nights that Tony spent with Sheila were their time to catch up on each of their lives. Sheila took a shower and went to meditate while Tony showered. Then they got dressed, all their preparations for their day happening in a seamless flow of efficiency.

They were making breakfast together: oatmeal, yogurt, and fruit. After some grumbling, Tony had adopted Sheila's eating habits, and she had to admit she felt better than if she'd eaten a doughnut, or bacon and eggs.

Tony was admiring Sheila's put-together look: pinstripe, gray tailored suit, and mint-green fitted shirt. She was off to the GHS board meeting later, and Tony was still wondering how much of the discussion she'd had with Ricardo, the supply-chain manager, she ought to reveal to her. This wasn't a case of confidentiality or proprietary technology. Tony wouldn't be violating her NDA, although, from what she'd gathered, anything to do with GHS about anything going on in the company and stated by anyone to anyone else could potentially send Erica into paranoid orbit.

Sheila would be sitting around in a conference room with her that very day, but Sheila was trustworthy and swore she wouldn't reveal anything Tony told her, and Tony believed her. She had spent her time in the shower obsessing about what Ricardo's information really meant. It was, she realized, too heavy to carry by herself, and she needed to discuss it with Sheila and get her opinion.

She told Sheila everything Ricardo had spilled.

"Hmph." Sheila snorted. "It's Mickey Mouse. It's bullshit. All except the part about putting the devices in drugstores. Yet sending the samples back to you to test if they don't work. *That's* significant. Roy told me the timeline was six months out. It seems she's pressing forward. I hope Erica plans to talk about that today."

"But don't you think their whole management approach is a bit wacko?"

"Honestly, for all you employees, I think it sucks, but it's not unusual, honey. These start-ups are under a lot of pressure to succeed—pressure that can make people lose their perspective and become paranoid. And don't lose your mind about the Graff project until you know more. Ricardo might not have the correct information. I wouldn't worry. I just want you to be careful and keep your head down. I don't want *you* to get fired."

Sheila gave her a hug and a tender kiss. Tony was mollified and mostly reassured. The devices-in-the-drugstores scenario still bugged her though, if it was indeed true. What she knew about the Leonardos made her throat constrict when she thought about them being used for testing patients. But she had always been a worrywart anyhow. That trait was appropriate for a lab scientist: the least little thing could make your testing results go south, and you had to keep vigilant.

Sheila swiveled her chair and looked out the big picture window of Global HemoSolutions' conference room. The distant hills, green from the recent rain, looked peaceful.

Erica was late to the meeting. Still playing the one-up-woman-ship power card, Sheila noted, sourly amused at her consistency. None of the other attendees said a word about it or even appeared to notice. They were busy chatting about golf, the stock market, and Valley gossip. When Sheila had introduced herself to them, they were cordial. To a man, they were remarkably alike—all from the Valley tech culture or from government, over sixty years old, and almost certainly Republican. It was probably the Stanford connection. That was an odd thing too. Erica had spent exactly two years at Stanford. She hadn't even acquired a degree, but she'd filed five patents that she touted in her prospectus. How did that work? Sheila had only the most superficial idea of the ins and outs of patents.

Erica arrived at last, and as soon as she was settled, Valley veteran and board chair John Derrault called the meeting to order.

"Any questions or concerns on minutes of last meeting?" He paused for the shortest of moments and then said, "In that case, let's—"

"I have a question," Sheila said.

Derrault looked pained but said, amiably enough, "Go ahead."

"Last quarter's minutes say, 'Erica to provide copies of legally vetted agreements with retail partners.' Are we to receive those today? Have other members received them by email? I check Roy's email every day but haven't seen anything. Please catch me up." Sheila formed her expression to indicate innocent curiosity and pitched her voice the same.

She heard no response but one or two throat-clearings and the movement of squeaky conference-room chairs. Derrault looked at Erica and asked, "Any update on that?"

Erica was studiedly neutral. "The lawyers are still reviewing them."

"When may we expect them?" Sheila asked, in the same mild tone. She recalled that's what Roy had told her, three months ago. Lawyers *were* slow, but not that slow.

"Oh, who knows? Lawyers," Erica said cavalierly. This remark elicited a few chuckles around the room.

"Let's go on," Derrault said. "You have some news for us, Erica?"

She beamed and made eye contact with everyone around the table. "*Fortune* has contacted me to do a profile. The reporter is coming in two weeks. *Business Insider* wants to write an article on me and being a woman in Silicon Valley and still succeeding."

There were murmurs of congratulations and approval around the room.

"You're going to be the toast of Silicon Valley. You are already," one of the gentlemen said.

Erica smiled in transparently fake modesty.

"Do you have new projections to share?" The publicity item was over. It wasn't even on the agenda, Sheila noted.

"I do," Erica said, proudly, and passed out some charts.

Sheila looked at her copy since she hadn't seen anything other than what Erica had provided the year before when they signed their agreement, nor did she know about any budget information. She'd found nothing in Roy's files and hadn't had an opportunity to check with him, so she decided to ask Erica.

"Could you send me some previous projections and a couple months' worth of budgets, along with the partnership agreements? I would really appreciate it. Roy isn't able to brief me at the moment."

"I'll take a look," Erica said. "But like I told you, the agreements are still being vetted."

"A draft copy is okay. It's just for my reference. I know it's not official or final," Sheila said, sweetly.

"Fine." Erica wasn't cordial anymore. What was up with that? Did Erica not have assistants to do these menial tasks like email documents?

The next two items were disposed of, and the talk returned to what Sheila considered superfluous fluff: the publicity Erica was receiving. She would be recognized for innovation and being a female entrepreneur at an awards dinner the following month.

After the meeting ended, Erica left as abruptly as she'd arrived, and Sheila had concluded the best thing to do was to embark upon a bit of schmoozing with Gary, her dad's old crony, and see what he might reveal.

"Hey. Do you want to grab lunch, and I can let you know how Roy's doing?" Sheila asked him.

They went over to Tanner's, a place Sheila knew Gary liked as much as Roy did. It didn't offer much Sheila could eat outside of salad and bread, but it would have to do. She wanted Gary to be comfortable and in a good mood.

Gary was old-school, just like her dad, and Sheila was glad he ordered a martini. She wanted him to talk unrestrainedly, and he mostly did, since he was a talker anyhow. She had only to provide gentle prodding, and his natural gabbiness along with a couple martinis did the rest.

Gary's bald head became a little pink as his second martini kicked in. Sheila caught him up on Roy's health and prospects and then gently brought the subject around to GHS.

"Do you like being on the GHS board?"

"Oh, hell, yeah. It's like the biggest thing in Silicon Valley right now. You heard all those magazines want to profile Erica. She's a rock star. And the company's valuation—it's five billion."

"She seems to be. Do you know how far along she is with the whatchamacallit—the blood-test machine?" Sheila was sipping, very slowly, a glass of white wine. She was determined to stay sober and not risk missing anything.

"Oh, she talks about how many companies are interested in it. She's going to start manufacturing. She's already renovating a factory space in Fremont. The demand for this is going to be through the roof. You know she's hired this big-shot ad agency in San Francisco. When they're ready to go, they'll do a full publicity campaign and website roll-out. This is going to be huge, Sheila. Huge."

"That sounds fantastic. Do you want another?" Sheila pointed at Gary's empty glass.

"Hey, why not? I don't have any meetings this afternoon." He winked.

"Erica can be a little short on the details of what she's doing that's not related to public relations, don't you think?" Sheila asked, mildly.

"Oh, I don't know. I think she has it under control. She's brought on a COO to take care of all that. Some Indian guy. You know, Sheila, we have to give her at least as much leeway as we'd give any man. We ought not to second-guess her. I'd think you'd understand that." Gary was another recent convert to feminism.

"I don't think anyone wants to treat her like she's some dumb woman. I didn't see that," Sheila said, and it was true. It was rather the extreme opposite.

"No. We try to be respectful. Early on, before Roy came aboard, there was this guy—I think he was another VC—and he was real aggressive with her. She got Derrault to can him."

"Aggressive how?" Sheila asked

"Oh, you know. He'd grill her. 'What about this, what about that?' He tried to trip her up. He'd go 'last meeting, you said this or that, and now it's changed?'"

"Uh-huh. He was booted?"

"And I was able to bring Roy in. That's good, right?"

"Right. Well, here's to all the money we're going to make." Sheila raised her glass.

Gary grinned, "You got that right, sweetie." Maybe not feminist quite yet. Sheila let it pass. She wasn't happy that the board of directors appeared to have completely abdicated their oversight functions. Erica had free rein to do whatever she wanted. Sheila was concerned about where that might lead, but, one, she could do nothing about it, and two, she didn't know of any bad consequences. Yet.

"Do you know who the COO is?" Sheila asked Tony later.

"Well, yeah. Of course. Huey."

"What's he like?"

Tony didn't answer right away. "He's kind of a jerk. Most of the employees don't like him. I told you about all that security junk. That's him."

"Yeah, right. You did. Do you think he's competent? I got the impression Erica has let go of hands-on management."

"I'm not sure."

Sheila decided to change the subject. "It was the most superficial board meeting I've ever been in. I need to ask my dad if this is normal for them. It's almost like they're a bunch of doting grandpas with their precocious granddaughter. I was the only one who asked a question, and I'm not sure I'm going to get an answer. Erica sloughed me off with some story about lawyers have to review this or that."

"Did they talk about anything to do with the company and what we're going to be doing with Graff?"

"Nada. Just the next-year income projections, and I still want to know more about them. Tony, honey, they'll tell you what you'll be doing when they tell you. Everything's always going to be last-minute. And you'll handle it, whatever comes."

Tony said no more. Sheila was right. She wasn't sure exactly what she ought to say anyhow. Talking with Ricardo had activated her foreboding, her manager Sanjay was in a cone of silence, and she couldn't even ask Gordon's replacement any questions about the progress of the Leonardo upgrades. She received monstrous amounts of lab supplies, as though they were going to be doing a lot of testing, and she dutifully signed for them, trained Tan, and organized the lab. Certain clinical lab supplies needed careful inventories. They couldn't use expired items, which would invalidate their assays.

About two weeks after her last talk with Ricardo, Sanjay walked into the lab with a man Tony didn't recognize. He introduced him as James, and then the two of them walked around the lab together discussing what, Tony didn't know. She was suspicious though, sensing there might be some sort of big change, and she was going to have to roll with it, like Sheila said. Well, she was getting used to the changes, which were frequent. She wondered if James might be another engineer and have something to do with Leonardo that they were supposedly going to test patient samples on, but Sanjay hadn't said anything yet.

Later in the day, Sanjay told Tony and Tan to move the stuff from the three back benches in the lab. It wasn't as though they needed the space, with only two of them working, and that didn't concern Tony. But *what* would take up the space?

She received her answer the following day. James, along with another fellow, entered the lab with no less than eighteen Leonardos on lab carts. They carefully placed them stacked two at a time on the bench, with a stand-alone centrifuge between each pair and connected to both.

It was quite a sight, and Tony first thought she was going to have to stand on a step stool in order to insert samples into the upper Leonardo. That wasn't ideal.

Finally, Sanjay sat Tony and Tan down and described what they were going to do.

Chapter Eleven

Sheila sat next to Roy in his hospital room. She was reluctant to dive into a detailed discussion about any business-related subjects because he was supposed to be resting and recovering. That was the theory, but in practice, he wanted to know what was happening at Pacific Partners with their various clients.

"How are things at GHS? Did you like the first board meeting you went to?" Roy's speech was close to intelligible, and he was seemingly in good spirits.

"Like" wouldn't be the word Sheila would use. Erica's lack of transparency disturbed her, as did the way the other board members seemed content to let her slide and cheerled as she embarked on what appeared to be a full-blown publicity campaign. On the surface, it was supposed to be about publicizing GHS, but essentially it was about Erica. All the while, Erica endeavored not to disclose any details to her own board of directors on what GHS was truly doing. And then there was what she gleaned from Tony's stories about her lab.

Sheila wasn't sure it was a good time to start quizzing Roy more closely about what he understood from his several months on the GHS board.

"Things are good. Erica is quite the PR whiz. She has a knack for attracting attention. Positive attention. We had a good meeting, though I'd like to know a bit more detail about these partnerships she's pursuing."

"She's all over that type of stuff," Roy said, cheerfully. "She meets with a CEO of some company, and the next thing we know, she's signing a contract with him and collecting another few million."

"It's all good. Hey, are you interested in anyone else besides GHS? Because I've got some news. Eric from Wolf Hunt says he's about ready to launch his IPO in a couple months."

"Whoa. Finally. That's good. He's confident it'll go?" Sheila was happy to see her dad switch gears easily from talking about GHS to discussing someone else.

❖

"How's Roy doing?" Tony asked as they wheeled their shopping cart around Whole Foods.

Sheila turned from the apple display she was examining and looked at Tony. "He's doing well. I'm surprised at how cooperative he's been about letting go of his involvement in the business temporarily."

"That's good to hear."

Tony had a myriad of concerns racing through her brain as they wandered through the high-end grocery store on Saturday. She'd been working so much, she and Sheila had scarcely had time to talk, even when she did stay over. Sex was much easier and more relaxing, anyhow, than discussing work.

The shopping trip gave them an opportunity to talk, but she had no idea which subject she wanted to tackle first.

"How's the lab?" Sheila asked. She had moved to looking at kale. "Red or green?" She held up a bunch of each, both looking insanely healthy if not exactly tasty to Tony, but she was learning to cope with the change in her diet.

"Either is fine. The lab's okay. We have to validate three tests for Leonardo before they send them to Graff's stores."

"Yippee. That's good, right? What's validate mean?" Sheila was peering into Tony's face with an inquisitive grin.

Tony gripped the handle of the cart far too tightly. The subject of the lab was anxiety-provoking, and she was still trying to work out what she should say to Sheila about it and what not to say. She was always weighing what was confidential and what was not.

"We have to run a whole bunch of tests to compare results with the Advia to make sure Leonardo works and spits out accurate results." Tony had been writing up all the protocols and had turned them over to Sanjay for approval.

"Sanjay told us we have to move as fast as possible. It's too boring to describe in detail, but I am going to be putting in some insane days."

"You can stay here however much you want to," Sheila said.

"Thanks. I appreciate it."

"You know I like having you. It's no sweat."

Tony knew she ought to be eager to move forward with their relationship, but she wasn't, and *that* triggered her nerves. She was hobbled by reluctance. If she gave up her San Francisco apartment, that would be final. She'd likely never be able to move back to the City because of the horrendous real-estate environment. Sheila's joke that she lived in the world's most expensive mailbox rankled her, even though she knew there was some truth to it She still had issues with the disparity in their incomes and how that was all supposed to work, but she hadn't brought up the subject because she was embarrassed to talk about it.

Finally, there was the lack of stability at GHS. Tony had no real fear of being fired, but an on-going general climate of uncertainty hung over the entire company in spite of the pep talks Erica and Huey routinely gave the entire staff. Tony would come away optimistic and energized, then crash hard the next day when presented with some abrupt change of direction or a fresh load of hearsay from Ricardo. She knew she ought not to talk to him all the time, but she couldn't stay away. He always turned out to be right. She managed to confirm things with other people and had concluded that, in order to survive, she had to pay attention to what people at work whispered about. And Tony wondered if she should disclose yet another thing to Sheila— Erica and Huey's relationship.

Ricardo had confirmed it. They lived together and came to work together, although they arrived separately in the morning. They always went out to lunch, and they always had their heads together. Tony didn't think the board knew about them, because Sheila would surely have said something. Maybe. Maybe she wasn't talking about GHS like Tony didn't talk about GHS as openly as she could. This made Tony uneasy as well, but she didn't have any solution.

They concluded their shopping trip and returned to Sheila's condo. Tony helped her put everything away, and they made lunch together—vegan tacos.

As casually as she could, Tony said, "I heard that Erica and Huey are an item."

Sheila's eyebrows flared. "Is that right?"

"Yep. It seems clear." In reality, it wasn't, but Ricardo was as confident as always that he was correct.

Sheila shrugged. "Well, that's tacky *and* icky. Not to mention questionable corporate behavior, but it's not illegal."

"Yeah. It's kind of disgusting. He's like twenty years older and is such a jerk." Tony munched her taco for a moment and asked, "Wouldn't the board of directors see that as, well, inappropriate?"

"Some of them might, but they wouldn't say anything. Wimps." Sheila laughed shortly.

"Can we go to the movies tonight?" Tony asked.

"Absolutely. Whatever you want to see, honey." Sheila beamed at her fondly, which made Tony feel guiltier than ever. Sheila was never short or irritable. She was sweet and accommodating, as well as sexy and affectionate. She was like this dream girlfriend, and Tony couldn't make up her damn mind to move in with her. Sheila didn't nag Tony about anything or make any passive-aggressive comments about anything, except for the mailbox crack. Tony felt like she didn't deserve her, and that was her last and most shameful reason for avoiding the subject of their living together.

Tony had learned the hard way to never question the enginerds' design decisions unless she had specific reasons to back up her misgivings. As soon as she saw the Rube Goldberg-like setup of the multiple connected Leonardos with one atop the other and the forest of cables connecting them and their peripheral centrifuges, she knew there'd be trouble. She ran a few preliminary tests to check, and sure enough, the top Leonardo yielded funky results. Heat rises, and heat, more than anything else, will muck up a chemical reaction.

She explained her results to Sanjay and James, and they were both hugely irritated, probably for different reasons. James reluctantly separated the paired Leonardos, and they were back to running one test apiece on them. It was a good thing the patient samples would come in by courier, and she and Tan had only to run the tests simultaneously on several devices to produce the required results. After, naturally, they had performed thousands of tests to be able to show everything worked. Tony was crossing her fingers this would be the case, but in reality, she was far from certain. At least they didn't have to make *all* the assays valid for *all* Leonardos, which would be logical, but Tony had a feeling that would never work.

The Leonardos had never been beta-tested. Each of them had to be good for just one test. Even though, to Tony, this seemed questionable, to say the least, she understood it might be necessary for the moment. She was willing to go along with the program, so to speak. They must have good reasons for doing it this way, but Sanjay hadn't, as per usual, given her any reasons. He hadn't even known enough about lab operations to tell the engineers to not stack Leonardos.

The central philosophy of the validation process was to make sure they could get the same result in the same way every time for each substance of interest they tested for across a range of quantities. They were supposed to test one hundred samples with predetermined quantities of the analytes of interest on several different Leonardos and on the commercial blood handler and compare them. The analytes that Sanjay and Huey chose were Vitamin D, gonorrhea, and potassium since these were among the most common tests that physicians requested. Tan and Tony had to recruit dozens of people to give blood to run their tests. They had to rope in their families and friends, including Sheila.

"Oh, baby, it's so sexy when you do this," Sheila teased while Tony pricked her finger and squeezed out two drops of blood.

"You say that now. Wait until you've had to do this a couple dozen times." Tony transferred the blood to microcaps and then to a cooler until she could take them to work in the morning. "Tell me this is sexy when your finger's so sore, you can't touch anything."

"You were able to use your fingers well enough the first time we made love," Sheila reminded her. "And I could tell they were covered with pricks."

"Yes, but I was highly motivated."

As Tony exited Sheila's car in the GHS parking lot and gave her a kiss, Sheila asked, "Shall I pick you up and we can go out to dinner?"

"I'd love to, but I don't know when I'll be done."

Huey was breathing down Sanjay's neck, and he in turn was hovering nervously in the lab while Tan and Tony toiled at their benches. Validation was the most labor-intensive lab project she had to do. And there was a deadline, Tony was certain, though Sanjay hadn't disclosed it.

Tony laboriously concluded one hundred runs for a test of Vitamin D at fifty milligrams per deciliter and then grabbed all the results to perform a coefficient of variation calculation. She'd set the target number at three percent, which was acceptable by clinical lab standards. This meant that the Leonardo could consistently return the same number with the same conditions every time, with only slight statistically acceptable differences.

This particular Leonardo had to render consistent results time after time in its measurement of blood spiked with a normal range of the vitamin D analyte. As she watched the results come out from the program that did the calculations for her, she realized this Leonardo wasn't going to pass validation for Vitamin D. The sample results had too much variation.

"Tan? What have you got?" Tony asked her coworker. He was doing exactly the same thing, except his target analyte was potassium. She knew, although Sanjay hadn't explained anything to them, that doctors requested potassium-level tests quite commonly, as potassium was a key health indicator. She and Tan were saving the gonorrhea tests for last, since that test had only a yes/no answer rather than a number, and it was easier to validate.

"No good. It's all over the place." Tony put the data from the Leonardo next to the data from the Advia runs. They had replicated all the conditions exactly, but the Leonardo's results bore no resemblance to the results from the Advia. Even worse, Tony knew that, though the Advia had been modified to be able to test the tiny volumes, she had no confidence in *its* numbers either. In lab parlance, it was being used in a manner not sanctioned by the manufacturer. But Sanjay had decreed the Advia was gold standard. Because he had a MD/PhD and was the boss, she shut her mouth and followed orders.

"Let me see," Sanjay said and took all their data and spread it out on a bench.

Tan and Tony looked at one another glumly as they waited.

Sanjay returned and handed the data back to them.

He'd check-marked a lot of numbers in each test printout with a red pen.

"Delete the values I've checked and rerun the analysis program. We'll report out the COV on the rest of the numbers. Do that for all the rest of the ranges." He meant for them to literally throw out the results that didn't fit. Tony and Tan looked at each other wordlessly, and Tony saw her alarm mirrored in Tan's face.

What Sanjay told them to do was scientifically dishonest and required them to manipulate statistics in an inappropriate way. Tony had never done such a thing, nor had she ever been asked to do anything like this in her work life.

"But couldn't we have some of the R and D engineering people take a look and see if maybe there's an obvious flaw they can fix to improve the results?" She knew the answer as soon as she asked the question.

"No time for that. Huey and Erica are waiting. Just do it the way I told you to." Sanjay didn't make eye contact with her or Tan. He walked out of the lab. The discussion was over, and it was clear they were under orders to validate the Leonardos as functional devices or else. And then they were going to send them out to be used on the public. Who knew what would happen next?

Tony and Tan took a break to eat some Chinese food Huey had delivered. He had brought it to them himself, all smiles. He clearly loved to see the lab staff chained to their benches for hours on end. It was seven thirty in the evening, and both she and Tan had been at work since eight o'clock in the morning.

"When are you two geniuses going to be done with this project? I feed you good so you can get more work done faster." He was both menacing and genial at the same time, and it was truly creepy.

"We can do maybe one more trial tonight," Tony said.

He appeared happy with that promise.

She debated with herself and finally blurted out her thoughts. "The Leonardos aren't performing all that well. Can we bring in a couple of engineers for consultation?"

"What? What are you saying? Does Sanjay know?" he demanded.

"Yes. He does, but he said—"

"I'll talk to him. You keep up the good work." He swept out of the empty cafeteria. It was hard for Tony to believe that Huey didn't know already what was going on, since he hovered over Sanjay like a hungry turkey vulture circling a corpse. But he wasn't that technically savvy, and Tony figured Sanjay could snow him and probably did, in the name of not getting in trouble with Erica. Tony didn't care if she got Sanjay in trouble with Huey. She had to at least make an effort to convince her bosses that they were headed down a dangerous road.

At Sheila's that night, Tony made her routine call to her dad. She listened listlessly to his recital of trivial bits of news and barely said a word back to him.

After she finished, Sheila asked, "How about I rub your head until you fall asleep?"

"Okay." Tony felt guilty about all she wasn't telling Sheila or her dad about GHS, *and* all she wasn't telling about herself. She was having trouble falling asleep at night. Her long hours at the lab didn't help either. But she convinced herself it was all temporary.

It was time for another board meeting, and Sheila had never received any draft partnership agreements from Erica. What should she do? She was being stonewalled and didn't like it. Gary's story of the board member who'd asked too many questions stuck in her mind. If she crossed whatever invisible line Erica had drawn, it would likely be her fate as well. It was curious that no one else on the board was at all worried. Maybe she shouldn't be either. She wanted to stay on, both because she needed to look after Pacific Partners' interests in Roy's absence, and, secondly, she wanted to see what was going to happen to the woman who was the most famous CEO in Silicon Valley and her much-lauded company. Sheila faithfully read all the news about Erica and GHS, and it was wondrous how positive it was.

Sheila concluded that discretion on her part was the ticket, even if she disliked Erica's arrogant approach to the people on the board, who were essentially her bosses. It was hard to question her since she was clearly doing something right. GHS was the most highly valued start-up in the Valley. And the ongoing undercurrent of sexism of the Silicon Valley culture sure made it look like *any* criticism of Erica Sanders was suspect. Between the astronomical paper worth of GHS and Erica Sanders's stratospheric fame, no one wanted to say the tiniest negative thing. Sheila recognized her unease and her suspicion, but she was reluctant to start causing trouble when she had no actual evidence other than her own dislike of Erica's management style. Even though board meetings were supposed to be confidential, things had a way of getting around.

For this meeting, Erica made her grand entrance with a tall, handsome, balding man in tow. He wore an expensive pinstripe, three-piece suit that broadcast "high-powered lawyer" loudly, though he sat by Erica quietly, smiling throughout her introduction.

"I'd like you all to meet my new corporate counsel, Harry Blevins. I thought it would be a good idea to have him join the board as well. I'm sure most of you are familiar with his reputation." Erica's smug expression irritated Sheila, but she diligently tamped down her pique and reminded herself that lawyers were always necessary in any company. Blevins *was* a catch. He'd had a hand in some of the highest profile legal cases of the past couple decades. His love of publicity was legendary as well, and he obviously knew it would benefit him to work with GHS.

Blevins made a boilerplate, mock-modest speech. The other board members, wide-eyed and worshipful, welcomed him, and they all settled back to enjoy Erica's optimistic news of more publicity and more potentially lucrative partnerships in the making.

"We expect to be shipping out Leonardos to the forty stores in the pilot project in two months," Erica announced with a certain amount of fake modesty.

That must be what Tony had been working on and stressing over, though she didn't say much. Well, that's how the start-up business worked, any business, really. When the boss said to the staff, "Jump," your only question was "how high?" And if she said, "This has to be done-yesterday," then Tony had to move as fast as possible. It was the way things were done.

Sheila reminded herself that she had to be sympathetic to Tony's plight, though she personally was several years away from being an ordinary worker and at the command of someone else. She was the boss's daughter, and the nature of her work was radically different than Tony's. She mused about the effect this all might have on Tony's agreeing to move in with her. It was not likely a good time to discuss that, unless Tony mentioned it, and Tony hadn't brought it up.

She tuned out of the board meeting—they weren't discussing anything of substance anyhow—and thought about how she could make Tony feel better about everything. She wished she could persuade her to practice Buddhism, but Buddhism didn't work that way. One chose the Buddhist way; one didn't get recruited into it as though it was some underhanded religious cult. To help Tony, Sheila thought she ought to at least start with the tried-and-true remedies: she would schedule a house-call masseuse, then some hot tub, a couple of drinks, and a tasty meal. Tony needed pampering, and if she didn't have to work on the weekend, then they could go somewhere romantic. Big Sur, maybe.

Sheila returned her attention to the meeting because Erica was talking, and she picked up on the word employee.

"I'm sure you know about my concern over leaks of proprietary information through our staff. We have a small number of disgruntled people, most of them gone, but some still employed, and Harry is going to help us manage them."

"Manage them? How?" Sheila asked.

"Let me answer that." Harry tapped Erica's arm gently.

"It's unfortunate but true that sometimes staff members don't take their NDAs quite seriously enough. They need gentle reminders and some incentives to return to the fold."

Harry's smile was predatory, and Sheila didn't care for it. She could imagine what sort of lawyerly "incentives" Harry Blevins might deploy in service of Erica's intense desire to control everything and everyone. Along with offering food, sex, and massage, Sheila was going to have to diplomatically again remind her girl to watch her Ps and Qs at work and maybe not gab with Ricardo or with anyone else, for that matter, about what was bothering her. And Sheila would tell her about Harry Blevins and his new role and his little speech.

"It really hurts my feelings that you would go over my head and complain to Huey," Sanjay said.

Though she wasn't sorry she'd done it, Tony had decided to placate Sanjay and pretend she was, though it was against all her instincts to lie about something like that. She was deeply concerned.

"Well, I know, but you weren't listening to me, and I thought about it, and that's the only thing I could come up with. I'm sorry, but what are we doing here? You ought to know that throwing out data points is just wrong."

Sanjay's expression looked even more pained. "I think you have an inflated idea of your own intelligence *and* an unrealistic view of how this all works. We have to be flexible, and we have to do what we're asked as best we can. The powers that be are determined to kick this thing out the door. We'll have time to fool around with it later, your ideas of perfection aside. You know the saying, 'Don't let perfect be the enemy of good.' *I*, for one, can't be insubordinate. Huey can revoke my work visa, and I'll be on the next plane back to Mumbai unless I can find another job pronto."

He looked hard at her, and Tony felt bad. She wasn't the only person involved in this conundrum, that was true. Sanjay had legitimate concerns about his job.

"Yeah. Okay. I'm sorry. I don't want that to happen to you."

"Thanks. Huey and I had a long talk, and we have got a new procedure I think will answer your concerns. And by the way, he wasn't overjoyed at you going over my head either. You know what can happen when you get on Huey's shit list. You better lay low and keep quiet—if you can, that is."

Tony swallowed at the implied threat. Then she composed herself to listen and be open-minded, though she wasn't optimistic.

Sure enough, Sanjay described a cockamamie protocol where they would collect data from six different Leonardos and then throw out the lowest and highest numbers and average the remainder and evidently pray that result would fall within the acceptable range. That was almost as insane as the first method Sanjay had cooked up, but there it was. Tony was a respecter of authority, and she would go along.

When Sheila came to pick her up at work, Tony climbed into the Volt and gave her a distracted kiss but said nothing.

"You okay?" Sheila asked, looking at her intently.

"Yeah. Just tired."

"Are you working this weekend?"

"Uh-huh." Tony tilted her head back and closed her eyes.

"What can I do?" Sheila asked.

"Nothing. Just take me back to your place."

"Are you hungry?" It was nine p.m., and Sheila truly hoped Tony had already eaten.

"Nope. Had dinner. Indian."

They arrived at the condo, and since asking questions wasn't working well, Sheila shut up.

Tony dumped her bag on the living-room easy chair, walked to the bedroom, and, without another word, took off her clothes, put on a T-shirt, and climbed into bed. It didn't seem as though anything romantic was going to happen, so Sheila put on her own T-shirt and slid into bed next to Tony, turned her bedside light down, and perused her smartphone.

Tony lay on her stomach, her face in her pillow. She groaned and flopped onto her back. "I'm too tired to sleep," she announced, put an arm over her eyes, and sighed. Sheila didn't find a need to respond. She stayed silent to see how this was going to play out. She scrolled through her emails, flagging or deleting them as needed. Tony flipped again and faced Sheila, who met her gaze but still stayed mum. Tony was clearly disturbed about something and had to make up her own mind to disclose it. Or not.

"I don't understand what they're doing. We don't have a viable product. Leonardo doesn't work, or it doesn't work in the way I would assume it should work, and they're sending them into drugstores to test actual people."

Sheila put her phone down and gave Tony her full attention. She remembered fleetingly what she'd heard in the board meeting and what she wanted to tell Tony, but this wasn't the time. It was time to let Tony vent, if that's what she wanted to do.

Tony continued. "It isn't right. At least I don't think it is, but I'm not in charge, and other people are A-OK with letting a crummy product out the door. We don't have any regulatory people to put the brakes on. There *are* no brakes."

"What are you afraid is going to happen?"

"Someone will get a wrong test result."

"The consequences would be...?"

"The patients could get a wrong diagnosis, or the doctor wouldn't know to check them out for an underlying condition."

"Are you *sure* that's what will happen?"

"No. I can't be sure, but based on my experience, it could."

"So, Erica is aware of this?"

"I would assume so. Huey knows. He's the one forcing my boss to do it his way, so if Huey knows, Erica has to know. They're—"

"They're in a relationship, and he's the COO, right?"

"Yeah."

"So, if Erica knows, then she's decided it's okay. And you have to accept that."

"Yes. I guess so." Tony was not agreeing, but she was resigned.

"You've made your opinion known, I'm certain."

"Yes," Tony said. "They know what I think, but they don't care. If they did, they would do it differently."

"Come here," Sheila said and spread her arms. Tony scooted over and nestled against her.

Sheila stroked her hair and kissed the top of her head. "That's the real reason, isn't it? They're not taking you seriously."

"No, they're not. But *you* do, right?" She turned her face up so their eyes could meet.

"Yes. Of course, I do, and I understand why you're upset. But think of it this way. You are not in possession of all the facts. Erica and Huey might know something you're not aware of."

"I suppose. But…" Tony told her what Sanjay had said.

She added, "He's trying to save his own butt. I don't trust him to do the right thing."

"Out of your control. You need to give people the benefit of the doubt. Maybe Erica has priorities you're not aware of. Maybe the Graff people know this is an experimental device."

Tony burrowed into her and said, "Yeah. I know. Maybe sometimes I take too much on myself."

"Yes, you do. The Leung code of honor." Sheila hugged her tighter. "Now you have to try and relax, darling, or you'll never get to sleep."

Tony let her body go limp. Sheila massaged her temples and said softly, "There you go. Let it all go. Sleep will find you. You will sleep and be at peace. The universe turns and the heavens are eternal. There is nothing whatever you have to do but sleep."

Tony had fallen asleep. Sheila kept her arms around her and pondered what Erica might be up to. It was maybe time to try to get some answers, if for nothing else than to reassure Tony. Maybe reassure herself as well. She didn't want to increase Tony's distress by sharing her deepening concerns about the board of directors.

CHAPTER TWELVE

"Thanks for making time to have lunch with me." Sheila favored Erica with a neutral smile as she placed her napkin on her lap.

Erica had been surprisingly open-minded to Sheila's invite, and here they were on the outskirts of Menlo Park in a shopping mall in a Japanese place removed from the hubbub (and prying eyes and ears) of downtown Palo Alto.

"Oh, my pleasure. I've been so caught up in everything I haven't had time for any socializing, but I thought, you know, I ought to get to know Sheila better. In this environment, you need allies, right?" Erica said, brightly. She pulled a water bottle filled with some sort of brown sludge out of her bag and set it on the table.

Sheila thought about asking her what it was but thought better of it. No sense in making her defensive right away. *That's sure to occur later.* They stuck to small talk until after they'd given their orders and the waitress was gone. Erica ordered exactly one thing—tuna sashimi. That was it. Was she anorexic or what? Apparently, the brown sludge was to serve as her lunch.

Erica's remark about needing allies sparked Sheila's curiosity. That could be meaningful or not. It wasn't a secret that women had it tough in Silicon Valley. But in Sheila's opinion, Erica had it easier than most. She was the CEO of a bona fide unicorn. She was a celebrity, literally, celebrated in myriad ways. But what was going on inside her company? Why did Erica not fulfill the most basic requests for documents? Were Tony's misgivings about the lab justified?

"I was wondering if you might have forgotten my asking for your draft partnership agreements a couple months ago."

"Oh, yeah." Erica smacked her head in an admirable display of remorse. "Yes. I'm sorry. That was dumb. I'll text Abby right away." She typed rapidly on her phone for several moments.

"There. You'll get them later today." Erica grinned. "Again, I'm sorry."

"Thanks. I wanted to be able to talk to you outside of the board meeting, in a more informal setting." Sheila hoped Erica would focus less on the performative and be more forthcoming without her cheerleading squad around her.

"Oh, absolutely."

Sheila said, "I'm curious. Why didn't you recruit any women to be on your board?"

Erica looked momentarily uncomfortable, but it was fleeting look. In a flash she set her expression to neutral, and then she looked away from Sheila into the middle distance.

"Oh, I couldn't think of anyone who could add value. I was looking for certain attributes."

"Such as? And what about—" Sheila named a couple prominent female Valley denizens.

Erica smirked, derisively. "Sure, Sheila. You know the Valley. I had to be taken seriously right from the get-go. The people around you are who give you credibility."

Sheila wasn't sure what bothered her more—the fact that Erica couldn't believe women could enhance her bona fides or that Erica thought she needed prominent men who could. It was all distasteful. She decided to drop the subject though. She had other questions.

She shrugged noncommittally. "Okay. I was just curious."

Then she asked, "How do you feel things are going in the company?" As Sheila was aware, open-ended questions often elicited the more revealing answers.

"My gosh. They couldn't be better. We launch in forty Graff stores this week. That's just the start. We'll have Leonardos in six hundred stores all over the West Coast by next year. In another year, we'll be able to place them in people's homes. I don't need to tell *you* what that means."

Erica stared at Sheila and fell silent. Sheila knew what she was implying: gigantic sums of money. Profit for investors. Rate of return. Sheila didn't know if it was more a reflection on Erica's focus or upon her perception of Sheila that she was homing in on the profit aspect. She usually talked about patients and the amazing transformation of blood-testing. In Silicon Valley terms, "disruption." GHS, Erica often said during her media interviews, would disrupt the blood-testing industry.

"Are you quite sure your Leonardo is able to do what is advertised it can do?" This was a risky shot, but Sheila wanted to put a dent in Erica's self-assured manner. What she'd heard from Tony was in her mind.

Anger flashed in Erica's black eyes, and then it was gone.

"Oh, yes. I'm sure. I've got amazing people. Brilliant scientists and engineers. I thought you knew that. Your…what is her name?"

"Tony."

"Yes, Tony. I remember. Her manager is one of them. He's a top pathologist."

Sheila nodded, pretending to take this information in as she thought rapidly. *I hope this works. I hope Tony doesn't get into trouble, and she sure doesn't have much respect for his expertise.*

"Tony tells me Leonardo isn't as efficient, I guess is the word, as she thinks it should be."

"Sheila. I don't want love to blind you or muddle your instincts. I want to be straightforward about this point. Tony is a very good worker, but she's not a PhD or an MD. She isn't that caliber, and she doesn't necessarily know what she's talking about. I don't mean to be offensive. If you want, I can talk to her, try to answer her questions."

Sheila *was* offended at Erica's condescension. Erica managed to be dismissive of Tony and of Sheila's concerns at the same time. But Sheila didn't react.

All she said was, "That might help. She's just worried."

"She ought not to worry. I'll take care of it." Erica's expression was serious and sincere.

And they went on to more innocuous subjects. If it wasn't for her misgivings, Sheila would like Erica much more. She was articulate and fascinating. The self-absorption, well, that could be excused. She was evasive though. As evasive in a one-on-one talk as she was at the board meeting.

Erica said brightly, "Thanks for lunch. I enjoyed talking to you. Let's do it again sometime."

On her way back to the office, Sheila thought hard about her next step. She was offended that Erica assumed or seemed to assume that she cared only about the money she and Pacific Partners stood to make.

On the other hand, expertise still counted for something. It could very well be that Tony didn't know everything that Sanjay, the pathologist, knew, and Tony *had* told her she held her tongue partly because she had only a master's degree and a medical technologist's license, and he had a doctorate and an MD. The biggest question in Sheila's mind was what possible benefit would it be for Erica to mislead all the investors, all the reporters, and all the potential customers she could attract? For her to do that would be stupid. Yes, she was grandiose and arrogant, but that was hardly uncommon for Silicon Valley executives.

Sheila didn't want to think her opinion of Erica was filtered through her own unconscious sexism. She didn't want to believe she thought like that. She'd sat through countless seminars on the subject and read tons of books. But she was still a child of the culture and Roy Garrison's daughter. Roy's view of and treatment of women was much improved in recent years, but she had still grown up around him. She couldn't say for sure, but she didn't think her view of Erica was biased, yet who knew what she'd unconsciously absorbed. Sheila hated to think *she'd* do anything unconsciously. Erica was annoying, but so what? She was well on her way to unimaginable success. Erica's own sense of self-preservation would have to dictate she wouldn't do anything to sabotage it. That would be insane. On the other hand,

Tony was deeply troubled, and she wasn't the sort of person who wouldn't pull the fire alarm if there wasn't a fire.

Sheila hoped Erica could talk Tony off the metaphorical ledge she was on.

❖

Tony was sure she was going to be fired. That was her first thought when she received the message to meet with Erica. Well. It was something if Erica was going to fire her in person instead of having Huey do it. As she walked up the stairs from the laboratory to carpet land, she could scarcely breathe from all the dread flooding her mind

Erica was smiling as she opened her office door and ushered Tony inside. *Smiling? What does that mean?*

Tony took a seat and attempted to calm herself. Erica took her time settling in her big leather executive chair.

"How are you?"

"All right. How are you?" Tony stuttered a bit,

Erica beamed. "I'm fabulous, but I'd even be more fabulous if I was assured that you were fine. I hear you're not. I asked you to come up here and talk to me. I want you tell me what's going on and how I can help."

Tony struggled to form her thoughts into coherent sentences. How did Erica know she was upset? Sanjay? Huey? Sheila?

Tony shifted in her chair and cleared her throat, thinking furiously how she could be honest without getting into trouble.

"I've put you on the spot. I'm sorry. That's not very nice." Erica looked remorseful. "Let me tell you what I've heard, and you can say if it's accurate."

"Okay," Tony said, barely able to articulate the word.

Erica leaned back and looked at the ceiling. "I understand you don't approve of how we are testing Leonardos for the Graff rollout."

"Ye-yes. Well, it's contrary to my experience and what I understand as standard lab practice. That's why I questioned it."

"I see. I understand. That's what I thought. Let me try to put your mind at rest." Erica leaned forward, elbows on her desk, and stared right at Tony.

"We have created something unique, something unprecedented. It's nothing like any similar device that's preceded it. You, I'm certain, are well aware of that from your long experience in clinical laboratories."

"Yes. I am," Tony said.

"Right. We have to treat the Leonardo in a totally new way. I've consulted the FDA and have sent them our validation plan. They signed off on it. That's one thing. The other is, Graff is aware this is an experimental device, and they're notifying the patients and getting their informed consent. That's why we don't have to have the Leonardos fully vetted and approved. You have nothing to worry about, Tony. You're a great worker, and your past experience tells you that things have to be done a certain way. I get that. But I want you to understand that this is an unprecedented situation. GHS is a radically different sort of company We're changing the world, and in doing that we have to find unique ways forward."

She paused and stared at Tony until Tony belatedly realized she was expected to speak.

"I thought you were going to fire me."

Erica laughed. "Oh, is that it? Well, I have no patience with people who can't give one hundred and ten percent, who aren't team players. But I don't sense that about you. You were worried, and you voiced your concern. That's acceptable, as long as you're telling the right people. I wanted to address those worries. Are you okay?"

Tony knew the correct answer. "Yes. I'm fine. Thanks for talking to me."

"Good. One more thing, though. I had lunch with Sheila the other day, and she was concerned about our technical progress. I'm not pointing any fingers, but she heard things from you. I hope you're not violating your NDA."

Tony's cheeks heated, and she was embarrassed and dismayed.

Erica stood up, and Tony followed her. She reached across her desk.

"Now you can get back to the lab with a clear mind." She shook Tony's hand and grinned at her benignly. She was dismissed.

Tony walked slowly back down the stairs, vastly relieved she still had a job, but uneasy that Sheila had said something to Erica. Sheila was right, as usual; Tony *didn't* know everything. She needed to back off her ingrained training and have faith in her company.

Erica's words had soothed her, brought her back into the fold. She was vaguely conscious of being manipulated, but it seemed like just normal boss behavior. Worse, she realized Sheila must have talked to Erica. She still wanted to believe—in Erica, in the GHS mission. Mentally she reviewed what Erica had said and didn't think the FDA would be as cavalier about the Leonardo as Erica had described. Erica was doing something underhanded. But, as Sheila would ask, why would Erica be doing something to harm her own business? There had to be another explanation, and Tony had to keep her eyes open and wait and see.

❖

"I'm somewhat better, I guess. I can get wound up so tight, it's like I have blinders on. I can't see beyond my own nose. I think sometimes I'm my own worst enemy." Tony paused. "Did you say something about me to Erica?"

Tony and Sheila were lying in bed, and Tony was tense and worried. The talk with Erica had mollified her only a bit. She was relieved she wasn't being fired, but that was all.

"I said I was concerned because I heard about the Leonardos and how they weren't functioning well from you."

"Well. Yeah. She reminded me of my NDA in not too subtle terms. Don't talk to her again, please, Sheila."

Sheila had her arms around Tony, and Tony felt her stiffen.

"I'm not trying to get you into trouble, but I have a duty as a board member. No one else is doing it. I had to have something to back up my speculation."

"But Erica is probably going to be spying on me from now on."

"Tony, baby, you tend to spiral yourself into a bad place when you feel under fire. You haven't done anything wrong. I'm sorry to cause trouble for you. I won't do it again."

"I need you on my side," Tony said.

Sheila patted her cheek. "Always."

They fell quiet for a few moments.

"Is it time yet for us to contemplate that Big Sur trip? Are you off the hook for working weekends for a while?"

Tony said sleepily, "Uh-huh. Yeah. Let's do it." Sheila had reassured her, and yes, they needed some time to themselves away from their routine lives. Away from GHS craziness. Some away time where they could renew their connection.

They took their time driving south on Highway One. That, Tony observed, was a function not only of needing to drive safely on the windy coast highway, but so they could truly enjoy the trip. She allowed Sheila to plan the entire thing from beginning to end, except for one thing. Tony said "no" to a bike ride. The Big Sur area seemed too daunting in terms of difficulty. She didn't have the chops to handle the hills, she said. Sheila acquiesced, though somewhat reluctantly.

"I wanted us to do the Seventeen Mile route near Carmel. We'll just drive it, I guess."

"I'm sorry. I don't want to be a drag for you, which is what would happen, literally," Tony said.

"Well, I'm fine with it. This is supposed to be fun for both of us. You definitely need some recreation. I'm thrilled you could take Friday off."

"I pointed out to Sanjay that I hadn't taken a single day off in more than six months. He agreed and ran interference with Huey."

"That's appropriate. You don't report to Huey, and he needn't have a say in everything you do."

They left in the morning, and their first stop was for lunch in Santa Cruz. Tony was familiar with it from her college days as a weekend destination. She didn't surf and didn't like roller coasters, but a pleasant *al fresco* meal with Sheila seemed just right.

Tony could sense a letting go in her mind and her body. She sat across from a smiling, Rayban-wearing Sheila at the Crow's Nest with an iced tea in front of her. Her perception of how relaxed she was at that moment made her aware of what a toll stress and overwork had been taking on her.

"I'm in the lab for such long periods, I feel like a mole. We have windows, but it doesn't help a lot. I forgot what sunshine and fresh air feel like."

"Touché. You will expire without light and fresh air, my dear."

She looked out over the wharf and then back at Sheila. "You always have the best ideas," she said fondly.

"I try."

"Tell me more about where we're going."

"Ah, yes. This place, Vedanta, has been around since the seventies. Hippieish, earthy-crunchy, but upscale." Sheila laughed. "I like it because of the views. Spectacular. Also, yoga and meditation classes."

"I don't have to do that, right?"

Sheila laughed. "No. You don't have to do anything you don't want to. This trip is for both of us, but a lot is for you."

"But you still won't tell me what it costs."

"Negative. I'll take care of it. The only thing I want you to do is not talk about work, think about work, or dream about work. This is about relaxation and sensual pleasures…of all sorts." Sheila raised her eyebrows rakishly, which made Tony laugh.

After they finished their sandwiches and salads, Sheila asked, "Ready to hit the road?"

"I am."

❖

When she planned the trip to Big Sur, Sheila was aware she was taking a risk. Tony tended to refuse to do anything she wasn't prepared to pay half of, and Ventana Inn would most certainly fall into that category.

Sheila pitched it carefully. "I want this to be a gift from me to you. Will you accept that?"

"I will, this time, because I'm ready to get out of town, and I'm too tired to quibble with you. It's a special occasion," Tony said.

"Good. This is for us. *We* need some downtime together."

That was true, but Sheila had even more in mind. They would have space to talk about their relationship and where it was going. Sheila wanted above all for Tony to agree to move in with her in her Menlo Park condo. They weren't in a second-date, U-Haul situation, to say the least. They'd been dating for over a year. It had been a difficult and busy time for Tony, and Sheila didn't like to press her on topics that made her uncomfortable while she was trying to cope with everything at GHS. But the pressure on Tony never let up, and they would never discuss anything if Sheila waited for the magical perfect time. If Sheila's questions could be answered, she would need to time them carefully and use a delicate approach.

Sheila had her own issues to deal with, especially in regard to her father. He was doing much better and was eager to get back to work. Sheila wanted to stay in his place on the GHS board of directors and keep a close eye on their progress and on Erica. Roy was very much the same as the other board members: worshipful of Erica and all too ready to accept whatever she said or did without question.

Sheila had private discussions with Roy's doctors, and they agreed he wasn't ready to return to full-time. She counted on them to be allies when Roy started agitating to be more active. She didn't know how long she could keep him benched, though. If he got into his stubborn mode, he could choose to ignore professional advice. She really hoped that didn't happen.

Meanwhile, it was time to put her own concerns about GHS and her dad aside and turn her full attention to ensuring that Tony was having a good time and creating the space where they could have the discussion about their future.

Fortunately for them, Ventana was a notably self-contained facility, with a fine restaurant and a spa and walking trails galore.

They could easily stay there all the time if they chose, but the Big Sur area offered a lot to see. Sheila decided to delay a trip to Hearst Castle for another time, since it was a bit of a drive. Instead, they explored the nearby state park and then went to Nepenthe for lunch.

One of Sheila's friends had introduced her to Nepenthe and its storied past. Sheila wasn't particularly enamored of old movies, but *The Night of the Iguana*'s use of its Big Sur locations was engaging. Nepenthe surely had one of the all-time great views of Big Sur scenery from its deck. Sheila had made a reservation to ensure they'd have a good table.

Fresh from a lovely morning's hike at the park and hungry for lunch, they sat down and opened their menus. Tony's face darkened, which alarmed Sheila. Tony had so far seemed carefree and cheerful.

"Yikes. This place is pricey."

"Yeah." Sheila agreed. "It kind of trades on its famous reputation, but the food's pretty good." She didn't want to start any sort of money discussion that could lead to an argument.

"I said I was okay with you paying for everything." Tony put the menu down. "I'm not going to argue about it."

Sheila heard a huge unspoken "but" at the end of that sentence.

"Good. Let's not do that. Look at that." She gestured to the vista of enormous green Santa Lucia mountains sloping toward the Pacific Ocean. It looked like one of those over-the-top landscape paintings from the nineteenth century, but it was quite real.

"I see it. It's amazing. Everything about Big Sur is great, and I'm glad to get to see it with you." Tony grinned and tilted her head.

That was much better. Sheila wanted Tony to key in on the positive and stay out of her head and in the moment. As much as possible anyhow.

Sheila took her hand across the table. "I love being here with you too."

Tony mirrored her smile, and they ate their lunch in peace and took a leisurely drive farther down the coast. Tony didn't make any more comments about money.

They went to the spa and had massages and rested before dinner.

By the time they sat down, Tony appeared to be completely relaxed and at peace, just how Sheila wanted her to be, and she looked good. If all went well, they would be sealing their agreement by making love a bit later in the evening.

"You do know I love you, don't you?" Sheila said to Tony over oysters on the half shell.

Tony's grin was tender. "Yep. I believe you do. And I love you too."

"And so…" Sheila dragged her index finger over the top of Tony's hand. "I was wondering if you were open to discussing moving in together."

"Now?" Tony looked alarmed. "I don't want to think about that right now."

Sheila struggled to keep her equilibrium. "I hadn't meant it to be an ambush, and I don't mean we have to decide tonight." Sheila had actually hoped that would be the case, but she was willing to forgo making a decision if the discussion could just start.

Sheila added, "You don't have to make a decision, sweetheart. I hoped we could talk about it though."

"It feels like you want to know right now."

"I haven't said that, have I?" Sheila asked, a little sharply. "I want to *talk*. Just talk."

She waited while Tony took a bite of poached salmon and could see the wheels turning in her brain.

"I suppose that it's a legitimate question," Tony said finally. "Can you let me think about it, and I promise I'll talk to you about it tomorrow."

And with that statement, the possibility of sex seemed to fly far away.

"Sure. Think about it. We can talk tomorrow. How's your fish?"

"It's good. How's your risotto?"

"Very good. I think I may want a fancy dessert tonight. You?"

"I could eat dessert."

They'd kept it light for the rest of the evening, shared a delicious, and in Tony's opinion, monstrously expensive peach and marionberry tart, and walked around the grounds admiring the starry skies. Sheila's question had thrown Tony for a loop, but she studiously avoided showing her shock. Sheila hadn't intended to make Tony uneasy, nor was it a complete surprise, but Tony was upset anyhow.

Back in their room in the king-size bed with its, no doubt, one-thousand-thread-count sheets and dozens of pillows, she wondered if Sheila would think she was deflecting if she initiated sex. What the hell? She wanted some reassurance, and Sheila willingly provided it.

But all it did was make Tony feel guilty. She was with a wonderful, gorgeous, sensitive, and smart woman, and she couldn't commit to her. Why? What the fuck was that about?

Sheila fell asleep right afterward, and Tony stayed awake trying to analyze her feelings. She felt "less than." She was smart too, but she wasn't pretty enough and didn't make enough money to be with Sheila. Yet here she was. Sheila was, at times, remarkably nonreactive to problematic issues. That in itself was irritating, and she always refused to get angry, which bugged Tony. It was stupid, but it was true.

She hadn't said any of this to Sheila. She'd sort of talked about her issues with their different financial levels, but Sheila always tried to talk her out of her concerns. This trip, for instance. Tony truly wanted to enjoy it and not think about expenses, as Sheila pleaded with her to do, but it was tough after a lifetime of watching her expenses all the time. True, she wasn't spending money, Sheila was, but it made Tony feel weird. The situation at work slithered back into her mind and didn't help her fall asleep in spite of a couple of orgasms and the happy hormones flooding her synapses.

At work, she was neither happy nor secure, and she had no idea what to do about it.

She needed to articulate all this to Sheila, and she had to agree to participate with Sheila in a discussion of their moving in together.

When they woke up the next morning, Tony was ready to make a stab at talking about herself. She waited until they had each drunk one cup of coffee and started on the Ventana's lovely complimentary breakfast. It helped that they could be alone on their deck, not in a restaurant surrounded by other guests. If things went south and they raised their voices, they wouldn't have to be objects of curiosity.

Sheila was patient, as always. She chatted amiably about their room, details about their trip, anything and everything, but she asked no questions and gave no sign of concern. She was uncanny. Tony almost wanted to do something to crack that façade, if that was what it was. Tony was sure it was real and not manufactured, but that made her resent Sheila's constant undisturbed calm even more.

"I don't want to disappoint you," she said suddenly.

"Disappoint me? How?" Sheila asked as she broke her pumpkin-spice muffin into manageable pieces.

"I don't think I'm ready to move in with you," Tony said, roiling in self-imposed shame.

"Fair enough, but why not?"

Here we go. I have to be honest. "We're not at the same place, financially." Tony knew that sounded lame and would probably never change.

"We haven't been from the beginning and aren't likely to be in the future. Though, who knows? If GHS goes public and you can cash in those stock options…" Sheila grinned.

"You know what I mean," Tony said, irritated.

"I do know, but what I don't understand why it bothers you so much."

"I'm not sure. I've always tried to live within my means."

"Which is adult and prudent, but so? With me, your means, as you call them, are increased."

"But it's not fifty-fifty."

"Why should it have to be? Look, say, for instance, you moved into the condo with me. For real. We can work out a fair split based on our salaries. It wouldn't be half and half, because that wouldn't be fair. We can negotiate, you know. We already do negotiate, love." Sheila reached for Tony's hand again.

"I know, but—"

Tony couldn't quite control her tongue and blurted, "I still don't understand how or why you're in love with me."

"I thought we worked through that a while ago, Tone." Sheila's voice was soft and pleading.

"Maybe you did, but I didn't."

Sheila sat back and blew out a puff of air, the first sign of frustration Tony had ever seen.

"Okay. What would help you get there?"

"More time," Tony said, knowing that was only partly true. She couldn't change Sheila's financial status or her own. She didn't know what had her spooked about commitment other than it was so…final. What if they broke up the following year, and then she couldn't move back to San Francisco? Finances again.

"Okay. Anything else?"

"I don't know." Tony was miserable. "I'm sorry I'm such a twit."

"Don't be," Sheila said, firmly. "We'll work it out. Take your time."

"Okay. I'll think about it some more."

CHAPTER THIRTEEN

It didn't help them to resolve their conundrum that GHS was in such a mess. Sheila was sure Tony could reach some resolution for herself if she were in a normal work environment and had the psychic space. Tony wasn't a gal who could compartmentalize her feelings. Sheila had no idea how long the company's frenzied growth and its accompanying turmoil could go on. She was grateful again how much her study of Buddhism had given her the tools to withstand life's vicissitudes. Tony didn't have that foundation, and Sheila reminded herself that she had be compassionate and, above all, patient with Tony as she negotiated her path and worked through her emotions.

They were quiet on the drive home. Tony stared at the scenery, and Sheila concentrated on navigating the curves. She hated the distance between them but told herself it was temporary. *Everything is temporary.*

She drove Tony to her apartment in the City, agreeing that they would meet later in the week. Tony's kiss good-bye was tender enough and gave Sheila hope. She did a short meditation before she started home to Menlo Park.

❖

Tony couldn't think of a single person to talk to about her conundrum with Sheila except her dad. He would scarcely be an expert on lesbian love problems. He seemed fairly clueless when it came to heterosexual marriage, considering how much he put up with from her mom. Still, he was the one person who knew her best and the one person with her best interests in mind. She asked him to meet her for dinner.

She chose a Chinese place on Geary Boulevard she remembered going to as a child, believing it would put them both more at ease.

"It's on me, Dad," Tony said as they poured out their cups of green tea.

"Don't be silly, honey. I'm your father."

"And that is why I asked you out. I need to talk to you about some stuff."

"Oh, are you in trouble? Do you need money?"

"Nope. Nothing like that. First, I'm sorry I haven't been around much." Tony had been telling him for months that she had to work overtime, knowing he wouldn't question her. But it was easier to stay with Sheila than come back to the City. Too easy.

He waved that apology away. "What's bugging you, sweetheart? If it's not work."

"It's Sheila or, rather, it's not her. It's me. She wants me to live with her. But I'm afraid."

"What are you afraid of? Does she treat you right?"

"Oh, better than right, Dad. She's amazing."

"Is it the money?"

"Well, yeah. But not how you think. She's very generous."

"Oh, then what's the problem? You love her? She loves you?"

"Yes. But I don't want to be 'less than' in our relationship. I want to be equal. Not like—" Tony stopped.

"Not like me and your mother?" Joe smiled at her sadly.

"I didn't mean it that way," Tony said, her face hot.

"Don't worry. I know what you mean," he said. Their dinners arrived, and they paused to fill their plates with moo goo gai pan and salted cod. Tony had ordered her father's favorites. The interruption allowed Tony to collect her thoughts better.

"I know she loves me, and the money doesn't matter to her. It matters to me, though. Mom always said I have to be able to take care of myself."

"Sure, sure, she said that. I think so too. But you can, and you do."

"Well, yes, but—"

The waiter came over and brought them a new pot of tea.

"Your mother and I…" Joe said. "You only saw parts. She was tough, but she helped make me tougher. You can't expect things to always be fifty-fifty or go around keeping score. It all works out in the end."

Tony thought about that advice for a moment.

"When you find the person who complements you, you need to accept that everything isn't perfect, but it doesn't have to be."

"So, I should move in with Sheila?"

"In practical terms, it's good, no? She has a fancy condo, and it's close to work?"

"I know all the practical reasons, Dad. It's the other things I worry about."

"What other things?" He looked a bit annoyed, surprisingly.

"You know, what happens over time. Is she going to change?"

"You want to know the future? No way, girl. You have to stick with the present. Yes. You will both change. Life changes, and you got to change too. Don't be afraid."

"She says things like that sometimes. She talks about Buddhist thought."

"Right. That can be helpful. Tony, honey, you don't want to miss out on love because you think things aren't perfect." Her dad reached across the table and put his hand on hers.

"I guess so."

"I know so. Do you want another pancake?"

"Thanks, Dad, but you take it."

Later, Tony looked around her apartment. It *was* really depressing. Four walls to contain her personal possessions and a bed to sleep in. And a place to have her mail delivered. Whoopee. She thought about Sheila's comfortable and stylish condominium but mostly about being with Sheila in it. She was nuts. She had to say yes. Perfectionism? Eh, maybe that wasn't working out well either in the lab or in her personal life. Maybe it was time to let go of all of it, and possibly she could be a happier person. There was a thought.

❖

"I have something to talk to you about. I think I can get off work at a normal time," Tony said.

"Well, thank goodness. We can't have any important conversations when you're too tired to even think. Should I cook?"

"Eat out, I think. But nothing fancy."

"Fine with me." Tony sounded good—not stressed or upset. This was encouraging. They'd had a few phone calls but no time together after their Big Sur trip, and Sheila had to struggle a bit to not call, not try to persuade. To not do anything. It seemed her discretion would be rewarded.

They went to their favorite Mexican restaurant and ordered burritos—the kind with all the bells and whistles.

Tony said, "I talked to my dad, and he sort of slapped me around metaphorically."

"Your dad?" Sheila had an image of Joe, based on Tony's descriptions and the few occasions she'd spent any time around him, that he was sort of milquetoasty. Not aggressive at all.

"Yep. Old Joe talked some sense into me. I'm a perfectionist—"

"No. My gosh. I had no idea." Sheila couldn't resist teasing Tony.

"Oh, shut up. You know what I'm talking about. Like you made me see that I had to let go of some of the crap at work, Joe sort of let me know my perfectionism doesn't work when it comes to us. I'm being a twit about it because I have issues with money, and trust too, I suppose."

Sheila stayed quiet, but her hope was rising. This admission was huge.

Tony pushed the burrito innards around on her plate. She liked to unwrap burritos and then eat their guts with a fork.

"I can't change the fact that you have way more money than me. And you like to spend it. Why not? You can."

"I like to spend it on you, sweetheart," Sheila said, gently.

"Yeah, and that's got to be okay with me. Not guilt-inducing. Listen…"

Tony reached for both of Sheila's hands and squeezed them between her own. "I want to commit to you. I want to live with you. But we have to work out an agreement about how we—you and I—spend money."

"Done. Or, rather, we'll work on it. I promise."

"So, there you have it," Tony said with considerable satisfaction.

Sheila was taken aback that, after all Tony's handwringing, she was acting like it was a simple decision, though it obviously wasn't. She was relieved and grateful.

Sheila leaned across the table, and they kissed. Next project—help Tony be more easy-going at work. That might be a touch harder to do than even getting her to agree to move in together.

After all the tense discussion around the validation testing, Tony wasn't looking forward to their group ramping up the lab to do actual patient testing, which Sanjay had informed her would begin soon. The Leonardos were in place around the Bay Area Graff stores. The press releases were sent out, and Erica had done another round of interviews in which, Tony noted, she made extravagant claims about the number of tests the Leonardo could do and, even worse, how much better they were than human lab analysts—like Tony. *That* galled her.

She, as much as anyone, appreciated how much human error could affect the outcome of a lab test. That was a given, but clinical specialists used ways, like quality-control checks, to prevent human errors. They weren't helpful, of course, when the instruments themselves were unreliable. The Leonardos were far more unreliable than even an incompetent clinical lab specialist. Tony mentally shook her head and went about making sure she and her lab equipment and reagents were all ready to go for patient testing.

Sanjay told her they had received a letter from the Medicare people who had regulatory oversight over clinical labs, saying they had to submit to proficiency testing, as did all clinical labs. Tony was fascinated to see how all this would play out, given how he and Huey had handled the validation test.

She was merely "interested," she sternly told herself. It wasn't her place to complain or question. Erica had made that clear. And she'd do what she was told.

Proficiency testing was a simple, though rigorous exercise that used plasma samples spiked with analytes for the various clinical assays, and GHS would test them. They didn't know the "right" answers. Only the College of American Pathologists, who sent them samples, knew the actual numbers. It would be something else, Tony realized, if they couldn't pass their proficiency testing. Then they would be inspected and might not get their license renewed. That would solve the whole problem.

The previous year, they had submitted results from the Advia machines for proficiency testing. This time, they had to use the Leonardos, and Erica and the company would have to stop and fix the Leonardos, which, Tony thought grimly, hadn't helped yet. This prospect soothed her considerably. GHS would be busted by an outside agency, and they'd have to clean up their act, and no one could blame Tony for anything.

When the samples came in, Sanjay told Tony and Tan to split them up and run half on the Advia and half on the Leonardo. Tony was surprised and pleased at his directive. She still hoped that real numbers could convince the management to halt the headlong forward motion that Tony knew was ill-advised.

When she showed the data to Sanjay, he shook his head. "Well, that's too bad."

Tony bit her tongue. Was that all he had to say? What a travesty. This guy surely had *some* level of integrity. "Which set of numbers will we report to CLIA?" Tony asked.

Before Sanjay could answer, they heard a booming voice behind them.

"So, what's the news?" It was Huey.

"Take a look at the results. They're right here," Sanjay said.

Huey muscled his bulk between them rudely. "What are these?" he demanded.

Sanjay explained to him which results were which.

"What did you do that for?" Huey was irate.

"Well, we wanted to see. And unfortunately, I'm sure the Advia numbers are correct, and the Leonardo's number are not."

Whoa. Sanjay was offering a real opinion. She watched as Huey glared at Sanjay, clearly trying to get him to back down. Sanjay didn't speak, but he kept eye contact with Huey.

Huey at last threw the printout in his hand onto the bench. "Report the Advia results to those regulatory people." He couldn't remember the name of the agency, and he likely didn't care anyhow.

"*That*'s what you think we should do?" Sanjay was incredulous. Tony was right there with him, thrilled he was doing the right thing.

"That's what I said," Huey nearly shouted. "Are you deaf?"

He turned and stalked out of the lab. Tony and Sanjay stared at one another.

"He just told us to commit fraud with the data we're giving to a federal agency," Tony said.

"Yep."

"Are you going to do what he says?"

"Yep." Sanjay wouldn't look at her.

"I'll move in as soon as the lease runs out on my place in the City," Tony told Sheila.

"I'll pay the penalty to break the lease if you want to leave early. I want you here as soon as possible."

"No. You have to let me do it my way." Tony followed with a hug to take the sting out of what she'd said.

"Right. You *are* right." They were busy talking about their future life together and how they would deal with questions of money and spending. Tony was struggling to stay calm about the latest happenings at the lab and keep her work and home life separated better than she had in the past.

She wanted to see how things played out before she told Sheila any of the latest lab shenanigans. The shit would hit the fan eventually, or it would all turn out fine, she hoped. Or the GHS board of directors would have to do something. Sheila wasn't on the board anymore. Her dad had come back to work and taken over.

Anyhow, Tony wanted to focus on what she and Sheila were doing and how they were doing. She had relinquished her sense of responsibility over what was going on in the lab. Once Tony had made that decision, she felt much better and was less anxious. She loved Sheila, which was the vital fact. They were going to live together. Tony even speculated a tiny bit about marriage but reminded herself to take it slow. First cohabit and see what that was like.

Sheila couldn't wait to talk to Roy after his first board meeting. She was deeply curious about what was going on with the company. Tony had stopped telling her stories about the goings-on at the lab, and she hoped that meant things had smoothed out.

As soon as she knew Roy was back from the meeting, she marched into his office. "Did they throw you a party?" she asked, making a joke to cover her eagerness.

"Ah, no. Gary wants me go out for a couple rounds of golf. I think I can get Doctor Whosit to sign off on that."

"Doctor Wen. What were they talking about this morning? What did Erica have to say?" How did he forget the name of his doctor?

"Oh, the drugstore thing is launched. If it goes well, she said they'd go national next year. Eight hundred stores. And that's just the beginning." Roy all but rubbed his hands together in glee.

Sheila grinned, but she thought of Tony and what she'd said in the past about the tenuous nature of the technology. No doubts were voiced at Erica's level, and no one on the board was asking because they didn't know *what* to ask. They still weren't told or didn't care about the colossal rate of employee turnover and why that was occurring. She wanted to check in with Tony and hear what she had to say.

"Did you meet Harry Blevins?"

"Oh, yeah. What a shark. But he's *our* shark." Roy grinned smugly.

"Did he have anything to say?"

"Nope. Oh, wait a second. He said they've got a new plan to make sure their ex-staff are adhering to their NDAs."

"Did he provide any details?"

Roy leaned back in his chair and tossed his nerf basketball and made his basket.

"Nah. He and Erica sort of cackled together evilly. Erica said, 'We're not going to have any issues with leaks of our discoveries. We're never going to let Quest Diagnostics or LabCorp get their hands on our tech.'"

"Hm. Well, that's been her worry from the beginning. I guess she's got someone like Blevins to take care of that."

Roy shot the basketball and missed, and he grimaced. He was already disengaged from their discussion. Sheila left, closing the door quietly.

❖

They stood side by side in Sheila's kitchen, chopping. This was what it was going to be like. Cozy domesticity, cooking dinner together. Tony caught Sheila's eye, and they both smiled.

"How are things in the lab?" Sheila asked.

"Eh, since you advised me to not get as involved, I'm better."

Sheila swiftly dismantled a turnip and threw it into the pot, then reaching for a sweet potato. Sheila was watching what she was doing and not making eye contact. Tony presumed she didn't want to cut her fingers off.

"I'm glad to hear that, but what *is* actually happening?"

"Oh. That's a different question," Tony said, sardonically. "We're about to lie to a federal regulatory agency."

Sheila stopped chopping, her knife poised, and turned face Tony. "Oh, really? That doesn't sound good."

"Nope, it's not, but I didn't have any say in it. It was Huey's deal. He's the one who'll have to answer for it if they find out, and they might or might not. They never inspect unless you plead with them to come out and inspect you. No regulator does that. They have no manpower. They're underfunded and busy."

Tony reeled off all this information like it was no big deal, but it made her stomach ache. "Oh, and the Leonardos are going out to the Graff stores, but they're pieces of crap." Tony turned back to her work and slashed savagely at the onion she was working on.

"I heard from Roy that the Leonardos are going out to the drugstores, not the part about them being pieces of crap."

Tony sighed. "Yeah. I can't wait to hear how that goes."

"Are you keeping your mouth shut at work?"

"Yep. Just like you told me to."

"Good, 'cause Erica has hired a lawyer who's famous for his aggressive tactics."

Tony threw her diced onion into the soup pot. "Nice."

She wasn't as carefree as she made out to Sheila, but she was determined to hold her tongue for as long as possible and wait to see what would happen.

"It's good to hear that you're keeping a low profile. I don't want you to get into any trouble."

"Nope. Not me. I'm like a little lab mouse. I'm barely making a sound above a squeak." *Before they kill me dead, which is what usually happens to little lab mice.*

"Great. Let's put the soup on and have a glass of wine, then sit on the couch and snuggle while we wait for it to cook."

"Sounds good to me."

A couple of weeks later, Sanjay, Tony, and Tan were in the lab looking over the patient test results, which didn't look good, and they were having a tense discussion to decide what to do about the situation. The door opened, and Huey stalked in, followed by a bunch of movers all trundling shrink-wrapped Leonardos on moving dollies.

The three of them watched silently. Huey was barking directions and cautions, and then he turned to the three of them. "These need to be fixed. I'll bring the engineers in, and you all get to work."

"What about the other units in the other stores?" Sanjay asked.

"They're fine. The stores these came from? They are going to be sending their samples by courier over to us, and you do the tests in house."

Sanjay, Tony, and Tan looked at each other. Something must have happened, and the Graff stores sent their Leonardos back. Since Huey was in a foul mood, they didn't ask him. Tony would ask Ricardo later. In spite of Sheila's admonition about yakking with him, Ricardo was still the one in the know.

"Are we testing the samples on Leonardos? Or on the commercials?" Sanjay asked, meaning the Advia machines.

"Advias, until we get this straightened out." Huey practically growled.

"Roger that," Sanjay said, smartly. "Will they be finger sticks or venipunctures?"

Huey looked even angrier. "Regular blood samples." He likely didn't know the word venipuncture.

Courier-delivered samples were problematical, which was one of the reasons the Leonardos were situated on site. The finger-stick-derived blood deteriorated, adding yet another layer of uncertainty to the results. In the meantime, there were still GHS devices out there analyzing the patients' blood. Tony remembered what Ricardo had told her months ago. Huey knew all along what they were going to be doing—yet another way they'd surely misled the Graff company.

Later, Tony visited Ricardo and asked him if he knew what had happened. "Oooee. It was a mess. I understand a couple of store managers called Erica and yelled at her. A couple of people who used their Leonardos then went and got some regular blood tests, and the results didn't match so the customers were upset, and the Graff store managers were pissed. I think a call came from Graff's project manager."

"Yikes." That was all Tony could think of to say.

"Uh-huh. It's ugly."

Sanjay told Tony to call him if any customer complaints came in while she was on duty testing patients' blood.

It wasn't too long before that happened, and Tony listened to Sanjay's soothing and utterly false reassurances to the doctor who hadn't believed the test results.

Tony finally spilled all of this to Sheila one evening while they were eating dinner.

"This isn't going to end well," she said. "Maybe you ought to talk to your dad, and he can try to pin Erica down."

"It doesn't sound good, and I don't think Roy would do anything."

Tony put her fork down, appalled. "Why not?"

"Tony, baby, I believe you, but it's going to take a lot more than that to convince him. I still think it sounds like typical start-up growing pains. Erica knows all about it, you said. Though I told you not to talk to Ricardo, you did anyhow."

"Excuse me, but I think my talking to Ricardo is missing the point." Since Tony knew that Sheila didn't like her to talk to Ricardo, Tony never mentioned him until then.

"Sorry. You're right, but I still worry. What are you going to do?"

"What am *I* going to do? What are *you* going to do? The company is going down the toilet. You told me to keep my head down. Fine. I still care, though."

Sheila tapped her fingers on the table and was silent for a few moments. Tony had never seen her show this much impatience.

"I'll talk to Roy and see what he says. You stay calm."

"Don't worry about me. I'm okay," Tony said, tersely.

She had a hard time falling asleep that night, though Sheila was out for the count, as always. It was irritating how well she could sleep when Tony couldn't. Tony hoped that, at last, somehow, Sheila and Roy would get Erica to what? Listen? Do something besides spin everyone on everything?

Tony received an answer the next day, but it wasn't the one she wanted.

Sheila said, "I'm sorry to tell you, but Roy isn't ready to step in yet. He said, quote, Erica has it under control, end quote."

"Huh. Well. Thanks for trying," Tony said, but she wasn't satisfied. There was *something* she could do, and she'd been thinking about it for a while. Sheila wouldn't likely think it was a good idea, but so be it.

❖

After Tony made her request, Ricardo looked at her for a long time without saying anything.

"Are you sure you want to do this?" he asked, uncharacteristically somber.

"Yes. I'm serious."

"Okay, then. I'll talk to Andy for you."

The scenario Tony had cooked up had two problems. The first was putting her hands on the proficiency results, which Sanjay had in his possession, and, second, making sure Sheila would be willing to go along with her plan.

She approached Sanjay a couple days later and asked to see the proficiency testing data. "I want to be sure the comparison calculation I performed was correct because I think I might have made an error." Tony willed her voice to stay steady.

Looking resigned, he said, "It's all over, so it's basically irrelevant."

"Yeah. I know. But I still don't want to leave anything wrong. In case."

He shrugged. It was easy, after all, to exploit how utterly beaten down Sanjay was and how little he even seemed to care. Tony felt somewhat sorry for him, but he was still a weenie.

She took the printouts of the proficiency testing results and the letter she had written and called Andy the programmer. He came over to the clin lab, and after she had printed the letter and copied the printouts, Andy erased the printer/copier's memory. No one would ever know she'd used the printer for the purpose she'd employed it.

At Sheila's that evening, Tony showed the documents to Sheila and explained what they were.

"I want to scan them and email them to the section of Medicare that regulates clinical labs, anonymously. Clinical Laboratory Improvement Amendments office."

Sheila read what Tony had handed her. Tony's letter laid out clearly how she believed GHS was violating the law. Sheila's eyes widened.

Tony said, "I can't do this at work, as you know, since they monitor our email. I want you to do it or let me do it from your laptop here at your house. I'm asking you to help me. I don't know what else to do."

Sheila read the letter again. "What do you think will happen?"

"I hope they'll do a surprise inspection and investigation and shut the lab down." Tony spoke as firmly as she could, but her voice still shook.

"You realize you're asking me to sabotage the company we both want to succeed."

"I'm not asking you to sabotage *anything*, Sheila. I'm asking you to help me right a wrong. GHS needs to put the brakes on, correct some of its behavior, and start behaving ethically. It doesn't have to be a death blow."

Sheila said, after a long pause, "All right. I'll do it, because I believe you, because I love you. You may be right that there is no other way. Erica won't do anything voluntarily."

"Nope. We have to force the issue."

CHAPTER FOURTEEN

Sheila knelt in front of her living-room altar, focused on her statue of Guan Yin, the goddess of wisdom and compassion, and said a silent prayer. She took the lotus position and meditated for a half hour. The experience was soothing and calming, but she still had doubts. She'd never done anything in connection with one of her start-ups as she'd agreed to do for Tony. It felt ethically slippery. On the other hand, Tony's certainty was compelling, and if she didn't give her lover the benefit of the doubt, what good was their relationship?

She prayed and meditated again in the evening after work was over. She could face Tony with a clear conscience.

"How long will it take, do you think, for them to respond?"

"Hard to say. It's a government agency."

"Well, we have to wait then."

"Yes," Tony said, grimly. "We wait."

It turned out to take only a month for the inspection to happen. Sanjay told Tony about it in a curiously noncommittal fashion, and she didn't find out why until the day of the inspection.

Huey came to the lab early in the morning. "You three just stay in here. Don't go wandering around. I'm handling it. I know somebody in here talked, so I'm going to find out who, and then we'll see what's what." He sounded menacing, and Tony was scared, even though she knew he'd never figure out it was her. Sanjay was ignorant, as was Tan. They couldn't get into trouble, nor could they name her as the culprit.

"What did the CLIA people say was the reason they were inspecting us?" Tony asked, innocently.

"Licensing." Huey bit off the word.

"Oh," Tony said. "Okay."

They were stuck in the office the whole day, and it was a major bore. Tony tried to read some journals, but she mostly fiddled with her phone. No inspectors showed up, however. They must have rescheduled for some reason.

She and Sheila went out to dinner, but she had nothing to report. They concentrated on their moving-in-together plans, a much happier subject.

"You didn't say anything to Roy about the inspection, did you?" Tony asked Sheila all of a sudden.

Sheila looked alarmed. "No. Of course not. I told you I'm keeping this strictly in confidence."

"You would think," Tony said, twirling pasta on her fork, "that Erica would tell them about a federal regulatory inspection, but you'd be wrong."

"She's certainly a withholder of info," Sheila said, tersely, wondering more than ever if this situation was sustainable. She wanted GHS to succeed, and she hoped it would for a lot of reasons. But there were more than a few red flags.

It wasn't just Tony's disclosures, though those were problematical. They seemed like technical glitches that could be resolved. But the lack of transparency around financial matters on Erica's part was just as bad, if not worse. She had seen for herself when she was subbing for Roy on the board what Erica was like, and nothing he'd reported from the two meetings he'd been to since his recovery gave her reason to think anything had changed.

Roy, for instance, had asked for the agreements that Sheila had been trying to get. He reported what Erica said, and to Sheila it sounded like a lot of non sequiturs and nonsense, and again, nothing happened.

Sheila hated to be in a holding pattern with her fingers crossed waiting to hear what happened next. It wasn't her nature. And though she was relatively new to the venture-capital game compared to her dad, she was apprehensive.

Roy was not being helpful at all. He still refused to confront Erica, and Sheila wondered if his medical crisis had taken some of the edge off his instincts.

Like most real news of GHS, the results of the CLIA inspection came from Ricardo. He didn't know all the details of what Tony had done. She wanted to protect him, but he was savvy and figured most of it out, and she'd ended up telling him all about it.

He shook his head sadly. "Well, it can't be a huge surprise to you, but Erica and Huey met the inspector and showed her some fake Leonardos and gave her a whole song and dance, and she was snowed and went away, leaving them with a few minor lab items to correct. They even had one of the R and D managers in to talk technical with her. You had a great idea, Tony, but it didn't work."

"You're fucking kidding me." Tony didn't like to use swear words. She was devastated though. It had seemed like such a fool-proof idea.

"Wish I were, Dr. Leung, but I'm not. Huey is still steaming about the inspection though. I hope you're not going to get found out."

"No," Tony said. "I was careful."

"These people are evil," Ricardo said, with feeling.

"Yeah. Makes me wonder why I stay. Why do you?"

"Good question. Well, for one thing, I'm insulated from the worst, unlike you lab types. And it's a good job." He shrugged. "Guess I have a high tolerance for bullshit. And unlike you, I don't have to deal with Huey's craziness."

Tony told Sheila what had happened.

"I hope this means you're going to give it all a rest," Sheila said.

"I don't know what the heck I can do, anyhow," Tony said, sadly. "I can get another job, I suppose."

"Is that what you want? If you do, I'm okay with it."

"I'm not sure. I'll take a little more time to think about it. I still hope for the best."

"Me too," Sheila said and laughed without humor. "Come here."

Tony slid over on the couch to get as close to Sheila as possible. If she could climb inside her skin, that would help.

It was time, past time probably to take action. Sheila picked the Pacific Partners' member she thought would likely be able to get through to her dad and convince him GHS had a serious problem, that he had to step in and persuade the other GHS board members to take action. The board members were the only people who had any leverage over Erica, the only ones who could bring her to heel. She was a global celebrity, not just a celebrity CEO. She ruled over the most famous "unicorn" in Silicon Valley. She was touted by women's groups and politicians. She had recently hosted a tour for the Obama administration's chief science-and-tech adviser, which the press covered with the usual fawning language. She was untouchable and answered to no one for anything, it seemed.

"What's this about?" Roy asked suspiciously when Sheila and Gary sat down in his office.

Sheila told him a sanitized version of Tony's disclosures, mindful of not exposing her by using her name. In fact, she told him Tony had nothing to do with it, and other GHS staffers had come to her on Tony's recommendation. Roy listened politely, but when she finished, he looked away—not a good sign.

"What sort of agenda do these people have going? Aren't they paid enough? These Valley techies are entitled little babies who ought to grow up. Erica's giving them the best jobs they've ever had." He sounded unusually irritated.

Gary spoke up. "Roy, this is a lot more serious than that. We don't have a good grasp on the technical details of GHS's product. To be realistic, we know nothing about the technology. We've relied upon Erica's assurances she has top people working for her. You have to admit there's been a lot of happy talk and promises from Erica and not a lot of results. And this latest thing? A visit from a federal agency? And why are the GHS employees talking to outsiders? We need to give them the benefit of the doubt and investigate their concerns and see if there's any truth to them. I think we have to take what Sheila is telling us seriously. You're a cagey guy. Talk to the other board people and see who else is harboring some doubts."

He looked from Sheila to Gary and back again at Sheila. "Okay. Fine. I'll talk to them."

Sheila reported her conversation with Gary and Roy to Tony. "You what?" Tony asked. "What did you say?"

"I kept your name out of it. No one will know."

"*Erica* will know. She's got Huey and HR spying on all of us. I told you."

"I thought it was a good idea. I thought you wanted me to tell them. I thought you'd be relieved. I'm surprised at your negative reaction."

Tony sat back in her chair, arms at her side. Then she rubbed her head as though she had a headache. Sheila looked chagrined.

"You have no idea what Erica is like."

Sheila spoke with some heat. "Oh, I have a very good idea. Remember? I went to a few board meetings. I tried to pry a legal agreement with some company out of Erica, and I couldn't do it. So no, I'm not totally ignorant."

"But you can't do anything about anything."

"Maybe Roy and some of the other board people can."

"I'm not holding my breath," Tony said sarcastically.

She went into the bedroom and lay on the bed. Sheila followed, sat on the edge of the bed, and stroked her hair.

"What can I do?"

Tony rolled over and their gazes met. She said, "This is probably not going to work out the way I want it to. I need to do what's best for me, for us."

Sheila said nothing, just continued to try to soothe her.

It was sort of odd how workdays somehow seemed to flow along in a normal way when nothing felt normal. Sanjay still had her testing samples with the commercial analyzers. She assumed the engineering group was, once again, trying to tinker with Leonardo and tweak it into some form of reliability. Meantime, Sheila's dad was supposedly going to confront Erica with the hearsay about her less-than-ethical behavior. And Huey's too, Tony hoped. That guy was something, the biggest asshole she'd ever worked for. Her view of Erica was highly tarnished as well.

Between the technical and regulatory shenanigans and her siccing Huey on everyone to beat them into submission, it was hard to maintain motivation for work and to feel any sort of trust. At the bottom what was there to really believe in? This vision that Erica had so marvelously articulated to her in her interview and continued to tout in all staff meetings was not materializing. Quite the opposite.

Tony brooded. She wasn't sure what she wanted to do. She could quit, as Sheila suggested. That seemed cowardly, but what about her own integrity that was being eroded more every day?

Her cell phone rang, and she didn't recognize the number, but she picked up anyhow.

"Hi, Tony. Gordon Ames here."

"Wow, Gordo. What a surprise to hear from you. How nice. How are you?"

"I'm good. I like my new job. The company is a normal sort of start-up. It's only berserk in the usual start-up way, but not nearly as much drama as GHS, thank God." He chuckled. "How are you? How's things?"

Tony wanted to tell him everything, but she hesitated to talk while sitting in her cube, where it was neither private nor safe.

"That is quite a long story, and I can't get into it over the phone. Do you want to have lunch or something?"

"That's exactly what I was hoping we could do. I have something to talk to you about, and I agree we need some privacy."

"Really? You don't say? Well, why don't we head over to that barbecue joint in East Palo Alto you love. We won't run into any GHS people there. Not their neighborhood." The place Tony had in mind was in a black neighborhood, East Palo Alto, and most techs from GHS were generally scared to go there.

"That'll work. Can you Uber it? I don't want to go anywhere near the GHS campus. I can't risk anyone recognizing me, and well, there's other stuff. I'll tell you later. Next Wednesday at one okay?"

"Yeah. I can make it.

When Sheila asked Roy if he'd talked to any board members, his response infuriated her.

"They know things aren't going that well, but they don't think there's a big issue. They think it's just the usual start-up growing pains."

"So, they're ostriches basically. They don't *want* to know. Dad, you know this is bad. Erica could be heading for a major disaster. The board has to step in. It's their job." Sheila emphasized the last word.

"Well. Yes. I know."

"So? No one is willing to step up?"

"I think one or two might."

"Well, work on them, Pops. Get some allies, make a plan next time you meet, confront Erica. You can do it. Do you agree we have some serious issues with GHS?"

"Yes. Some of the people I talked to agreed that all wasn't copacetic, and Erica could be problematical."

"Great. Work on them. Come on. You can forge a consensus. You know how to do that. You've always been good at it."

"I forgot how tasty the food here is," Tony said as she devoured a barbecued pork sandwich. "I basically never go out to lunch anymore."

Gordon picked at his plate of baby-back ribs. They stuck to innocuous subjects at first: Tony and Sheila moving in together and Gordon's new job. Gordon told her the story of how he was fired, and, sadly, it was all too familiar. At least he seemed happy in his new job.

After a beat of silence, Tony said, "So. What did you want to tell me about?"

Gordon pressed his lips together. He'd never been especially open about what he was thinking. He was kind and friendly to her when they worked together but was never a big talker. Except that one time when he told her how Erica had faked the Leonardo 1.0 results. That had turned out to be a huge sign of things to come.

"I got a call about three weeks ago. It was a reporter from the *Washington Post*." He paused.

"What did he or she want?" Tony asked reasonably but had already begun to feel tense. Funny how the term 'reporter' could have that effect. Gordon seemed terribly uncomfortable as well.

"He. He told me he'd heard from this medical blogger that all may not be as it seems at GHS. This blogger said to the reporter, 'Maybe you ought to look into it.' Meaning GHS. Long round-about meander through various former employees and Stanford folks and whatnot, and he came to me. I decided to tell him what I knew from when I worked there."

"Wow." That was all Tony could come up with.

"Yeah." Gordo looked unhappy. "This reporter, Avery's his name, knew the right questions to ask. I spilled."

"Why?" Tony was genuinely curious about his motivation. At the time they were working together, Gordon had been a straight arrow, to all appearances a loyal company man.

"This blogger guy—he's a doctor—and he knows what he's talking about. He told Avery there's no way this type of technology is ever going to work. The laws of physics and chemistry make Leonardo inoperable. It's all a sham."

And with those words, Tony's heart froze, and her stomach turned over. It was as though she had this truth buried in her subconscious and was afraid to let it free. Gordon's statement busted it open, and it flew straight into her waking brain. She'd been trying to ignore it for over a year, but it was time to stop playing around and accept reality.

"Do you think that's true?" she asked Gordon.

"Yeah. I read the doctor's blog about it. I always said I didn't know squat about biochemistry and lab science and all. But I'm an engineer, and I thought there had to be a reason all the fixes and tweaks and tinkering weren't cutting it. It's really simple chemistry."

"It doesn't work," Tony said flatly. That thought had been waiting in her brain all along and had just needed the right moment or right motivation to come out. There it was—what Tony had been denying to herself for months. She had always thought Erica was brilliant, and she'd been awarded patents for the Leonardo, and *that* meant the technology worked.

Tony said, wryly. "I always figured it was an engineering problem, not a chemistry problem."

"Nope. It will *never* work, no matter how much engineering is applied. And the worst, most horrifying thing is that Erica has everyone convinced the Leonardo does work or will shortly. She's lying, to everyone. To the public, the patients, the investors, the employees. She's got us all fooled."

They sat silently for a few moments.

Gordon said, "When I was unemployed, I read a biography of Steve Jobs. Remember how Erica always quoted him like he was God or something?"

"Yeah, I think so." Tony said.

"Well. The bio said that one of Steve Jobs' superpowers, maybe his biggest, was he could create a reality-distortion field around himself. He could convince everyone he knew to buy in to what *he* thought. That's what Erica did too."

"Right. Now I see that. It worked to some extent."

"Yes, but Jobs actually produced a viable product, a lot of them. Erica, so far, has not."

"That's true."

Gordon said, grimly. "This is all going to come out sometime, probably soon."

"What did you tell the reporter?" Tony asked.

"Everything I knew, every last detail. He put me on background, and he's not using my name. He promised."

"So, your NDA doesn't matter anymore?"

"I looked stuff up on the Net and don't think they can do anything to me. I don't care. They won't know it was me anyhow. But I wanted to talk to you to ask you to meet the reporter. He asked me for names, and I thought of you."

"I can't do that," Tony said automatically.

"Well. Yeah, it's dicey because you still work there. If GHS finds out you talked, yep, they can sue you."

"You are really not concerned?" Tony asked.

"No. My conscience is what I care about."

Tony didn't think too hard but abruptly said, "I made an anonymous complaint to CLIA about the lab."

"What's CLIA?"

Tony explained the whole thing to him, including the fact that her plan didn't work. His shocked expression said it all.

"Wow. You did that? And nothing happened? This is really bad, Tone."

"Yes. It's the worst. I've been wondering what to do since then."

"Talk to the reporter and tell him what you know."

"I'll have to quit GHS first. I can't do it while I still work there. They'll find out."

"They might still find out anyhow. Think about it."

Instead of trying to think it through by herself, Tony told Sheila. They were in the hot tub, supposedly relaxing before dinner. Instead of admiring her body as she usually did, Tony watched Sheila's face. Sheila sat still, her blank, neutral expression not registering any emotion. That scared Tony more than any outburst ever would. Sheila said nothing for a long time, and when she finally spoke, her voice sounded unfamiliar. It was tight and flat, absent of any compassion or understanding.

"You cannot talk to the reporter," Sheila said finally. "That would be the worst thing you could do."

"Because?" Tony thought she knew the answer, but she needed to hear Sheila say it out loud.

"The perception of a company by the public is as valuable as its actual monetary value. Something negative, whether it's true or not, something that damages the public value or opinion, has a snowball effect. GHS will never recover. It will be done. Over."

"You'll lose your investment," Tony said dully.

"Yes. We will. All of it."

"But if what Gordon says is true, and the reporter writes it that way, you'll lose it anyhow. Fraud. That's what it is, honey. I've come to believe that. Based on all I know, Erica is going around touting technology that doesn't exist, that doesn't do what she says it does. She's faking it, and I don't think she's going to make it. I've been trying to tell myself that we just hadn't hit upon the right methods and it would all work out in time. I was willing to believe that it was all start-up shenanigans, like you said. But it's not that. It isn't going to happen, sweetheart."

"We don't know that, and it still makes no sense." Sheila was looking into the middle distance, and Tony grew even more afraid but also bit angry at her obtuseness.

"It's true," Tony said in a near whisper. "I suspected it already, but now that I talked to Gordon, I know it's true. I found the blog he told me about, and the guy knows what he's talking about. I understand now why we can't get the Leonardos to work correctly. And I can say it out loud. Honey, you can't just keep saying Erica is only being a typical Silicon Valley CEO and she wouldn't purposely screw up her own company. I don't think that's what's going on. She doesn't want to admit that it will never work."

"Please don't talk to the reporter." Sheila fixed Tony with a pleading expression.

"I'm not going to, at least not yet. How is this going to end? Sheila, the way Erica and Huey screwed around with that inspector—doesn't that mean anything? I mean what do *you* think? With all the stuff I told you about..."

"If you talk to the reporter, that will start all sorts of trouble. At least let's find out what my dad can do."

To Tony's chagrin, Sheila still maintained her maddeningly even tone. She was beginning to wonder what her true feelings were. All that Buddhist junk Sheila absorbed: what in the end did it mean? Tony wanted Sheila on her side, all the way. But that was likely not possible. Sheila was stuck in the middle of a huge conflict of interest, for sure. Tony felt sick. This made what her dad had said way back when they first met true. *Be careful.* That what he'd said.

"You don't believe me," Tony said.

"It's not that. I don't—"

"Nope. You don't believe me. You think I'm wrong."

Sheila, who'd been looking down at her feet, raised her eyes. "No. I don't think that. I don't know what I think."

"It's all screwed up. It's a sham. I know it, and I think you know it too."

Sheila raised her voice for the first time ever since Tony had known her.

"No. I don't, and you don't either. It's totally counterintuitive for Erica to sabotage her own company. She wouldn't do that. She has absolutely nothing to gain by doing that. There's got to be another explanation."

"But that's what she's doing. I have the proof."

Sheila said nothing more. Tony felt sick to her stomach.

Tony climbed out of the hot tub and put on her robe. She scarcely noticed the chill night air on her still-wet body. She didn't care if Sheila's eyes were following her as she slipped her feet into flip-flops.

"Where are you going?" Sheila called after her.

Ah-ha. I hear a tinge of pique. "I'm going inside to get dressed. I'm going back to the City. If you would drive me to the train station, I'd appreciate it, but otherwise I'll take an Uber." Tony was happy *she* could speak without apparent emotion. That was gratifying. Not that the emotion wasn't there, but she didn't want to show it. She wanted to match Sheila's dispassionate delivery.

❖

Sheila sat in the hot tub watching the ripples in the night-darkened water. Tony was upset. She needed to cool off, and she'd be okay. She was smart and wouldn't do anything rash. Of that Sheila was convinced. Tony was the opposite of impetuous. She abruptly stood up and threw her own robe on, and, with her towel in hand, she walked through the living room to the bedroom.

Tony was nearly dressed except for her shirt and shoes. She was stowing clothes into her overnight bag.

Sheila said, "Give me a minute or two, and I'll drive you. Unless I can persuade you to stay."

"No. I need to go home right now. It's pointless to try to talk about this. You're not going to change your mind."

"Right." It was useless to argue. Sheila mechanically pulled on some sweats.

In the Volt, Sheila didn't try to make conversation. Tony didn't kiss her as she exited the car in the Palo Alto train-station drop-off zone. She didn't look back either.

She'll come around. Once Roy can get the board involved and rein in Erica, it'll be better. She'll feel better and cool down.

Tony tried to put aside her conflicted feelings and behave normally at work. Sanjay was apparently on autopilot. He no longer seemed to care, or maybe he just didn't want to ask any questions that would invite the notice of Huey and his bad temper.

They still had weekly all-hands meeting where the staff would look at each other blankly as Erica and Huey attempted to generate enthusiasm for whatever little snippet of news they imparted. Tony no longer believed a word they said, nor, it seemed, did anyone else. She had watched the sitcom *The Office*, and her coworkers' expressions reminded her of the paper-company staff as their idiotic boss blathered on about whatever. The GHS staff faces had exactly the same expression while Huey and Erica were touting the company's progress or, more often, what new publicity Erica had garnered. They even gave each other side-eyes the same way *The Office* staff did.

Tony was supposed to give notice to her landlord in a matter of days when it came time to renew her lease. She had no idea what to do. She was no longer sure she ought to live with Sheila. She still loved her but…Sheila was unable to wholeheartedly get behind her. And in a perverse way, Tony understood. Sheila was genuinely conflicted. But in the end Tony thought Sheila ought to believe her and take her seriously. And take action.

She had no clear answer to any of it. She didn't know what to do about her job or about her girlfriend—two situations in flux. It was like being adrift on the ocean and having no way to navigate, not even having an oar to paddle with, and it was horrible. She hated any kind of uncertainty or ambiguity anyhow, and she was stuck in massive uncertainty in the two most important areas of her life: her job and her lover.

Sheila was on edge, and no amount of prana breathing was going to bring her down to a steady state. She told the receptionist to call her the second her dad returned. He was typically back from GHS board meetings within a couple of hours, but she suspected this board meeting would take longer. She halfheartedly tried to focus on some other projects. She made a few calls but found it hard to concentrate. She and Tony had exchanged texts a couple of times during the past few days, but not about anything significant. They were mostly about items Tony had left at her house that she wanted back. Tony hadn't offered to come over or meet to talk. Nothing.

It was suddenly obvious to Sheila that her future might hinge on the result of the board meeting. That was a bone-chilling insight. If the board voted to depose Erica and replace her with someone else, or put some serious restrictions on her, then Sheila could honestly say to Tony that the problem was being handled and that she hoped it would all work out in the end. Maybe that would reassure Tony. But…she and Tony were coming from opposite points of view. Sheila could never do a thing to jeopardize a company they were heavily invested in. That would be not only silly, but a breach of trust for the investors in their firm, who put their confidence in Sheila's father and his partners' investment acumen. They could initiate legal action against GHS, but that would be greeted with an uproar and would likely effectively end the possibility that they ever would make any money. The fallout of such an action would be dire.

Tony was concerned with ethics and the scientific and medical soundness of the technology. Sheila herself could effectively do nothing to make any difference in this situation. This was a classic dilemma. Buddhist thought would definitely counsel doing nothing.

Tony, on the other hand, could do something radical. She'd already tried with her complaint to the regulatory agency. Sheila knew Tony wanted her full-throated agreement that basically GHS had to be shut down. She couldn't do that, and she couldn't offer any effective counterargument to prevent Tony from talking to that reporter. Tony was upset enough to do just that, but she hadn't yet, and Sheila still had a chance to dissuade her. Maybe If Roy came back with good news such as Erica being deposed as CEO.

Her phone rang. The receptionist said, "He's back." She leapt up and raced down the hall to Roy's office. His chair was empty. She looked back down the hall toward the entrance. No sign of him. She went to the front office. "Is he here?"

Mari said, "He came in and said, 'No calls.'"

Sheila wheeled and went back to Roy's office. It was still empty.

She sat down to wait. In a couple minutes, her father strolled in and sat down behind his desk.

"So?"

He played with a letter opener and didn't meet her gaze. "You're not going to like it. Don't be mad at me, honey."

"Tell me."

He swiveled his chair around and reluctantly spun out a story that infuriated Sheila. A couple of the members had raised concerns that they tried to articulate in the most diplomatic fashion. Erica pushed back and then slowly worked them around with a combination of flattery and contrition. She had a plausible explanation for the inspection results and for all the delays and missteps. In the end, she was still the CEO, and her board members were still wimps.

"Dad, I think I ought to tell you something, but it's really important you keep this confidential. Tony called that inspector in, and she knows GHS has serious internal problems that could amount to fraud. I don't know that this is true, but Tony is positive that the problems are going to bring GHS down, and she has no incentive to lie about anything."

"Oh, Sheila, that's not possible. Erica's got some issues, but she's not that dumb. That can't be true. Does your girlfriend have some kind of ax to grind? What's her deal?"

His dismissive attitude struck her the wrong way. "She's an honest, straightforward person, Dad. She has no axes to grind, as you put it. And you need to back off."

"All right, all right. Sorry." Sheila went back to her office and sat in her chair trying to calm herself, but it was useless.

Filled with dread, Sheila texted Tony and asked to her to come over after work and have dinner, and she agreed.

Sheila watched Tony as she entered the passenger seat of the Volt and said nothing beyond, "Hello, darling." Tony mumbled something that might have been hello. Sheila didn't lean in for a kiss, nor did Tony initiate one.

They didn't speak beyond the necessary discussion for obtaining dinner. It was Italian, and they spread it all out on Sheila's dining-room table.

"Well. What's the news?"

"Not good, I'm afraid. The board wimped out. She's still the big kahuna. No reprimand even. I'm sorry, baby."

Tony put her fork down and glared at Sheila. "You're kidding."

"Tony, I really am sorry. I don't agree with this, but there's nothing I can do."

"Did you talk to your Dad?" Sheila endured a stab of guilt at what she had actually said to Roy. She had broken Tony's confidence, and it ultimately made no difference anyhow.

"Yes, I did, but there's not a lot I can say to him that doesn't violate your confidence. I told him about the inspection."

"Yeah. You didn't have to use my name. Just amazing that they aren't already up in arms about what Erica's doing."

"Well. It's hard to do something if no actual crime is involved. We tend to let CEOs run their companies. Market forces—"

"Okay. No actual crime? What about fraud? Isn't actually lying to people a bad thing? Erica must be some kind of genius hypnotist or something. She's got them all fooled. As a matter of fact, Gordon has a theory…" Tony told Sheila about her conversation.

"Tony, baby. I know how what I'm telling you sounds. I cannot do anything. I'm not in charge. Are you—?"

Tony had stopped eating and was staring at her plate. "Are you not even the least upset? Can anything break through your façade? Are you just immune to emotion? Maybe you can't influence the board of directors, but you could be upset. You could say, "'Tony, I understand you have to talk to the reporter. I support you doing that because I love you.'"

"What good is getting upset over something I can't change? I'm not going to tell you something that isn't true. That would be worse."

"Well, maybe I *can* change something. I can go talk to that reporter."

"Tony…" This was what Sheila had feared would happen.

Tony stood up and threw her napkin on the table. "I'm going home. By train. Don't bother to get in touch with me."

"Tony—please. Sit down and talk to me."

"I'm done talking to you." She walked out the front door.

Sheila didn't follow her. Strong emotions washed over her—anger, fear, and grief. Was this over? What was going to happen if Tony followed through?

CHAPTER FIFTEEN

His name is Tomas Avery. His number is 212-555-5555. I told him to expect your call. He'll fly out here to interview you. I'm glad you decided to talk to him. You have a perspective that I don't, facts I don't know. He's the real deal. I looked him up."

Tony sat in her old SF apartment and stared at the paper where she'd written the name and number Gordo gave her. The *Washington Post*. Holy crap. Sheila. Jesus Christ. When had she turned into this automaton with no emotional affect? She could at least commiserate with me, tell me that I ought to do what I think is right. Hold my hand. All she said was don't talk to the reporter. At least she did say "Please." That was something.

Tony was miserable, but at least she'd made a decision. And she was convinced she'd made the correct choice. She could clear her conscience and know she'd done what she could. She would no longer represent a conflict of interest to Sheila. She intended to resign from GHS. That was the only honorable thing to do if she was going to blow them up by talking to a reporter. She thought about the NDA. *Screw it. They can come after me if they want, if they even know I've talked.* She'd ask Gordo if anything had happened.

She called and left a message for Tomas Avery, then one for Gordon, and then she went to sleep. The next morning, she dropped off a resignation letter to Sanjay. It was short. Two sentences. It was no surprise that Huey came to her cube an hour later and said, "You can go ahead and leave today. Security will escort you out." She nodded, didn't say anything more, and left quietly. She checked her phone every hour, but Sheila hadn't texted. She went home and called her dad.

❖

It was an odd feeling—not knowing what she was going to do—and Sheila hated it. A forty-five-minute meditation didn't clarify anything either. She'd go to the dharma talk on Thursday, and maybe that would help. She tended to her other clients and went to two pitch meetings. Roy didn't seek her out, which wasn't a surprise. She hoped he was feeling as bad as she was. Tony didn't contact her, and she was determined to follow Tony's order not to get in touch with her and wait for her to cool down. But Tony *wasn't* a hothead. It felt like she'd made a final, irrevocable decision, and Sheila couldn't blame her. Both her decisions, to go to the reporter and breaking up with Sheila, were the correct choices. For her.

It looked like they were over. Sheila didn't want to believe that. She wasn't ready to practice acceptance around it, for sure. Buddhist practice was of no value at this moment. She'd made a request of Tony based on what she believed would best serve the needs of her company. She didn't feel guilty for that. She was sorry Tony had to leave.

I'm just going to be miserable for a while. Doesn't the Dalai Lama say pain is inevitable, but suffering is not? I don't have to suffer. I have to locate my compassion for Tony and her pain. I must trust and wait. But Sheila didn't seem to be able to embrace that advice at all. She was devastated. Unbalanced wasn't an accurate term for what she felt.

At the dharma talk, it seemed some universal forces were at work, because the leader, Acharya Robert Stevens, announced that he planned to discuss anger. Hope for relief and hope for progress briefly raised Sheila's mood.

"Thich Nhat Hanh says anger is habit energy. We are angry as a culture and as individuals, and it takes only an event or word from someone to trigger us. Our anger is old. It is in our bodies, and it will always flare under the right circumstances."

Sheila thought about that point. She had thought she was free from anger, but it was clear she wasn't. Even though she hadn't said it to Tony, she was angry with Tony for her actions at GHS, considered them counter-productive and foolish. If viewed from Sheila's vantage point, they were. But not from Tony's. Tony had the right to expect her girlfriend to wholeheartedly support her. Sheila couldn't do that, and therefore they broke up. It made sense, but she still felt horrible.

Stevens continued. "We identify the three poisons as greed, delusion, and anger. We know anger is destructive both to ourselves and to our society."

Sheila took that in. *Boy, is that ever true.* After Tony left her via Uber, she had felt physically sick.

Stevens went on. "Anger and fear are closely connected. In fact, I would assert that behind *all* anger is fear."

What am I afraid of? Losing things that are valuable to me, and one is the success of GHS. The other is Tony's love. Which is most vital to me? Money or love? That's easy to decide. Or it ought to be.

She forced herself to refocus on what Stevens was saying. He was describing how to handle anger, what to do with it. At the end of the talk, she approached him and signed up for his three-day intensive meditation workshop. She would take some time off and take care of herself. If Tony returned, she wanted to be ready and have her feelings under control.

After talking to Avery and setting up a meeting with him, Tony breathed easier. Tomas Avery promised everything she told him was on deep background and her name wouldn't appear. Tony was reassured and believed him, but she figured the facts, when revealed in the *Washington Post*, would likely direct Erica and Huey to conclude she was the one who provided them. What would they do? She didn't know, but she thought she was okay with the consequences.

She still had, however, the problem with Sheila or, rather, her view of Sheila's behavior. The pain was like a low-level but insistent background noise, and she slid in and out of regret for leaving Sheila in such a dramatic, final manner. Sheila was never going to be wholeheartedly behind her; her conflict of interest would make that impossible. Sheila also would never show the depths of emotion most people would succumb to. Tony ruefully concluded that one thing she'd come to love most about her girlfriend was part of the reason they weren't together. She couldn't expect Sheila to be other than who she was. Tony was certain Sheila cared about her and probably knew Tony was right, but Sheila couldn't change what was going on any more than Tony could, and Tony vaguely felt she'd been unfair and possibly way too impetuous to insist Sheila not get in touch with her. They were practically living together, even if it wasn't official, and they were supposedly in love, and they hadn't talked or broken up officially. It just…was. Tony wasn't sure she was finished yet, only that she *wanted* to be finished and move on.

She pounded her kitchen table. She had committed the cardinal sin of leaving a job before she had obtained a new one. She'd walked away from her lover with whom she was about to move in. In an extremely short time, she could no longer afford the apartment she was living in because she had no income. She had to talk to her father and get his help.

Gordon called her a couple of days later, terrified. "Tony, I think we're in trouble. I got a letter from a lawyer. Someone named Blevins. I—"

"Wait a sec, Blevins? I know that name." Tony remembered that Erica had brought this guy to the staff meeting and introduced him.

"And what did the letter say?" she asked.

"That I'd violated my NDA and they were going to sue me. I can't afford a bleepin' lawyer." He was near tears, and Tony was suddenly scared for herself on top of feeling bad for Gordon. So much for his optimism that he could handle whatever came his way.

"There must be something you can do," Tony said.

"I'll ask Avery about it. I'll call you. But be careful. They might be following him. Or you."

❖

Tony had moved back in with her dad. It wasn't ideal, but for the time being it was for the best. She was looking for a new job and wondering what to do about Sheila and their shattered relationship. She'd talked to her dad, but although he was sympathetic, he'd only listened without offering any suggestions. He wasn't too positive about her talking to a reporter either, but he agreed it would at least move things forward.

She met Tomas Avery at a place in the Richmond near her childhood home. She told him it was safer than meeting in Palo Alto, and he agreed.

An unassuming fellow in a sport coat, he wore old-fashioned horn-rimmed glasses. But when Tony sat across from him and really made eye contact, his gaze was level, direct. He asked great questions and was clearly self-assured and experienced.

"They have tried to shut me down, but the *Post* has lawyers as good or better than that dude Blevins. They tried to play hardball with us, but it won't work."

"Blevins sent a threatening letter to Gordon."

"I heard. He doesn't want to talk to me anymore. I can understand."

"You're going to keep my name out your article, right?"

"Yes. We've agreed, and I'll honor that deal. But I think I'm being tailed, and most likely by people GHS hired."

"Tailed?" Tony choked out the word.

"Yes. I want to be totally up front with you. And *you* may still end up hearing from the GHS lawyers. Are you still up for this?"

Tony didn't answer right away. Telling the reporter her story warred with her fear at the consequences.

He added, "You may want to hire a lawyer who knows whistleblower law."

"A lawyer?" Tony stuttered.

"Yes. I'm truly sorry, but these people do not play nice. I've already lost Gordon, but he did spend some time talking to me. I'd be grateful if you could help. I've interviewed a ton of people and am publishing as soon as I can, but I still need some more details on the laboratory operations. Can you help?"

"I want to, but I need to think about it—twenty-four hours?"

"That's okay."

Tony told her dad what she was considering.

"I don't have money for a lawyer, honey. Unless I take out a loan. Can Sheila possibly help?"

Tony slumped in her chair, defeated and having no idea what to do.

"Sheila didn't want me to talk to the reporter. That's why I'm here. We had…an argument." *And I stormed out of her car telling her not to call me.*

Joe drummed his fingers on the table, then paused. "I can see why, but from what you say, this reporter is going to write an article with or without your help."

"Yes, but my information would be huge. And I want him to get what I know out there."

"You ought to talk to Sheila," he said.

Yes, that was true, but how could she talk to Sheila after what she'd done? And if she did, how would that solve anything? Sheila wasn't prepared to help her. Sheila cared about GHS's bottom line. She'd made that clear. She thought what Tony was doing was wrong. No. She wasn't going to ask Sheila for help.

Weeks went by, and nothing happened with GHS, that Sheila was aware of. That was good. Erica continued to regularly appear in the media, bright-eyed and full of solemn pronouncements about her "mission."

But there was still no word from Tony. Sheila wanted desperately to call her, but Tony had been clear about what she *didn't* want. Sheila had no reason to think she'd changed her mind. That would be out of character. Sheila didn't even know where she was living or if she was still at GHS. She had disappeared, and Sheila couldn't say that Tony was entirely unjustified in wanting to not be found.

Sheila was no longer sure she'd been right to tell Tony *not* to talk to the *Washington Post* reporter. That had been her automatic response. Even worse, she'd begun to suspect that all her responses to both the problems at GHS and Tony's difficulties were oriented toward her business concerns and mastering her emotions via her Buddhist practice, not responding to what Tony needed or what would be good for the two of them. She'd essentially left Tony out of her thinking, and she'd been right to finally leave Sheila. It was a miracle Tony had stuck with her for as long as she did.

Sheila looked at the last text she'd received from Tony to let her know she was ready to be picked up from the train station for dinner. Sheila stared at her phone, wondering what would happen if she texted Tony? How would it be if she took the initiative? *Just wanted to see if you were okay.*

No, it was a bad idea to do something someone had expressly asked you not to. Sheila missed Tony so much she felt like she'd had her leg amputated, and she realized she was mired in grief. She was mourning the end of their relationship. At least she assumed it was over. Unless she received information that said otherwise, it was time for her to work through her grief and go on.

Maybe at some future point she could see Tony and tell her how deeply sorry she was for her failure to support her. She attended the anger workshop and was left with even more regret that she hadn't recognized her own anger and instead had tried to suppress it.

❖

Tony had emailed out a dozen résumés, hoping for a response from someone. She was sitting at her dad's, wondering what to do with herself, when the mail arrived. She didn't think she'd be getting any responses to her resume submissions via snail mail, but she shuffled through the mail anyhow.

It was such a nondescript envelope, legal letter size, white, with her name neatly typed on front with "care of" her father's name and address. "Hand-delivered" was stamped at the bottom. But it provoked such fear in Tony she couldn't move; she was frozen in place.

It had no return address, but Tony had a foreboding about who it might be from. Her curiosity overcame her fear, and she tore the envelope open. A letterhead at the top contained a bunch of names, but the body of the letter gave her an instant upset stomach and tight band of headache in her forehead. She had to read it twice to be able to absorb everything.

They must have known she talked to Tomas Avery. They certainly must have followed him, as he had said, and observed her talking with him in the café on Thirty-sixth Avenue.

We have reason to believe you made false and defamatory statements about Global Health Solutions to others. You spoke in direct violation of your non-disclosure agreement. You must cease and desist immediately. We demand you appear at the offices of…for interview.

Tony sat on the couch, the letter in her hand. She hadn't actually told Tomas Avery anything, but it didn't matter. She was still in hot water. She shook, and it took several deep breaths to quell the nausea that threatened to send her running to the bathroom. *Breathe. Think.* She was clearly in deep trouble, and she needed help, probably of the legal variety. Her dad had made it plain he'd try to help her, but she didn't want him to go into debt. She had some savings, but they were rapidly dwindling as she used them to partially support herself while she looked for work.

Sheila. No. Sheila would never want to give or lend her money for this purpose. Not after she'd pleaded with her not to do it and she'd gone ahead and gotten in touch with the reporter anyhow. She had basically left Sheila weeks before. As far as Tony was concerned, they weren't together anymore.

She called Gordon, not knowing who else to talk to. "I've gotten a letter from Blevins." She read it to him.

"That's what mine said too. Avery told me to try to hang on, that they were bluffing because they can't strong-arm me since I'm no longer an employee. Neither are you."

"But what can they do?"

"I'm not sure. Do you think I ought to hire a lawyer anyhow? I'm scared."

"I'm scared, too. Even if I think they can't do anything to me legally, I don't know what they will do. I told Avery I couldn't talk to him, and he was disappointed, but he said he understood."

Gordon was silent for a beat. "Maybe you ought to get a lawyer too, Tone. If they have a reporter followed and then have us followed, who knows what *else* they'll do?"

CHAPTER SIXTEEN

Tony stared at Sheila's number for a long time. It wasn't just that she needed help. She realized she wanted to talk to Sheila, and she regretted cutting her off so abruptly. She tapped the number before she could think about it too much and not follow through. She recalled that this was exactly how she felt when they first began to date.

"Hello." Sheila's cool voice came over the Wi-Fi, sounding the same as it always did.

"Hi. This is Tony." Of course, she knew who it was since she knew Tony's number. *Idiot.*

"Yes. Hi. I'm glad you called." She did sound pleased.

"You are?" This was good news.

"Well. Sure. You told *me* to not get in touch. I was hoping *you'd* call me. I respected your request. But that doesn't mean I didn't very much want to hear from you. I'm so relieved."

"Yes, I did, and I'm sorry I said that. I was angry."

"I was too. But I'm not now."

"You?" Sheila? Angry? Holy shit.

"Yeah. Uh-huh. Me." Sheila's voice was steady.

"I have to talk to you about something. It's kind of an emergency," Tony said, desperately.

"Shall I come to the City or you come here?"

Tony thought about it. She was the supplicant. She ought to go to Sheila's turf. "I'll come over there. By train."

"Of course. Tonight?"

"Yes. I think I'll take the four o'clock Caltrain, if you can meet me—"

"Absolutely. Text me when you're here."

❖

They sat in the Volt for a long time in the station parking lot. For one thing, Tony might merely need to turn around and get right back on the next train. If Sheila turned her down, that's what she'd do.

Tony told her what had happened, and Sheila listened without comment.

"I know this a big ask, considering how you feel about me talking to a reporter—who I didn't say anything to, after all. I lost my nerve. But it didn't matter. They're still coming after me. I need to hire a lawyer and—"

"I'll pay for it," Sheila said. That was all. Only four words, and Tony relaxed. Sheila continued talking though. "I was wrong to not take you seriously. Very wrong. There are some other things you ought to know."

A few weeks after the last board meeting and Sheila's unhappy conversation with Roy, Gary came to her office.

"I've heard things about GHS," he said. "But first I need to talk to you about Roy. He isn't well, and he's trying to hide it. He's asleep a lot of the time. I've caught him. He's forgetting things. We have to get him to quit Pacific Partners. He's not able to handle working. He's going to make a mistake, a big one, at some point."

Sheila and Roy had kept away from one another since their last talk. This was no way to run a family relationship, let alone a venture-capital company, but Sheila hadn't wanted to deal with the situation or with Roy. Yet she couldn't avoid it any longer. She had to step in.

"I'll talk to him. But tell me. What did you hear about GHS?"

"Well, for one thing, there's a Stanford prof who knows Erica and who's been telling a lot of Valley people that she, for one, didn't think Erica had the faintest idea of what she was doing."

"Who?" Gary told her it was someone who'd known Erica when she was at Stanford.

"What else?" Sheila asked.

"Oh, you know, it's kind of hazy and non-specific. Like someone told someone else 'there's no there, there.' That they haven't got the technology they've been touting for the last few years. The rumor is that the Graff deal is messed up, and they may be about to sue her. But it's all whispers. Erica is still on top, and no one wants to sound like 'the sexist pig who can't handle a woman being a celebrity' CEO. But this prof, she's something else. She's the research person who turned Erica down when she asked for help. She tried to tell Erica she was on the wrong track, but Erica wouldn't listen. Doesn't that sound familiar? Geez, Sheila, think about it. As of right now Erica has literally nothing to show for all the money she's gotten thrown at her. It sure makes me wonder."

"Well. You're not the only one. Hm. I'm going to tell you something, Gary. And it's another example of how Roy is losing his grip, in my opinion." Sheila told Gary the story of Tony and GHS and what Roy's response had been.

"So, there is something to this. We ought to, one, stage an intervention with Roy. Two, we need to know more about what's going with GHS. We may have to let the other partners know. But not until we have more facts, not just rumors."

"I hear you. Let's deal with Roy first."

After she finished her story, Sheila said, "So I've broken your confidence. Twice. And I apologize for doing that, but I want you to know I'm sorry for doubting you. I want to help you deal with this situation, in whatever way I can, financially, emotionally. And Tony, love, I want us to be together. I want you to come live with me like we planned."

Tony sat quietly for a few moments. Sheila was okay with silence, and she didn't hurry as she gathered her thoughts.

"I'm glad you said something to your dad and Gary. I'm not at GHS anymore, and I'm tired of hiding. I'm sorry I walked out on you the way I did. I was totally stressed out by what was happening to me and so furious with you about how supportive you were *not* being, even though I understood intellectually where you were coming from."

Sheila laughed a bit. "I was angry with you, too, for leaving me. Mostly I was mad at myself for having tunnel vision. Of all people who ought to know you knew what you were talking about, it ought to be me. I was focused on GHS and what could happen if the publicity started to get bad, not on you."

Sheila stopped for a moment and swallowed. "And I've gotten so used to controlling my emotions that I didn't let *you*, of all people, see how I felt. You were right to leave when you weren't getting what you needed from me. I've trained myself to take my emotions out of my work. Buddhism helps me do that. But I didn't stop to think how that would look to you. I didn't want to deal with the fact that I was angry with you for not listening to me and going ahead with your plan to talk to the *Washington Post* reporter. I was already ticked off that you made that anonymous complaint to those federal people. Then I went to a dharma talk about anger…and it became obvious what was going on with me. But it was too late, I thought, since you'd already left and told me to not contact you. I didn't think it would be a good idea for me to try to call you. I hoped you would come back."

"Thanks for saying that." Tony meant it. "Ironic, huh? I didn't tell the reporter anything after all. But it didn't matter. GHS is after me anyhow. It's that guy Blevins."

Sheila shook her head. "Yep. That guy, Erica's attack dog. Let me look into hiring a lawyer. I'll get a referral for someone who's experienced in this type of law. If you decide you want to talk to the reporter again, it's fine with me. It's time for me and everyone else to stop pretending everything's okay. It's time for you to do what you and I both know is the right thing. I need to stop being an impediment. I'm behind you one hundred percent. I love you."

As they embraced, an enormous sense of relief washed over Tony, and she started to cry. Sheila hugged her tighter and whispered, "It's going to be all right. Don't worry. We'll deal with this together. Shh. It's okay, sweetheart."

After picking up some food, they went back to Sheila's condo Tony calmed. She felt liberated, released from the burden she'd been carrying alone.

"I wasn't sure what would happen with you, so I didn't come prepared to stay overnight, but I, um, want to."

Sheila grinned slightly. "I hoped it would all work out for us, and it seems it has. How about you?"

"Yes. We've both apologized enough. I'm fine."

Sheila touched Tony's cheek. "I have a new extra toothbrush for you."

Tony took Sheila's hand, kissed it, and then leaned over and kissed Sheila on the mouth. The kiss seemed to go on endlessly, and Tony nearly started to cry again, but another feeling was taking over—arousal.

Tony broke their kiss. "Can we skip the hot tub?"

Sheila laughed. "Yes, we can. Absolutely."

They walked to the bedroom hand in hand. Without breaking eye contact, they took off their clothes, heedlessly dropping them to the floor.

Tony hadn't let herself dwell on the idea that after her angry departure she'd never see Sheila again, let alone touch her. When they were finally together in bed, naked, they hugged, both seeming to want to go slow and savor the moment. The full import of what she'd nearly lost struck Tony hard, mingling with her relief, and she held on to Sheila so tight that Sheila winced.

"Sorry," Tony whispered. "I didn't mean to hurt you. I can't believe I almost let you go. That was so wrong." She teared up again.

"I'm okay. Shh. Don't worry. We're here, together. The present is the only thing that matters. We've made our apologies. We can talk more later." Sheila moved away so she could stroke Tony's breast, slowly at first and then more firmly. Tony relaxed into Sheila's touch, which was soothing and stimulating. Her inconvenient feelings of remorse drained away. By the time she reached orgasm, her mind was blissfully empty of everything except Sheila.

"I remember how this feels," Tony said. "I'd tried not to think about it when we were separated. That would have made me hurt worse."

"Self-protective reaction. I did indulge in some sensate memories though. I told myself that all was not lost...yet."

"You are always the optimist," Tony said, drily.

"Yes, I am. That's an outgrowth of my work, and Buddhist practice, of course. Not always the best path, but I'm not ready to let it go. Here we are talking and..."

"Yeah, I guess, but I'm ready to stop talking again."

They were lying close together, and Tony gently rubbed Sheila's thigh as she recovered from orgasm. She rolled over on top of her.

"Who's the dead beetle now?" She bit Sheila's neck.

"That would be me. Happy to be."

"Good," Tony said and made love to her as though her life depended on it. Maybe it did.

It was not going to be easy to convince Roy he had to step away from his company, but it was the only route to take. Sheila gathered Gary, her mother, and one of Roy's other close friends, and they sat him down.

At the end of all the speeches they made, Roy didn't say anything for a long time, but when he finally spoke, he was surprisingly cooperative.

"You all have a lot of nerve treating me like I'm mental, but I guess it was the only way to get through to me. I don't feel that well, but I haven't wanted to believe anything was wrong with me. I wanted to be back in tip-top shape, but the doc told me to not be overly optimistic. I'm going to do what you ask and retire. I'd like to still be in the loop, but I will not try to tell you what to do at Pacific Partners. I'm done. There's one thing. Gary, can you lobby the other partners about elevating Sheila to full partner? It's time. But it ought to come from you and not me."

"Dad—"

"It's what I want," Roy said with a spark of his old stubbornness.

Gary grinned. "I don't think it'll be a problem."

❖

As Tony laid out her situation to the attentive and kindly man sitting behind the big desk, she held on to Sheila's hand. She wasn't afraid anymore, or uncertain. Whatever this man thought she ought to do, she'd do it and stop having second thoughts. About anything, really. That was over. She was going to move into Sheila's place in a few days.

He listened, and Tony admired his listening skills. He took notes as she spoke, but he made eye contact, nodded, and smiled a few times. Being heard gave her a great feeling. Sheila and Tony had spent a few more hours talking over the unraveling of their relationship and acknowledging again the part each of them had played.

"First of all, no one can sue you for talking to a reporter. Your NDA isn't enforceable if a potential crime or a regulatory violation is involved."

Tony was so relieved, she almost fell off her chair.

"I'm going to respond to that letter you received with all that scary nonsense. From now on, they have to talk to me, and I'll talk to them. You are not to reply to any communication, written or verbal, from GHS. That's my job."

Tony squeezed Sheila's hand, then smiled at the attorney and said, "By all means, please. You can take over. I don't ever want to talk to them again. I don't want to see them."

She emailed Tomas Avery, and they spent a good amount of time on the phone as he interviewed her. He expressed his gratitude unreservedly and promised he would still regard her information as on background and only refer to her as an employee. Tony thought that anyone in the know who read the article would likely be able to tell what her job was and who she was, but she wasn't worried.

She talked to Gordon, who'd hired his own attorney. They agreed that it was better for them to tell what they knew rather than be frightened and try to hide. Gordon's attorney told him the same thing as Tony's. They'd done nothing wrong. Global Health Solutions, in the person of Erica, had done some truly bad things, and no amount of bullying from them ought to be tolerated.

Sheila and Tony, along with the rest of Silicon Valley, watched and waited to see what would happen next. With the publication of Avery's article in the *Washington Post*, it was as though someone had flipped a switch. The news coverage of Erica Sanders abruptly stopped being laudatory.

Right after the *Post* article broke, Erica appeared on a cable-TV investing show. She was defiant and combative as the show host coaxed her to take some measure of responsibility and explain what the reporter had written. She would not in any way admit that her vaunted technology was worthless. She blamed the messenger, i.e. reporter, and she blamed her employees.

Sheila and Tony watched from the comfort of their couch, glasses of wine in hand. They looked at each other and shook their heads. She was never going to change.

"It ticks me off that she's blaming us for what she did, or didn't, do."

"Yeah. That's kind of unsurprising though," Sheila said.

Erica dropped out of sight. The news about her continued though. The Security and Exchange Commission charged her with fraud.

"That's good, right?" Tony asked Sheila.

"It is, but the SEC is notoriously lenient when it comes to penalties and holding people accountable. It's only a civil violation."

"Oh," Tony said, deflated.

"Cheer up, love. The latest gossip says both she and Huey are going to be criminally indicted."

"Oh, great," Tony said, upbeat again.

Sheila was philosophical about losing the investment in GHS, which she considered inevitable.

She told Tony, "You win some and you lose some" is the motto of the VC world." The loss hadn't actually officially happened yet, but it was coming as far as Sheila was concerned, and she wouldn't be blamed for the debacle. The rest of the companies in her portfolio were doing fine, and one went public to the tune of a couple of billion. But the SEC verdict resulted in a drastic devaluation of GHS's worth, which, as Sheila explained to Tony, was all on paper anyhow.

The other partners were understanding, and most of them said it could happen to anyone. They agreed with Gary and Sheila, that even Roy, with all his experience, wasn't able to tell something nefarious was going on. Incompetent CEOs were one thing, but criminal fraud was something else. They knew about Sheila's attempts to raise an alarm about Erica and GHS. They were contemplating a lawsuit to try to recover some of their investment.

Sheila was elevated to full partner on Roy's recommendation, and he retired. He showed up at the offices only sometimes, as he had agreed.

"I'm sorry, sweetie. I guess I should have known Erica was too good to be true."

"Dad, nobody knew. It wasn't just you."

A year elapsed, and Pacific Partners took their investment loss as a tax write-off. Everyone mostly wanted to try to forget about it. Sheila dove into working with brand-new start-ups. There was never any shortage of people with big ideas. Sheila was stricter with her starry-eyed CEOs. She gave them more reporting requirements and more benchmarks to meet, and she made them take an ethics class, then incorporated all of it into their investment agreements.

Tony had almost recovered from what she identified at last as a form of PTSD. Though it went against her principles, she allowed Sheila to persuade her to go to therapy.

"Why would I want to relive all this? I want to forget it."

"You just think it's over, that it's gone, but it's not. Trust me."

Yet therapy was much different than she'd imagined. The therapist explained to her that she'd experienced trauma and would heal from it, but she had to talk. Over time, therapy worked, and she stopped feeling as though she'd lost her mind and like something terrible was about to happen to her.

From being in the news practically every day, Erica became invisible. She was just gone.

Sheila joked, "It's not like I miss her or anything. She's not a friend. She almost made us break up."

"Yes. Let's blame her. I like that. She made my life miserable for almost two years. The beginning was good. Also, she's why we met. I guess I can be a little grateful."

"But only a little," Sheila said, grinning.

A new biotech company from Mountain View recruited Tony, and she happily returned to a workaday life that had her commuting fifteen minutes from their condo to a laboratory that was far more about science and scheduling testing than drama and lies.

Tony wasn't surprised, but she was still a bit unnerved when she was served with a subpoena to appear for a deposition. Richard, her lawyer, had told her it was likely. She and the rest of the world heard on the news that Erica and Huey were indicted for fraud in US District Court. It turned out as Sheila predicted. Tony thought wire fraud and conspiracy to commit fraud were oddly innocuous names for what Erica had done.

"These are felonies," Sheila said. "This is some serious shit."

Tony laughed. But then she asked, "You won't get any of your investment back, will you, if she's found guilty?"

"That's unlikely. All that money she was getting will go for lawyers' fees."

On the day of her deposition, Tony sat with Richard beside her. She was nervous, but it was okay. After all, she wanted to see Erica held responsible for what she'd done. Sheila couldn't be present, but she was close by, in another part of Erica's lawyers' office.

Erica sat across the table from her, with Harry Blevins. Richard had told her this might happen.

"It's not usual, but it's a sign what you're going to say makes them nervous, but don't let it bother you," he'd said. "They're trying to psyche you out, intimidate you. I'll make sure they don't. I can tell you not to answer a question if I don't like it."

To say the least, Erica lacked her usual verve. Truthfully, Tony thought she looked defeated, drained, and barely even acknowledged Tony. She didn't even seem to recognize her.

The deposition was grueling, but Tony wasn't afraid anymore, and when Erica's lawyer, the fearsome Harry Blevins, interrogated her and tried to make her waver or trip her up, Tony was very grateful that Richard answered.

At dinner with Sheila and Richard later, Richard told them that when he saw a video of the government attorneys questioning Erica, he was struck at the time by her demeanor.

"It was a lot like how she looked in your deposition, but she actually had to answer questions. Most of the time her answers were 'I don't know' or 'I don't remember.' I didn't think it was a great strategy. She could have used the Fifth amendment."

After Tony looked at the videos, she and Sheila had been fascinated at the change in Erica.

Tony said, "For someone who always projected extreme self-confidence and was so talkative, it was eerie."

"She was amazing. She was one of those people who they say can talk the birds down from the trees," Sheila said. "I was dazzled by her, like everyone else. And, like everyone else, I was fooled."

"Isn't it funny?" Tony said. "After all of Erica's efforts to protect the GHS 'trade secrets,' there weren't actually any trade secrets to protect. She was just hiding the fact that she had nothing."

"And we bought it," Sheila said, sadly, shaking her head. "What does that say about us?"

"Most people want to trust others, believe people have good intentions and integrity," Richard said, "But often, people don't. We're not well equipped to tell when other people are lying. That's a number-one concern for lawyers but not most folks. We want to trust."

"But I still don't understand why she did what she did," Tony said

"I don't either," Sheila said.

They both looked at the lawyer, who shook his head and shrugged. "I don't have any insight, if that's why you're looking at me."

"We should have asked a lot more questions or demanded a lot more background information to back up what Erica was telling us," Sheila said thoughtfully.

"Yes. I'll agree to that." Tony smiled. "Trust but verify is a rule I've always applied to my lab work, and I think I'll apply it to everything and everyone from now on."

"Me too," Sheila said. She, Tony, and Richard clinked their wineglasses.

"Here's to honesty and transparency in all things," Sheila said.

Looking at Sheila fondly, Tony said, "Here's to us."

About the Author

Kathleen Knowles grew up in Pittsburgh, Pennsylvania, but has lived in San Francisco for more than thirty years. She finds the city's combination of history, natural beauty, and multicultural diversity inspiring and endlessly fascinating.

Other than writing, she loves music of all kinds, walking , bicycling, and stamp collecting. LGBT history and politics have compelled her attention for many years, starting with her first Pride march in Cleveland, Ohio, in 1978. She and her partner were married in July 2008 and live atop one of San Francisco's many hills with their pets. She retired last year after working for twenty years as a health and safety specialist at the University of California, San Francisco.

She has written short stories, essays, and fan fiction. She is the author of nine novels.

Books Available from Bold Strokes Books

A Love that Leads to Home by Ronica Black. For Carla Sims and Janice Carpenter, home isn't about location, it's where your heart is. (978-1-63555-675-9)

Blades of Bluegrass by D. Jackson Leigh. A US Army occupational therapist must rehab a bitter veteran who is a ticking political time bomb the military is desperate to disarm. (978-1-63555-637-7)

Guarding Hearts by Jaycie Morrison. As treachery and temptation threaten the women of the Women's Army Corps, who will risk it all for love? (978-1-63555-806-7)

Hopeless Romantic by Georgia Beers. Can a jaded wedding planner and an optimistic divorce attorney possibly find a future together? (978-1-63555-650-6)

Hopes and Dreams by PJ Trebelhorn. Movie theater manager Riley Warren is forced to face her high school crush and tormentor, wealthy socialite Victoria Thayer, at their twentieth reunion. (978-1-63555-670-4)

In the Cards by Kimberly Cooper Griffin. Daria and Phaedra are about to discover that love finds a way, especially when powers outside their control are at play. (978-1-63555-717-6)

Moon Fever by Ileandra Young. SPEAR agent Danika Karson must clear her werewolf friend of multiple false charges while teaching her vampire girlfriend to resist the blood mania brought on by a full moon. (978-1-63555-603-2)

Quake City by St John Karp. Can Andre find his best friend Amy before the night devolves into a nightmare of broken hearts, malevolent drag queens, and spontaneous human combustion? Or has it always happened this way, every night, at Aunty Bob's Quake City Club? (978-1-63555-723-7)

Serenity by Jesse J. Thoma. For Kit Marsden, there are many things in life she cannot change. Serenity is in the acceptance. (978-1-63555-713-8)

Sylver and Gold by Michelle Larkin. Working feverishly to find a killer before he strikes again, Boston Homicide Detective Reid Sylver and rookie cop London Gold are blindsided by their chemistry and developing attraction. (978-1-63555-611-7)

Trade Secrets by Kathleen Knowles. In Silicon Valley, love and business are a volatile mix for clinical lab scientist Tony Leung and venture capitalist Sheila Garrison. (978-1-63555-642-1)

Death Overdue by David S. Pederson. Did Heath turn to murder in an alcohol induced haze to solve the problem of his blackmailer, or was it someone else who brought about a death overdue? (978-1-63555-711-4)

Entangled by Melissa Brayden. Becca Crawford is the perfect person to head up the Jade Hotel, if only the captivating owner of the local vineyard would get on board with her plan and stop badmouthing the hotel to everyone in town. (978-1-63555-709-1)

First Do No Harm by Emily Smith. Pierce and Cassidy are about to discover that when it comes to love, sometimes you have to risk it all to have it all. (978-1-63555-699-5)

Kiss Me Every Day by Dena Blake. For Wynn Evans, wishing for a do-over with Carly Jamison was a long shot, actually getting one was a game changer. (978-1-63555-551-6)

Olivia by Genevieve McCluer. In this lesbian Shakespeare adaption with vampires, Olivia is a centuries old vampire who must fight a strange figure from her past if she wants a chance at happiness. (978-1-63555-701-5)

One Woman's Treasure by Jean Copeland. Daphne's search for discarded antiques and treasures leads to an embarrassing misunderstanding, and ultimately, the opportunity for the romance of a lifetime with Nina. (978-1-63555-652-0)

Silver Ravens by Jane Fletcher. Lori has lost her girlfriend, her home, and her job. Things don't improve when she's kidnapped and taken to fairyland. (978-1-63555-631-5)

Still Not Over You by Jenny Frame, Carsen Taite, Ali Vali. Old flames die hard in these tales of a second chance at love with the ex you're still not over. Stories by award winning authors Jenny Frame, Carsen Taite, and Ali Vali. (978-1-63555-516-5)

Storm Lines by Jessica L. Webb. Devon is a psychologist who likes rules. Marley is a cop who doesn't. They don't always agree, but both fight to protect a girl immersed in a street drug ring. (978-1-63555-626-1)

The Politics of Love by Jen Jensen. Is it possible to love across the political divide in a hostile world? Conservative Shelley Whitmore and liberal Rand Thomas are about to find out. (978-1-63555-693-3)

All the Paths to You by Morgan Lee Miller. High school sweethearts Quinn Hughes and Kennedy Reed reconnect five years after they break up and realize that their chemistry is all but over. (978-1-63555-662-9)

Arrested Pleasures by Nanisi Barrett D'Arnuck. When charged with a crime she didn't commit Katherine Lowe faces the question: Which is harder, going to prison or falling in love? (978-1-63555-684-1)

Bonded Love by Renee Roman. Carpenter Blaze Carter suffers an injury that shatters her dreams, and ER nurse Trinity Greene hopes to show her that sometimes love is worth fighting for. (978-1-63555-530-1)

Convergence by Jane C. Esther. With life as they know it on the line, can Aerin McLeary and Olivia Ando's love survive an otherworldly threat to humankind? (978-1-63555-488-5)

Coyote Blues by Karen F. Williams. Riley Dawson, psychotherapist and shape-shifter, has her world turned upside down when Fiona Bell, her one true love, returns. (978-1-63555-558-5)

Drawn by Carsen Taite. Will the clues lead Detective Claire Hanlon to the killer terrorizing Dallas, or will she merely lose her heart to person of interest, urban artist Riley Flynn? (978-1-63555-644-5)

Every Summer Day by Lee Patton. Meant to celebrate every summer day, Luke's journal instead chronicles a love affair as fast-moving and possibly as fatal as his brother's brain tumor. (978-1-63555-706-0)

Lucky by Kris Bryant. Was Serena Evans's luck really about winning the lottery, or is she about to get even luckier in love? (978-1-63555-510-3)

The Last Days of Autumn by Donna K. Ford. Autumn and Caroline question the fairness of life, the cruelty of loss, and what it means to love as they navigate the complicated minefield of relationships, grief, and life-altering illness. (978-1-63555-672-8)

Three Alarm Response by Erin Dutton. In the midst of tragedy, can these first responders find love and healing? Three stories of courage, bravery, and passion. (978-1-63555-592-9)

Veterinary Partner by Nancy Wheelton. Callie and Lauren are determined to keep their hearts safe but find that taking a chance on love is the safest option of all. (978-1-63555-666-7)

Everyday People by Louis Barr. When film star Diana Danning hires private eye Clint Steele to find her son, Clint turns to his former West Point barracks mate, and ex-buddy with benefits, Mars Hauser to lend his cyber espionage and digital black ops skills to the case. (978-1-63555-698-8)

Forging a Desire Line by Mary P. Burns. When Charley's ex-wife, Tricia, is diagnosed with inoperable cancer, the private duty nurse Tricia hires turns out to be the handsome and aloof Joanna, who ignites something inside Charley she isn't ready to face. (978-1-63555-665-0)

Love on the Night Shift by Radclyffe. Between ruling the night shift in the ER at the Rivers and raising her teenage daughter, Blaise Richilieu has all the drama she needs in her life, until a dashing young attending appears on the scene and relentlessly pursues her. (978-1-63555-668-1)

Olivia's Awakening by Ronica Black. When the daring and dangerously gorgeous Eve Monroe is hired to get Olivia Savage into shape, a fierce passion ignites, causing both to question everything they've ever known about love. (978-1-63555-613-1)

The Duchess and the Dreamer by Jenny Frame. Clementine Fitzroy has lost her faith and love of life. Can dreamer Evan Fox make her believe in life and dream again? (978-1-63555-601-8)

The Road Home by Erin Zak. Hollywood actress Gwendolyn Carter is about to discover that losing someone you love sometimes means gaining someone to fall for. (978-1-63555-633-9)

Waiting for You by Elle Spencer. When passionate past-life lovers meet again in the present day, one remembers it vividly and the other isn't so sure. (978-1-63555-635-3)

While My Heart Beats by Erin McKenzie. Can a love born amidst the horrors of the Great War survive? (978-1-63555-589-9)

Face the Music by Ali Vali. Sweet music is the last thing that happens when Nashville music producer Mason Liner, and daughter of country royalty Victoria Roddy are thrown together in an effort to save country star Sophie Roddy's career. (978-1-63555-532-5)

Flavor of the Month by Georgia Beers. What happens when baker Charlie and chef Emma realize their differing paths have led them right back to each other? (978-1-63555-616-2)

Mending Fences by Angie Williams. Rancher Bobbie Del Rey and veterinarian Grace Hammond are about to discover if heartbreaks of the past can ever truly be mended. (978-1-63555-708-4)

Silk and Leather: Lesbian Erotica with an Edge edited by Victoria Villasenor. This collection of stories by award winning authors offers fantasies as soft as silk and tough as leather. The only question is: How far will you go to make your deepest desires come true? (978-1-63555-587-5)

The Last Place You Look by Aurora Rey. Dumped by her wife and looking for anything but love, Julia Pierce retreats to her hometown, only to rediscover high school friend Taylor Winslow, who's secretly crushed on her for years. (978-1-63555-574-5)

The Mortician's Daughter by Nan Higgins. A singer on the verge of stardom discovers she must give up her dreams to live a life in service to ghosts. (978-1-63555-594-3)

The Real Thing by Laney Webber. When passion flares between actress Virginia Green and masseuse Allison McDonald, can they be sure it's the real thing? (978-1-63555-478-6)

What the Heart Remembers Most by M. Ullrich. For college sweethearts Jax Levine and Gretchen Mills, could an accident be the second chance neither knew they wanted? (978-1-63555-401-4)

White Horse Point by Andrews & Austin. Mystery writer Taylor James finds herself falling for the mysterious woman on White Horse Point who lives alone, protecting a secret she can't share about a murderer who walks among them. (978-1-63555-695-7)